ARCHITECTURE AND ARTISTRY

GREEN VALLEY LIBRARY BOOK #11

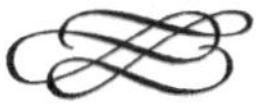

NORA EVERLY

COPYRIGHT

To Carolyn.
With all my love.
Thank you.

*"My life and heart have been forever transformed.
You are the architect and artist of my own personal paradise.
Now, when I close my eyes, I won't need to imagine what heaven feels like.
I'll know."*
- Penny Reid, Beard Necessities

CHAPTER 1

SADIE

Monday mornings could kiss my ass. In fact, every morning could kiss my ass. Like usual, my blaring alarm had jolted me out of a dream. There was nothing like waking up in a state of confusion coupled with a near heart attack to get you going in the morning. Today, the jolt of doom had been preceded by my bi-weekly stress-induced nightmare and followed by my usual clumsy-handed pawing at the snooze button on my cell phone until I finally gave up and rage-flailed my way out of bed to face what would inevitably be just another day to trudge through.

All night long, I had been out of control, free falling into nothing as I spiraled between awake and asleep. I had no memory of the nightmare other than the super fun exhausted feeling it had left me with.

I much preferred the dreams I had about my brand-new neighbor, the beautiful Barrett Monroe. He also happened to be my co-worker, our siblings were now married and expecting, and unbeknownst to anyone but my closest friends, he was also my secret teenage crush. Our lives had become crazily intertwined of late, which was why my naughty dreams about him had started back up again. But, I had to say, the dreams I used to have as a teenager had nothing on the ones I'd been having lately. Grown-up Sadie had a way better imagination and hadn't had sex in over a year. And let's face it, dreams were useless unless you woke up with a happy tingle and left-over dirty thoughts to take with you to your morning shower.

Seriously, did dreams ever come true? For anyone? I would really like to know.

Now nightmares, on the other hand, were real. I could always count on a good nightmare to keep me on my toes.

Obviously, I was going through some things.

My life was an utter mess. I knew I was drowning when the only thing to get me out of bed in the morning was the promise of coffee and the tragic knowledge that I woke up every morning already in need of a nap. Or maybe a brief coma.

I rolled my eyes at my overly dramatic thoughts and rubbed the steamy face of my cell phone to check the time. As usual, I was running late. *Surprise!*

I had no time for coffee, or my hair dryer. I had to wake my boys up straight away or they'd be late for school, and they couldn't miss school because I couldn't afford to miss work.

Since their father had left us a few months back, dealing with those two could sometimes be tricky. They'd become prone to acting out at home and sometimes at school, or faking sick so they could be with me all day. And I had loads of guilt about it, their lives had been upended just as much as mine.

I used to be a stay-at-home-mom, able to be there for them whenever they needed me. Now I was a working single mom trying to do my best. We had moved from our house in Knoxville to Green Valley, Tennessee—back to my small hometown. Before, they'd had a father, who despite being a shitty husband, had been a good dad. They were in a new school, and we'd just moved out of my nightmare mother's place—a farmhouse on the most picturesque lavender farm you could possibly imagine, called Lavender Hill—and into town with my sister. Our new house was a sprawling ranch on a cul-de-sac. They had their own rooms and a big back yard to play in, but they'd been hit with change after change lately and none of it had been easy, even if it was ultimately for the best.

With a quick reach, I switched off the shower and wrapped myself in a towel, stumbling over the bathmat as I entered my bedroom.

"Flynn, Rider, time to get up!" I shouted. Yes, I had named them after *that* Flynn Rider. I'd had a mild obsession with the Disney movie *Tangled* while I was pregnant and had named my twins accordingly.

I bent to rifle through one of the stuffed boxes of clothes lining the back wall of my new room. Sighing in frustration, I mentally added unpacking to my to-do list for when I got home from work. I'd moved into this house over the weekend with my sister and my boys. It was still a mess, with boxes and moving debris everywhere.

I was afraid Clara had no idea what she was getting into when she'd insisted we live together. But she didn't want to be alone, I couldn't afford a house like this on my own, and I was way over living with my mother, who on her best day could make Mother Gothel cry. So we went for it. On paper it was an awesome idea, but in practice? Identical second-grade twin boys were no walk in the park, and I'd leave it at that.

Where was Clara, anyway?

I darted back into the bathroom and pulled my wet hair into a ponytail to deal with after running the boys to school. Getting dressed could wait, too. *No one will see me in the drop-off line*, I reasoned as I slipped back into my pajamas. The only thing that mattered to me about morning drop-off was getting there first. I mean, freaking rats could figure their way out of a maze, but grown-ass adults couldn't manage to just pull the frick up to keep the dang line moving. *Do not get me started.* I would have them ride the bus in the morning but that would make our wake-up time move up by a half hour—no thank you.

"Come on, boys! Let's get a move on. Get up right now and I'll order pizza for dinner!" I hollered. They were probably going to start judging me down at the Pizza Hut if I showed my face in there again this week, but I didn't have time to care about that.

Flynn poked his head out of his door. "I've been ready for a million hours. Can I keep playing Minecraft until Rider gets up?" Flynn, just like his twin, Rider, was a mini version of me and my three sisters. Blonde hair, big blue eyes, tall, slim, and covered with freckles.

I stopped in my tracks, mid-hallway. "Do you know where your backpack is?" His eyes darted to the side. Of course, he didn't. *I* didn't even know where it had ended up. "Find it, then you can play. Where's Auntie Clara?"

"She went to the gym. She gave me Oreo Pop-Tarts for breakfast. I asked her for four of them and she gave me the whole box. Living here is gonna be great. My tummy hurts and I don't even care." I located the Pop-Tarts on his dresser and snagged them. I laughed to myself as the ridiculous thought that she could have at least chosen a fruit flavor crossed my mind. "Find your backpack, Flynn."

He huffed out a breath. "Fine. If I find Rider's too, can I have five dollars?"

"What do you need five dollars for?" He was eight. Money should be useless to an eight-year-old.

"I need more Minecoins." In-game purchases, of course. Buying a videogame was an investment nowadays. Like buying a house—the money never stopped flowing into it.

"Sure, okay, yeah. Find y'alls shoes too," I added after noticing his bare feet.

He smirked. "Ten dollars."

"*Gah!* Deal," I agreed, "But just this once." Nipping burgeoning extortionist behavior in the bud was now added to my to-do list. Maybe I should work on my mom-guilt too, while I was at it. It would probably make life cheaper in the long run.

"Yes!" He ran off down the hall toward the living room.

I shoved Rider's door open and entered. "Time to wake up, sweetie pie."

He rolled over with a grunt.

"Rider!" I sat on the edge of his bed and shook his shoulder.

"I'm not a morning person," he grumbled without opening his eyes.

"It's time for school."

"I'm not a school person either. I already know enough stuff." He flopped to his side, facing away from me. "Ask me what two times four is," he mumbled into his pillow. "It's six. Wait, no, it's seven. Wait, no, it's eight. See?"

"I'm sorry, honey, but you have to go to school. Life is all about learning. One day you'll realize that you will never know enough about anything. Which is kind of sad now that I think about it." I paused to consider what I was saying to my small child. *Yeesh.* "Never mind. I'll order pizza tonight if you get a move on." Pizza made everyone happy. I should stick with that.

He turned over and opened one eye. "Fine. I am a pizza person, but I'm too emotionally exhausted to get up today." Hey, that was my line! I'd said it to Clara last night after dinner. My theory that Rider was an eavesdropper had hereby been proven. I'd have to be more careful what I said around him in the future.

"How about five dollars for Minecoins or whatever? Will that get you out of bed?" I reluctantly offered. My day had barely started, and I was already in the hole. Bribery was expensive, but it was hard to turn back once you'd ventured down that path.

"Okay, I'll get up. But I want Robux instead, and I need seven dollars to get what I want in my game."

"Deal. And this is only going to work today. Keep that in mind tomorrow morning before attempting a pre-breakfast shakedown." I kissed his forehead and he smiled.

"Okay, Momma."

"All right! Get up! Get dressed! Let's go, go, go! It's your lucky day, Pop-Tarts are on the menu this morning!" I tossed over my shoulder as I breezed out of the room on the hunt for my keys and wallet.

The mirror in the hallway gave me pause as I passed it. Dang it, what if I ran into Barrett outside? He wasn't the problem. I saw him every day whether I wanted to or not, and I always wanted to see him—*so bad.*

Except for right now.

I didn't want to see him in the state I was in; or rather, for him to see me. I studied my reflection in the mirror with a scowl. Bare face, wet hair, pajamas. I knew for a fact he would look like pulled together suit and tie perfection if he happened to be out there when I had to leave with the boys. I imagined there wasn't a moment in Barrett Monroe's life where he hadn't been on point.

I liked looking sexy around him; it made me feel like I had the upper hand. We had chemistry between us—the bickering kind. I was hot for him and couldn't have him for all the reasons that drew us together, so picking fights with him was the only way I could think of to fight my attraction. It was juvenile, yet also fun. Barrett gave good banter. Banging a co-worker and your sister's brother-in-law was never a good idea. And now that we were neighbors? Forget about it.

Whatever.

I had no other choice than to load the boys up for school outside. My minivan was assigned to the driveway, while Clara's BMW got to live in the garage. It was only fair since I got to have the downstairs bonus office space all to myself. Clara claimed she could do her nefarious plotting from anywhere in the house and my design table needed a designated space. Thus, giving up the garage to her was the least I could do.

Once the boys were ready—lunches shoved in backpacks, shoes on feet, bellies full of Pop-Tarts—I took a careful peek out my window. Barrett's truck was parked in his driveway, but the coast was clear. "Come on boys, let's get a move on." Maybe I could get out of here before he left for work.

Rider bolted around me in a mad dash through the garage, laughing all the way. Suddenly I regretted letting him have the Pop-Tarts. Rider plus sugar was always an interesting combination.

Adding to the disaster, our garbage and recycling totes had been tipped over at the curb—before pick-up, thank you very much—and someone had decided to load up my recycling tote with a million liquor and wine bottles that had rolled all over the street in front of the house. We'd been here for two days; my neighbors were going to think a couple of lushes had moved in. *Dang it.*

Flynn stopped at my side. "It's going to be one of those days." He sighed and leaned against my side.

"Seems like it," I agreed. I brushed a kiss to the top of his head before moving aside to let him pass. "Get right in the van, honey, no dilly-dally." I turned the lights out and set the alarm, then stealthily made my way to the driveway, hoping Barrett wouldn't hear us and come out.

"Hey, Momma!" Rider all but shrieked. So much for stealth. He stopped in front of me, panting and jumping down. "Listen, this is so important. If I was invisible and shut my eyes, would I be able to see through my eyelids?"

I bit my lip, trying not to laugh. "I want to say yes, but I'm no scientist. Ask your teacher when you get to school."

"'Kay!" he shouted. He then commenced running laps around the minivan.

Thankfully, Flynn was in a mellow mood. He had loaded up and boarded the express van to Green Valley Grade School with zero problems. Rider on the other hand . . .

"Momma! You can't catch me! I'm invisible."

Crap!

"Rider! Open your eyes!"

"Ouch, stupid van." He turned to glare at me, deliberately widening his eyes like the little smartass I had inadvertently raised him to be. "I *cannot* see through my eyelids! You were wrong, Momma!"

"She told you to ask Mrs. Shaw at school." Flynn hung his head out of the window to defend my motherly honor. "She said she's no scientist, dummy."

I spun toward the sound of Barrett's garage door lifting. My heart raced out of control. "Okay. All right. Stop. Rider, get into the van. We have to go. Right now! Move it! Move it!"

"Sorry, Momma, I can't. Me and this van are now mortal enemies. We must duel to the death! *Pew pew pew!"* His laser fingers took aim as I stood there horrified.

Good lord, Barrett was going to see me.

Not the sexy, got-her-shit-together MILF I always pretended to be—with the clothes and the hair and the makeup.

The real me.

I shoved my wet hair back with a grimace.

Frick! Not only would he see me in all my morning glory, but he would also see my invisible son shooting at my minivan. Swallow me up, earth, please!

CHAPTER 2

BARRETT

"Dad, are you ready?"

"Coming," I shouted back. Monday morning was here, bright, early, and right on schedule. But this one would be different.

My alarm had woken me as usual but today I got up with a smile on my face rather than dragging my ass out of bed with coffee and a hot shower being the only things to look forward to. My daughter, Lizzy, had moved back home over the weekend, which meant I would no longer be alone in this big house. I slipped into my sport jacket with a grin and adjusted my tie in the hallway mirror before heading into the kitchen.

I'd once been the guy who'd had it all. Straight As, student body president, captain of the debate team, steady girlfriend. I graduated college with honors, and I had always known what I wanted.

The job? Architect.

The wife? Leeann.

The life? Big house, big family, all the love.

Sure, my daughter was born way before schedule but all that meant was an earlier start for Leeann and me. We got married in college and moved into an apartment off campus. I thought we'd made it, that we'd beaten the odds. We'd had our difficult moments, but we were happy. Or so I had thought.

She left us when Lizzy was in kindergarten, took off without giving me even a hint she wanted a divorce. She moved to Knoxville, enrolled in law school, and became an attorney, the high-powered, mostly mean kind. A real shark. Eventually we divorced and Leeann gave me primary custody of Lizzy. That was until Lizzy decided to graduate high school early and move in with Leeann to attend college in Knoxville. But for reasons I did not yet know, she had dropped out and come back home. I was overjoyed she was here, but worried about why. I knew all about what rushing through life could cost you—heartbreak and peace of mind. Well, that's what it had cost me. I didn't want that for Lizzy.

"You're going to wear a tie to work? Even with jeans?" She wrinkled her nose as she poured a travel cup of coffee and slid it across the butcher block island counter to me.

"Thanks." I placed my briefcase and keys down and smoothed my hand down my chest before taking a sip. "What's wrong with my tie?"

"It's stuffy, you look like an old man," she replied as she poured herself some orange juice. "You're lucky I'm going to be home with you in the morning. We can work on your clothes."

Frowning, I answered. "I am a stuffy old man. I'm almost thirty-six, a grown adult human male who works in an office eighty percent of the time. Business attire is—"

"Well, according to Mom, the thirties are the new twenties," she shot back with an eye roll. "You should loosen up a bit, Dad." Mischievous eyes met mine over the rim of her glass and I could tell she had ulterior motives. "Then maybe you could finally meet someone new," she added under her breath.

"I guess I could try life without a tie. At least for today." Deliberately ignoring the last part of her statement, I slipped the tie over my head and set it on the counter. I was unsettled; this felt odd.

As an architect and sometimes project supervisor at my family's contracting company, I could dress how I liked, and unless I was at a site, I preferred to look professional. Monroe & Sons had been a fixture in my hometown of Green Valley, Tennessee, for over sixty years and we were still going strong. I took pride in my work, the company, and my family's reputation, and I liked to look the part.

I sipped my coffee and sighed. I felt weird without the tie. Then I felt weird about the second half of Lizzy's statement. "What did you mean by 'meet someone new?'" Leeann and I had been divorced longer than we were together. I had moved on a long time ago. I had met plenty of "new" women, none of whom I had introduced to my daughter, for various reasons.

She set her glass down and looked me in the eye. I braced myself; the last time she looked me in the eye like that was to inform me about college and the move to her mother's place. "It's obvious to me that you still love Mom. Maybe not full on *in love*, but you'd go back to her if she asked you to. Am I wrong?"

I hesitated before answering. Was she holding out hope? Because—no. Leeann and I were over in every way that could exist on this planet and every other planet in the universe. "It's more complicated than that," I carefully answered. "I will always have love for her, she's your mother. And for a long time, I did want to get our family back together—for you." Had I been lying to myself back then? Sure, I had wanted our family back for Lizzy, but I had also wanted it for myself. I didn't like the fact that I couldn't make my marriage work, and I still didn't.

I had dated off and on over the years, but nothing had ever stuck for more than a few months. No one had ever made me come close to the intense feelings I'd had when I was with Leeann. Was it because she was my first love? Or the fact we had a child together? I didn't know, and I never examined it too closely. I felt what I felt and left it at that. I had been content to raise our daughter and while I hadn't been deliberately waiting around for Leeann to come back for those first few years after our divorce, I hadn't *not* been waiting for her either. But those days were long over. Too much time had passed between us, and she'd moved on and on, and on again. She had just finished divorcing her fourth husband, so yeah, I was well beyond the days of pining over my lost marriage. It was over and it would stay over.

"Dad, you don't want to ever go back to her. Trust me."

I had always avoided speaking ill about Leeann in front of Lizzy, so I sidestepped her statement. "Don't worry about me. Tell me what happened."

She looked away, effectively shutting down the topic. I knew better than to push her, so I decided to let it drop—for the moment. "I don't want to talk about it now. We have to get to work. Do you think Uncle Garrett is really okay with me being his assistant?" This Monday would be Lizzy's first day on the job with the family, back where she belonged.

Two of my brothers and I worked for Monroe & Sons. My youngest brother, Garrett, had been a crew leader but was now training to take over. Everett, son number two, was our carpenter. Only one of us didn't join the company: Wyatt went to Nashville to play college football, then became a police officer. Now he was a deputy sheriff right here in town.

"Yes. Don't worry, sugar, it was his idea." My father had recently suffered a mild heart attack, which prompted a restructure of the company. Garrett had stepped up to take charge of the day-to-day decisions, while my father remained on board to guide his eventual transition to head of the business. Change was afoot, but it was all good things.

"I'm just nervous, is all," she muttered to the countertop. "My stomach has been in knots all morning. I even threw up."

I tipped her chin up. "Hey, it's going to be fine. I promise you."

"I know, I know, you're right and I'm being silly. It's just Uncle G. Not like a real boss. I mean, he is a real boss, and I'm going to do my best, for sure. But most bosses never gave you piggyback rides when you were a toddler." She pulled away with a sideways smile. "But still, let's hurry and get out of here before I chicken out and get back in bed to hide." She opened the door leading to the garage and pushed the clicker to open it. Immediately we heard a ruckus coming from the house next door.

"What in the world . . .?" I mumbled as I grabbed my things to head outside.

"Our new neighbors," Lizzy answered with a laugh. "Good morning, y'all! Hey, Sadie!" she shouted.

Sadie and I were old acquaintances from high school. Now she was my co-worker, her sister, Willa, was married to my brother, Everett, and this was the first Monday with Sadie as my neighbor. She'd moved in over the weekend with her sister and her twin sons. Fate kept slamming us together for some reason. Probably because I thought she was gorgeous and funny and smart and a brilliant interior designer. And due to my admiration of her many magical qualities, I continuously made an ass of myself around her. The smooth moves I'd enjoyed in my youth seemed to have disappeared after my divorce.

"Mornin', doll," Sadie hollered back, stopping to wave at Lizzy. "Rider, quit hitting your brother! Get in the van. We're running late." I stepped onto the driveway to see that Rider had not listened. Currently he was running laps around the van, laughing as he hit his brother's outstretched palm on every pass. Flynn was currently buckled in, backpack on his lap, ready to go. I knew the boys were in second grade. I also knew they'd gone a bit wild after their father had left the family a few months back. Sadie had her hands full with these two.

"Morning, Sadie. Hey boys," I greeted them over the top of my truck as I opened the back door to stow my briefcase.

"Barrett, hey," she gasped. Her breath floated like a cloud over the brisk morning air behind her as she chased after Rider. She wore pink and white polka dotted pajamas and a hoodie. Her wet blond hair flopped around in a ponytail on top of her head, while her slippers slapped angrily over the pavement of her driveway. Rider was fast. She was too, but she was nowhere near catching him. "Dang it, Rider," she yelled. "We don't have time for this today!"

"You look different," I said without thinking. I'd never seen her like this; she was always immaculately put together. Whether in office attire or casual in jeans, she was always a stunner. I found myself staring. She was on a whole other level of beautiful right now, incandescent in the early morning light with her fresh face, pink cheeks, and her wet blond ponytail flying behind her as she attempted to catch Rider.

"Dad—" Lizzy hissed.

"Really, Barrett. Are you being serious right now?" Sadie stopped to glare at me. I winced when her hands hit her hips. I'd said the wrong thing again.

"Uh—" It hadn't been an insult, but I couldn't exactly tell her how lovely I thought she looked when she was so clearly frustrated. Timing was everything and right now was terrible, for obvious reasons. "Let us help you. Lizzy, come on."

"On it." We crossed the strip of dirt that divided our two driveways, then split up to corral Rider toward his mother.

"What are you up to, Rider?" I held my hand out for a high five of my own.

He smacked it as he ran past me. "I'm running off my excess energy like my teacher makes me do sometimes. I'm thinking of jumping around next. What are you up to?"

"Trying to get another boring day started. Are you ready for school?"

"Nope." He dodged a laughing Lizzy then giggled as Sadie made a grab for him and missed. "This is fun!"

"I'm going to take the PlayStation away!" Sadie hollered.

"Hey, no fair!" Flynn shouted from the inside of Sadie's minivan before getting out to glare at his mother. "I play it too and I'm being good."

"*Gah!*" She flung her hands in the air. "I can't take this anymore. Herding cats would be easier!"

"Freeze!" I boomed. Everyone froze and stared at me. Dogs stopped barking. Birds ceased their chirps. The entire street was now quiet.

"Jeez, Barrett, your dad voice is impressive." Sadie briefly quit being irked and grinned at me. "Thank you."

"Do it again." Rider said in an awed voice.

I shot Sadie a quick grin before addressing Rider. "Maybe later." I held my hands out for our secret handshake. I had taught all the kids in the family the secret handshake my brothers and I used to do together as children. I knew Sadie's boys well. Ever since my brother Everett had married her sister Willa, our families had been spending time together—holidays, barbeques, weddings, and random get-togethers. In fact, Sadie and her sisters were now part of my mother's group text. There was no escape for them now.

"Y'all two boys better watch out or he'll teach that trick to your mom," Lizzy said with a laugh.

Rider grinned up at me. "No way. Teach it to me, Barrett."

"I'm sorry, Momma." Flynn returned to his seat in the van with a pointed look at Rider.

With a shrug, Rider followed his brother into the van. "Let's blame it on the Pop-Tarts and leave the PlayStation alone. You said sugar for breakfast is a bad idea," he called out to Sadie.

"If you behave all the way to school then you have a deal."

"Deal." A tiny hand shot out of the window. Sadie shook it.

"Thanks, y'all." Sadie straightened her wet ponytail with a sheepish grin while a blush rose over her neck to color her cheeks red. "Mornings can get away from me sometimes," she confessed.

"No problem, Sadie. See you later." Lizzy darted back to my truck and got in.

"We'll see you at the office. Don't worry about being late. Take all the time you need," I offered.

She scowled at me, back to being irked. "Have I ever been late before?"

"No, that's not what I meant. I, uh—" What was it about her that attracted my foot to my mouth so much? At first, I'd thought it was her looks. She was so gorgeous it almost hurt to look at her and she knew it too. But not in a way that made her conceited; it was more like something she had to make peace with. I saw how people, especially men, sometimes reacted to her, like she wasn't even human. Ever since I'd first laid eyes on her, way back when we were kids, she'd always been the girl I would look at a little too long. It was never a crush, never about lust. She was too young for me back then and as kids, even a couple of years can make a world of difference. But she sure was beautiful. Now that I knew her a little bit, she had surpassed beautiful. She was stunning and so much more than a pretty face.

"I will see you at the office," she declared. "*On time.*" With a huff, she turned and got into her minivan. If it were possible for a vehicle to express anger, hers did it as she backed out of the driveway, leaving me standing there wondering if I would ever be able to say the right thing to her. Dejected, I got into the driver's seat.

"Dad, what was up with that?"

"I have no idea." I decided to be honest. "I can't seem to talk to her without making an ass of myself at some point in the conversation."

"You like her," Lizzy deduced, glancing at me out of the corner of her eye as she texted someone.

"Well, yeah, she's a great designer—so creative. She's beautiful, of course, but that's not all. She's smart too. I see her every day chatting with Garrett or with your grandpa and grandma at the office, but whenever I try to talk to her . . ." I turned, taking my eyes off the road for a second to catch Lizzy grinning knowingly at me.

"You *really* like her. I could tell by how you watched her chasing the boys around."

"Well, uh, sure—"

"Don't worry, it's all good. You don't have to say any more. I get where you're coming from."

"I don't see how it's possible, since I don't get where I'm coming from." I chuckled. "I'm just going to avoid her today so I don't piss her off any more than I already have."

"You do that. Great thinking." One quick look showed she was still texting. Good. The subject of Sadie and whatever my feelings were for her was better being dropped than being discussed with my teenage daughter.

As usual, confusion filled my thoughts as I contemplated the enigma that was Sadie Hill. She was sassy, smart, and always bold as brass. Her sheepish smile and blushing cheeks this morning coupled with her apparent vulnerability threw me for a loop. It intrigued me.

After a stop at Daisy's Nut House to pick up the weekly doughnut breakfast for the crew, I turned the corner onto Main Street. The Monroe & Sons office was in an old Victorian mansion set on a corner lot in downtown Green Valley. You couldn't miss it if you tried. The driveway and front yard had been converted into a parking lot years ago and the main entryway and parlor were now the waiting room and main office for the business.

Lizzy was hired to work the reception desk in the entrance, answering phones and greeting anyone who came in. Garrett and my father shared the office, but Garrett preferred to be on-site, so he was rarely there. My office was upstairs in what used to be a sitting room. Sadie worked in the dining room when she was here, but she was usually on a site with me or Garrett.

The rest of the house was just a regular home. I grew up here and my parents had continued living here up until my father's heart attack and partial retirement. Now, my brother Garrett and Molly, his new wife, were in the process of moving in. I could work at home, and sometimes did, but I preferred coming into the office.

It was less lonely that way.

I parked in the garage then turned to Lizzy. "You got this," I encouraged.

"I got this," she repeated with a nervous smile. "Thanks, Dad."

I would have ruffled her hair with my palm like I did when she was a little girl, but her hair was in a bun, and she was too grown up for that anyway. I sighed. Why did today have me thinking of each time I had ever dropped her off for the first day of school? Why was my heart constricting like I was letting her go again when I had just gotten her back? Maybe because she was eighteen and it was only a matter of time before I would lose her to the world. "I'm proud of you," I said, finally finding words again. "Let's go, sugar."

I got out of my truck in time to see Sadie pull up in her van. "See you inside," Lizzy grabbed the doughnuts and ran through the interior garage door, leaving me alone with Sadie.

A black spike-heeled shoe hit the driveway followed by a long, gorgeous leg encased in a pair of slim cut black trousers. My eyes traced her curves as she exited her van then turned to grab her things. I gulped as I tried to force my eyes to land on hers, rather than follow the enticing form of her body as she stood straight again. She wore a white pinstriped oxford blouse, a tangle of gold necklaces, pearls in her ears and she had styled her gorgeous blond hair in a high sexy bun. How had she turned into *this* in a matter of a half hour?

"Good morning," I stumbled over the words as I struggled to keep my eyes on hers. "I was about to fix myself some coffee in the kitchen before we go. Can I get you a cup?" Today was a Bandit Lake site workday. We usually drove up there together but today, I had my doubts. She had started the day off mad at me instead of it happening later in the afternoon like usual. I sighed.

Her eyes narrowed on mine. "You never offer to fix my coffee. And what's that in your hand, Barrett?" She pointed to my travel mug, and I gulped. *Shit.*

"I—I'm just trying to help," I stammered. "I mean, it looked like you had a tough morning—"

"I don't know what you're talking about. I'm *fine*. My morning was *fine*. I had coffee at home." Now she was outright glaring at me and probably fibbing because there was no way she had time to drink coffee, eat breakfast, then show up to work looking like a modern-day Marilyn Monroe bombshell.

"What about breakfast?"

"Don't. Just don't, Barrett. I can take care of myself. I've been doing it since I was a kid, okay? Let's get to work. Can we please just do that?"

"I didn't mean to infer that you couldn't take care of yourself—" I started.

"Work. Please. Now. The Bandit Lake site needs our attention. Meet me in the dining room after you *get your coffee*." She whirled and with a final glare at my travel mug marched to the front door and entered the house to gather our materials for the day.

"Smooth." My brother Garrett said from the interior garage door. "We've all been wondering what's been going on between the two of you. I guess I'm the first to actually witness it."

"I don't know what you're talking about," I grumbled.

"You never figured out how to read a room, Barrett. You're the guy people go to for help, to fix their problems, and you're great at that. You take care of everyone and it's been going on for so long that it's become your default reaction. Try listening for a change. You and Sadie aren't as opposite as you think."

"What is that supposed to mean?"

"Lizzy just told me about the driveway drama. How would you feel if someone offered you help after a hard morning when you were used to handling everything yourself? Think about your own pride. If you're going to offer to help her out, don't be so obvious about it." He chuckled before going back inside.

Huh. He may have a point.

CHAPTER 3

SADIE

The dining room at Monroe & Sons did double duty as my workspace and as a huge family dining room big enough to seat twenty. More could fit if folding chairs were added. And if what I had heard was true, Everett Monroe had built the gorgeously massive and intricately carved table for his mother at her behest —after taking a demolition hammer to the wall that separated this room from his father's study. It took the already big dining room to cavernous levels of huge and created a humorous bone of contention between his parents. After my sister had married his brother, me and my boys were often included in the family functions held here and it did a lot to explain the perfection that was Barrett Monroe.

His family was wonderful. He was blessed with two parents who adored each other. His three brothers were kind, sweet, and charming—and I'll just say it, hot as hell. Each one was tall, dark, and as handsome as could be. There was no way anyone in this family could take a turn to the dark side. They were all too good to be true, and that started at the top with his awesome mother and sweetheart of a dad. Bill and Becky Lee Monroe were parenting and relationship goals.

"Good morning, Sadie honey!" Becky Lee called out as she glided into the dining room with a huge smile aimed my way. She was all big, southern dyed blonde hair, perfectly made-up face, pearls, and pink pantsuit perfection. She was gorgeous, sweet, and fun. She was everything I had ever dreamed a mother could be when I was growing up and what I wanted to be for my boys.

"Morning," I returned as I gathered the materials Barrett and I would need today.

"How's that accursed house coming along?"

I laughed. The Bandit Lake site had been a thorn in Monroe & Sons' side for well over a year, even before I had started working for the company. "It's coming, slowly but surely. If the owners could ever manage to agree on something it would go much faster. That, and if stuff would just stop breaking. No matter what we do, something falls apart and we discover something new to fix."

"Those people." She winked at me. "Bless their hearts."

"Bless them all the way to infinity," I agreed.

"Uh-oh, who are we blessing?" Barrett strode into the room, sans coffee mug, and started helping me load up our things.

I managed to curtail the annoyed scowl that threatened to cover my face. Okay, it was one quarter annoyance and three quarters hunger and lack of coffee. I hadn't had time for breakfast, not if I wanted to show up looking hot . . . and like I hadn't actually needed his help this morning. Also, I was mad at myself for noticing his sexy forearms in his rolled-up shirt sleeves, damn it. And where was his tie? The top two buttons were undone, and it made me want to rip that shirt the rest of the way off. I grew flustered as I checked him out. He was extra hot today. Usually, he was buttoned-up-suit-and-tie hot. Today he was jump-him-in-the-supply-closet hot. Though, if I were being honest, I'd jump him in a suit too. *Freaking damn it.*

"Good morning, my sweet boy." Becky Lee greeted him with outstretched arms, hugs and kisses, and her sweet smiling face. And as usual, my heart felt it like a jab. He was so lucky to have a mother like her. "We're blessing the Sandersons and the nightmare they have wrought upon us up at Bandit Lake," she answered as she patted his cheeks with her French manicured fingers.

He chuckled. "It will get done and it will be perfect because I will make it so. Don't worry about a thing."

"Oh, I'm not worried about the two of you. I was there with your daddy yesterday and it's looking gorgeous. Sadie, we're lucky to have you working for us! You're so talented. You have an amazing eye for design. I just love your work up there."

My cheeks heated. "Thank you," I answered, at a loss for any other words. Until working for the Monroes, praise of this kind was foreign to me.

"I'll see y'all later, I'm meeting your daddy for breakfast." We said our goodbyes to Becky Lee. She left, taking the sunny vibe in the room with her.

"I'm ready when you are," I said, hefting my box of materials onto my hip and trying not to grunt at the effort.

"I'll take that. It looks heavier than usual," he offered.

"I've got it. Let's go." Why did he bring the stubborn out in me so much? I found nothing wrong with accepting help—except from Barrett.

He shrugged in answer and grabbed his small stack of boxes, rolled up blueprints, and his briefcase.

We crossed through the huge dining room into the foyer where Garrett stood at Lizzy's desk chatting with her. "Sadie! Let me get that." He took the box from my arms and shot Barrett a glare. "What's wrong with you, man?"

Barrett said not one word but the tightening in his jaw told the story.

Unfortunately, I was now officially past hungry and well into hangry territory, so I didn't say anything either lest it come out way bitchier than I would ever intentionally speak to anyone. I needed food and was beginning to worry about my temperament and the likelihood of me staying awake throughout the day.

Oh well. I'd made a bad choice; one more bad decision and I'd have the whole set.

We followed him to Barrett's truck, loaded up, and took off toward Bandit Lake. I watched as downtown Green Valley rolled by in the side view mirror as he drove. He switched on the radio to break the silence that filled the truck.

"Oh, you have to change the station. I can't listen to that."

"Why? I thought every woman in her thirties loved Adele. At least that's what Molly said the other night."

"Thanks for pointing out my age," I huffed. "And yeah, Adele is awesome. The problem is I always sing along, and I commit, Barrett. You don't want to hear that. If I could sing like her I would literally never shut up. You're lucky."

He switched it back off with a chuckle. "Whatever you want."

"Thanks."

The streets and buildings began to meld into one bright blur as the sun parted the clouds. It shone in my eyes, so I closed them against the glare with a sigh.

Would I ever not be tired?

I'd forgotten I had sleep instead of dinner last night. I hadn't been hungry when I'd fed the boys and after they went to bed, I crashed instead of fixing a meal for myself. Clara had been out, or I would have eaten with her.

I decided to keep my eyes shut for just one more minute because it felt so good. The sun was warm on my face and Barrett was a good driver. He knew how to stop and make turns without jolting me or making me slide around in my seat. Just one more thing he was perfect at. I sighed again and let my cheek rest against the window.

"We're here." His deep voice roused me.

I turned to focus on him but was still halfway stuck in wherever my thoughts had wandered off to as he drove. "What?"

"Wake up, sleepyhead, we're here." He passed me a Starbucks bag. "Eat this."

I took the bag without thinking. The breakfast fumes shooting out of it were glorious and I wanted to stuff whatever was inside into my face immediately. "What?" I repeated. I was confused straight out of my brain. My stomach growled and I scowled at the bag.

"Do you want me to whisper it in your ear?" His lips lifted in a teasing smile.

I rolled my eyes. "No, thanks." *Yes please . . .*

"I stopped and got you some breakfast. Your stomach started rumbling after you fell asleep."

"I didn't fall asleep," I argued before unwrapping and taking a huge bite of the breakfast sandwich he'd bought me. "I was resting my eyes." I covered my mouth with a hand as I spoke with my mouth full. It was rude, but winning an argument trumped manners every time in my opinion.

One of his big hands rested on the steering wheel while the other tapped on the console between us. Even his hands were beautiful—broad and strong. I bet he was good with his hands, which looked capable of doing great things. "Then who was snoring in my passenger seat if it wasn't you, silly?"

I tore my gaze away from his sexy hands to answer. I swallowed the bite and wrinkled my nose at him. I had never snored in my life. *Hmph.* "Well, that I do not know. But it wasn't me. I may have closed my eyes for a second, but I was awake the entire time. And I do not snore."

"I guess I must have been hearing things." He chuckled.

"Yeah, you should get that checked." But my heart wasn't in the argument, and I turned my focus back to my food and took another delicious bacon, egg, and cheesy bite. "Oh, my freaking gosh, I'm going to marry this sandwich after I divorce Stephen's stupid ass," I moaned. "I'll make you happy, sandwich, I swear." I took another bite and closed my eyes as I chewed.

He laughed and pointed to the cup holder. "I got you some coffee too. It's black, one sugar, splash of cream, correct?"

"Yeah, that's how I drink it." I took a careful sip. "This is perfect. Thanks." I turned to thank him properly. But I got stuck staring for a second at his beautiful dark, velvety brown eyes with their black spiky lashes, sumptuously arched brows, and adorable tiny crinkles at the corners. Damn it. "Seriously, thank you, Barrett."

"You're welcome. Is that coffee going to turn you into a bigamist? Or are you just going to secretly cheat on your breakfast sandwich?" he teased again, mouth quirking into an almost irresistible half-smile.

As long as I had this sandwich to love, I could resist him and his grins and his sexy hands and his rolled-up-shirtsleeves-and-perfectly muscled-forearms of my fantasies. At least, that's what I was trying to convince myself of.

"I might just cheat on it." I smirked. "I'm pretty sure the sandwich is my one true love." *Other than this house. Could one fall in love with a place?*

He laughed and opened his door. "We should get to work. This wretched house isn't going to finish itself." When we first started here, it was falling apart—a total disaster. We had come a long way.

Despite the trouble this place was causing the company, I loved it. Set on eight acres, this Georgian style home was the biggest I'd ever seen up close, almost big enough to be a mansion. It was three sprawling stories tall including the attic, with a gorgeous brick wraparound porch, stately columns spaced evenly along the front, and urns which I had planted liberally with ivy, begonias, petunias, and dahlias. It was painted a white stark enough to make it glow against the deep evergreen of the trees that filled the acreage around it. My suggestion to add some color to the doors and shutters had been accepted and they were now stained a deep hunter green to match the trees.

Aside from its astonishing beauty, Bandit Lake was a special place. You couldn't buy property here; you had to inherit it or, if you were lucky, find a place to rent in order to live here. It was also one of the cleanest lakes in the country. As part of the Great Smoky National Park, it was environmentally protected.

"Is the kitchen on the agenda for today?" I bagged up my food and went around to the back of the truck to gather my things, balancing the bag and cup of coffee on top.

"The kitchen from hell, you mean." He smirked as he grabbed the heavy box Garrett had given him crap about with a pointed look. I rolled my eyes in response.

"You and your mother, I swear. This house isn't cursed. It just needs some extra love. She has good bones, Barrett." He went ahead of me to unlock the door.

"She's a harpy, hell bent on destroying the company and my sanity," he shouted over his shoulder. "I mean, I don't know what my father and Garrett are thinking by sending us out here all the time. We're working on things that don't make sense for us anymore—"

"You mean, the great and powerful Barrett Monroe, heir to the Monroe & Sons dynasty of illustriously brilliant contractors is going to let a simple little lake house beat him?" My heels clicked over the newly installed slate tile of the entryway as I followed him inside. I stopped, dismayed when I spied a tile with a crack in it. It hadn't been cracked when we were here a few days ago, dang it. "There's another crack in the floor, Barrett!" I set my stuff down on a custom-built console table by the front door so I could get a closer look at the tile.

"Are you kidding me?" he shouted from the kitchen.

He entered the room, following my pointed finger to the busted floor tile. "I'm serious. Look for yourself. I inspected the floor before we last left, and it was perfect. Maybe your mother is right, and this place is cursed. Or maybe it's ghosts! Or even aliens. Molly said—"

"It's not ghosts or aliens. And please don't listen to Molly and her theories." Molly, Garrett's wife, and one of my life-long friends, often let her imagination get the best of her, much to everyone's amusement.

"You don't know that. No one can know for sure. The universe is a wide and vast place, Barrett. Oh! Remember what happened to the dock last week? Now *that* could have been aliens. I was watching *Ancient Aliens* with Molly the other day and it turns out that aliens like large bodies of water. We need to be careful out here, maybe we should invest in some security cameras—"

"Sadie. Seriously? It wasn't aliens. There are no aliens in Bandit Lake. Wyatt or Beau Winston or Hank Weller or one of the many people who go fishing out there would have caught one by now if there were."

"Fine. You might have a point about aliens." I answered. "But this place is at least jinxed by something. It's hexed or it's cursed, just like your mother says. We should smudge it with sage next time we're here and chase out the bad vibes."

"If we tried that, it would probably catch the damn place on fire," he muttered under his breath.

"Ha! See?"

"What's going on with you today, anyway? Are you okay? It's almost like you're inventing things to argue about. When we got here you were all about the good bones of this place and giving it extra love."

Heck yes, I was inventing things to argue about. It was either fight or flirt. Argue or jump his sexy bones. He brought me breakfast and coffee. He was being too sweet for my own dang good. I needed him to act like a hard-nosed jerk, like the perfectionist butthead he could sometimes be. But nooo, lately he'd been adorable and sweet and when his foot went into his mouth it was funny and cute instead of annoying. Damn it.

"Okay. Then what in the world is going on here? You tell me." His lips flattened and he looked away without answering.

"Weird shit, Barrett." I pointed at him. "That's what's going on here. Every week it's something strange and random, believable as accidents or whatever. But the cracked tiles seem deliberate, Barrett. And what about that broken window last week? I do not believe for one minute that the branch we found on the floor caused it."

Skeptical eyes returned to mine. "It's probably a bunch of punk kids, pulling pranks and causing trouble. It happens all the time on construction sites. I'd believe that over aliens or ghosts. I'll tell Garrett to call the sheriff's department. He can handle it."

Now I was the one to look away. "Fine, be logical. Bo-ring!" He chuckled in response.

I wouldn't admit it to him, but every time I hung out with Molly, it took a solid week to get aliens out of my head. I let the subject drop. A good argument with him was always interesting, but I preferred the kind I could win.

"There is no sense taking someone off a crew. I can replace one tile by myself." I headed to the covered stack of tiles in the corner. We had ordered extra supplies of almost everything due to the bad luck we'd been having here and stuff was piled up everywhere.

I stood on tiptoe, reaching for a tile from the top. "Crap!" I lost my balance, laying a hand on the middle of the stack to steady myself. The tile tower wobbled, and a few slid off the top to crash on the floor. "*Ahhhh!*"

"I got you!" Suddenly I was no longer wobbling on my high heels in front of a precariously piled up stack of slate tiles; I was in Barrett's arms halfway across the room instead. My jaw dropped when the entire tower of tiles collapsed to the floor with a huge cracking slam.

"Oh my god! You just saved my entire life." Startled, I wrapped my arms around his neck and held on.

His chest heaved and his eyes were huge on mine. He blinked, once, twice. "That was too close," he finally said.

"Yeah, stupid alien booby traps," I cracked.

Laughter burst forth and he hugged me tighter into his body rather than set me down. I wasn't mad about it. In fact, I could stay here all day.

"Well." He cleared his throat.

"Yeah . . ." I whispered. My body tingled in awareness of his.

"I should, uh probably put you down." Instead of doing that, he shifted me higher up his chest, tilting my body such that I was plastered against his wide chest. At six feet tall, I was no lightweight. The fact that he held me so effortlessly was a major turn on.

"I guess so." His eyes were on mine and our lips were so close together if I puckered up, I'd be kissing him. I was so tempted to close that little inch that separated us, but I didn't.

In fact, we were also close enough that when his eyes dropped to half-mast and his cheeks flushed a light shade of pink, it made me wonder if he'd had this reaction to me every time he turned away during one of our bickerfests—because I sure did. I inhaled a deep sigh, silently willing him to kiss me. There was no way I would do it first.

But he shook himself out of our mutual lust trance and let me slide down his body. The second my feet hit the floor, he turned away with another nervous cough. "Take a break. Finish up your breakfast. I'm going to head into the kitchen and get started."

"Okay . . ." I breathed as I stood on my now weak knees watching him walk away. That was a close one. I couldn't help but wonder if I should have kissed him.

CHAPTER 4

SADIE

Things had thawed between us after that fateful day at Bandit Lake.

The first few weeks in the new house breezed by in a blur of hectic morning school runs where sweet Lizzy made it a point to help me load up my boys every day and Barrett annoyingly and awesomely started bringing me coffee in a travel mug—which I both resented and appreciated. I couldn't help but feel it crossed a professional line. But since we were neighbors, I let it slide and added finding the time to meal-prep something for breakfast to share with them to my ever-growing to-do list of things I would most likely never have time to actually do.

But evenings here were the worst.

My kitchen window had become both the bane of my existence and my secret shame.

Each evening at precisely six-thirty, no matter how hard I tried to avoid it, I found myself right here at the sink doing the dinner dishes by hand. Forget about the freaking brand-new dishwasher Clara had bought us. I needed to take my time.

I never thought I'd be the type to peep on a neighbor. I also never imagined I'd have a neighbor as good-looking as Barrett Monroe. But worse, he wasn't only my neighbor, as my co-worker this pervy peeping I was doing probably violated some sort of sexual harassment law. I knew I was really the one crossing a line, not Barrett with his delicious morning coffee.

As an architect and project leader for Monroe & Sons, detail oriented was the kindest way to describe him. Precise, inflexible, and kinda rigid were the not-so-nice ways. But at home, the qualities that sometimes annoyed the crap out of me at work, worked for me.

I'd been here long enough now to have learned a few of Barrett's routines. In a close second place was his shirtless Saturday afternoon truck washing session in his driveway. No matter how cold it got, there he would be cleaning that dang truck. But my favorite was his evening jog. If I was late by even a minute, I would miss his glorious evening warm up around our cul-de-sac which was always followed by a quick stretch on the sidewalk in front of my house. Don't even get me started on his butt when he bent forward to stretch his delicious hamstrings. I had tried and failed to quit my peeping tomfoolery, but I feared I was now irrevocably addicted to that booty, and, dang it, I hadn't been this aware of my kitchen sink in . . . well, ever.

To keep it real, as a teenager, I used to have an on and off, hero worship type of crush on him. He was a senior when I entered Green Valley High as a freshman and believe me, I wasn't the only girl with a crush on the beautiful Barrett Monroe. But in recent months the crush had come back, and it had intensified.

We worked together so I had decided in my own wishy-washy way that it was imperative that I fight it. He could never know how much I admired—okay, lusted after—him. But somehow, despite my best intentions, our interactions had morphed into that strange bicker-flirting work relationship that I knew for a fact neither one of us understood. He got my goat but good, I was almost always flustered and kind of angry around him.

Basically, I wanted what I couldn't have, and it pissed me off.

I liked working for Monroe & Sons and I wanted to keep my job, and I had kids to raise. Plus, how often was a person lucky enough to find a job they not only liked, but were also appreciated and respected at? I needed that in my life. Respect was something I'd never had growing up and it was addicting.

"Bless his heart because the good lord up above sure did bless him everywhere else. Look at that ass. Just look at it."

I jumped about a foot, letting the blinds crash to the windowsill. "Dang it, Clara. You scared the crap out of me." My pushy younger sister couldn't keep her mouth shut about my newly rekindled Barrett crush.

"Better to be startled by me than by him. Although, it would be entertaining to watch you blush to death when he finally owns the fact that he wants you to watch him jog around the block and busts your pervy peeping ass. It is not a coincidence that he stretches every day right there." Her hand flung out, gesturing in amusement to the window.

"Hush. He has no idea I watch him, and he won't. The bushes block his view," I hissed. "Talk quietly or the boys will hear you."

"Okay," she whispered. "Is this better?"

I rolled my eyes. "Yeah, it is. Thank you very much."

"You're welcome very much. I think you should go outside. Be out there when he jogs back this way and flirt your ass off. I'll watch the boys for you."

"No way! Are you nuts?"

"Of course I am. But that's not the point."

"I'm not even divorced yet."

"Only because you can't find your dumbass husband to have him served with papers."

"We work together."

"They don't have rules against that at Monroe & Sons."

"How do you even know that?"

"I asked Everett."

"Fine. Maybe I don't want people thinking I slept my way into my job."

"Since when do you give a shit what people think about you?"

I huffed out an annoyed sigh. "I don't."

"Then what are you waiting for? Barrett is husband number two. Go get your man."

"We both know I'm a hot mess and he is utter perfection. We're total opposites."

"He is no such thing. Yeah, you hero worshipped him in high school, but he's just a man, Sadie. He's more than whatever fantasy you've built of him in your mind, and he has problems like we all do. The fact that he's divorced proves it."

"I guess so. But marriage? I can't picture myself ever getting married again."

"Oh yeah? What would it take to get you down the aisle again?"

"A blue moon and a big ass diamond?" I joked.

She rolled her eyes. "Don't be stubborn and don't be blind. That's all I'm going to say, you big poop."

"Momma!" Flynn and Rider were currently playing video games in the living room. "Flynn won't let me have a turn!" Rider shouted.

"We're not done with this," she insisted. "Come here you two." Clara dashed to the pantry, unearthing a soccer ball still in its package. "Auntie Clara got you a present today."

Present was the magic word. When they heard it, they came running. Hence the reason why I couldn't seem to stop bribing them to do stuff. I tried to rationalize it by telling myself I wouldn't get up and go to work for free, but I wasn't quite a believer in that line of logic.

"Can we play?" They barreled into the kitchen and excited energy filled the room the second they saw the ball.

"That's why I called you in here," she answered with a grin. "Let's go."

I held my hands out in protest. "What are you doing? It's almost bath time."

"This is a better idea." She grinned at the boys, then turned to whisper in my ear. "It will wear them out and we might run into Barrett the normal way instead of you being served with a restraining order for stalking and spying on him through the window like a sad little creeper."

"*Hmph*," I snorted and pulled away. "I'm not going outside like this." I gestured to myself. Pink cut-off sweatpants, black baby T-shirt with "Genie's Country Western Bar" printed across the boobs, and a messy ponytail. "No way." I mean, I had standards to uphold, and he'd already caught me in my pajamas several times.

"Oh, you're fine. Get your shoes and a hoodie. Come on boys."

They looked up at me expectantly with their beautiful big blue eyes that always triggered my mom guilt and made it hard to say no to them. "Please, Momma," Rider asked with a studiously perfected hangdog look.

I glanced at the clock above the stove in consideration. If Barrett kept to his schedule—and he always did—I had thirty minutes before he'd be back home. It was plenty of time to play with the boys and get back inside. "Okay, fine. A few minutes outside, bath time, then bed. Got it?" I held my hands out for a double high five. A high ten? We smacked palms then headed to the front door. "Hats, hoodies, socks, shoes. Move it, move it!" I clapped my hands as I spoke, making them laugh as they got ready.

Moving in here with Clara had been the best decision I had made in years. I smiled at her as we herded the boys out the front door. She grinned back and tossed me the ball. Each day spent here was like a balm to my soul.

"Kick it to me, Momma," Rider shouted as he jumped up and down in front of Barrett's driveway. I obliged, sending the ball straight to him. "Ooh! Good kick!"

"Your momma has skills, boys. Better watch out!" Clara shouted. Rider laughed and kicked it back. I dribbled the ball between my feet before kicking it to Flynn. "She used to play soccer in the Green Valley Junior Soccer League just like you, Rider," she added.

"Really?" He was impressed. "That's awesome!" There was only a boys' team back then, but my mother had raised such a colossal fuss that they had to let me join.

"Yep, I sure did. I was a bit older than you, though." Clara and I exchanged sad glances. I had played for years and would have kept right on playing, but my daddy left us the next year, Clara and I had gone a bit wild after that, and our momma hadn't been willing to drive me to practice after he left anyway. She was too busy raising us "good-for-nothing Hill offspring," she'd said. Momma had a way with words that could cut you like a knife.

"Can you do this?" He took the ball and bounced it off his head, passing it to me. I dribbled it then kicked it high to bounce it back to him, laughing when my ponytail flopped to the side. "You're funner here, Mommy!" He grinned with delight then kicked it to Flynn who quietly passed it to Clara.

"Thanks, bud." The unintentional back-handed compliment both hurt and healed. I had been miserable at my mother's place and my boys knew it. Before we'd moved in with her, I had warned her about treating them right. But when she actually did, it hurt because her love had never been given to me the way she unreservedly gave it to my boys.

Flynn was taking his father's absence harder than Rider. Or maybe he was just more expressive. Every time I tried talking to them about it, they shut down, each trying to process it in their own way. I was ashamed to say that, for me, his leaving was a relief.

Stephen and I were not a love match, even though I was sure when I first met him that I had found rainbows and butterflies, hearts-and-flowers-true-love when we first got together back in high school—coincidentally, not long after my father had left. Upon retrospect, it was obvious I had been looking for love in all the wrong places. And he had been looking for a convenient piece of ass with low self-esteem who would do anything for him. Luckily, I was no longer that girl. That girl had died during my pregnancy with the boys when I'd discovered he was a jerkface cheat and a big dumb liar. Whether he had cheated on me during the years we'd spent together before the boys, I did not know.

"What's a blue moon?" Rider asked.

"Uh, you say that when you're talking about something rare or that hardly ever happens, and how much did you hear?"

"Not a lot. Blue moons sound neat."

"Hey, Barrett!" Clara shouted, wrenching me out of the storm cloud of bad memories and useless speculation I was about to get lost in.

"Barrett!" the boys shouted. "Play with us!"

I spun on my heel then checked my watch. He was early; he'd only been gone about fifteen minutes. "What's wrong? Did something happen to you?" I asked without thinking, then froze. *Damn it.*

His dark eyes met mine and he grinned knowingly. "I got a cramp in my side." He inhaled a deep sigh, his broad chest expanded on the intake, and it was all I could do not to gawk at him—muscles . . . so many muscles. He addressed the boys. "I'll join you next time. I kinda hurt myself tonight."

I could see his abs through his shirt, for the love of heck—but I managed to force my eyes into submission and snapped them back to his. "Oh, that's too bad," I breathed, at a loss for words.

"Yeah, I like to get at least thirty minutes in." He raised his hands over his head in a stretch. I almost died at the sight of the strong corded muscles of his neck as he tipped his head back. And that jawline? It was absolute perfection, sharply defined and covered with the perfect amount of dark stubble, exactly how I liked it.

My eyes, of their own accord, drifted lower as his shirt lifted ever so slightly baring a sliver of his defined stomach. Then it became a battle between my eyeballs and my brain. I needed to avert the traitorous orbs but before I could, I caught a glimpse of the happy trail leading down to the bulgy good stuff.

I inhaled my own deep breath as I gave up and allowed my gaze to go on a journey over his hot-as-hell form. Six-foot-four inches of Barrett Monroe were taking my eyes on a trip, and I was in danger of embarrassing myself at the sight.

"Boys, bath time. Come on inside." Clara took the ball from Flynn, tossed it to me, then led the boys inside the house.

"What—?" She couldn't have planned Barrett's side cramp. But she sure as heck planned the rest, leaving me out here alone with him like this. I scowled and clutched the ball to my chest instead of hurling it at her retreating back. I glanced sheepishly back at Barrett.

His grin had softened to a small smile. "I'm going to say this again, and hope-fully it will come out better than that first Monday morning here in the driveway. You look different."

"Yeah? Well, I don't wear heels and makeup at home, Barrett. I'm a freelance hot mom and I make my own hours." I couldn't help but crack a defensive joke as I grumbled and adjusted my ponytail with one hand. "I don't have time to get dolled up every time I go outside—"

"It wasn't an insult, Sadie. You're adorable right now, stunning in an entirely different way." His eyes softened on mine, just like his smile had.

I found myself fighting a big dopey grin that was threatening to pop out and give my crush away. "Oh. Okay then. Well, thank you." Unfortunately, I couldn't control the red flush that rose over my cheeks or his knowing reaction to it.

He backed up a few steps, gesturing to the ball. "I'm feeling better. Show me what you got, stunner."

"Stunner?" I allowed a small smile to cross my face. It was a non-flirty, totally neutral smile. *Yeah, you keep telling yourself that, dummy.*

His lips quirked sideways in a grin as he nodded. "Every time I get to see a different side of you, it stuns me." He gestured to his heart and made the cutest mock-surprised face I'd ever seen in my life.

Instead of keeling over dead from being stunned myself and the resulting sudden heart palpitations, I spun the ball on my finger, let it go, then kicked it to him. He passed it back with a knee and my small smile turned huge. Barrett had skills too. "I used to coach Lizzy's soccer team when she was little," he informed me.

"That's right. They finally let the girls have their own team in the league."

"Sure did. I had to yell at a few people on the city council and threaten to unleash my mother on them, but it was worth it."

"Lizzy is lucky to have you, Barrett."

"I try."

A brief burst of melancholy clouded my thoughts. I wished my own father had tried instead of leaving us. I shook it off and smiled at him. His return grin hit me in the heart, and I decided to keep my eye on the ball and not in the past.

We continued passing the ball between us, up and down and around the cul-de-sac, laughing like kids the entire time. I'd never had this kind of fun with anyone aside from my sisters and my boys and I loved it. I didn't think it was possible for a man to be this way with me. In other words, most men usually hit on me, ogled my ample chest, got up into my space, and generally propositioned me to do unspeakable things with them. Very few had ever seen me as a human. I know, I know—not all men, *blah blah blah*—but my lifelong experience had taught me otherwise. I was an early bloomer and a natural blond, and I'd been in a D-cup since age twelve. I was scarred for life.

We came to a stop, grinning and laughing together in Barrett's driveway. He bent, picked up the ball, and handed it to me. Our fingers brushed and I shivered. Our eyes met and I found my body swaying toward his. He reached out and ran a fingertip down my forearm then took the ball back to let it drop to the grass on his side of the driveway.

Anticipation flooded my veins, but for what, I did not yet know. We had never been able to say the right thing to each other before tonight. Funny how saying almost nothing at all had caused something indefinable to shift between us as we stood there staring at each other in the amber tinged glow of the early evening sunset.

"I had fun with you." His voice was warm, his eyes were hot, and I was about to lose control of my crush and jump him as my feelings burned an out-of-control trail through my body.

This man drove me insane and had been doing it for years. "Me too. I mean, with you," I murmured.

"Good." His face lowered a millimeter closer to mine and I swayed a half an inch nearer to his big, gorgeous body, tilting my head back, the better to gaze into his magnetic chocolate brown eyes.

My lips parted, exhaling in amazed desire at his proximity, at this second chance at a possibility that I couldn't help but covet. Since our Bandit Lake near-kiss I'd been thinking about what I would do if presented with another opportunity and had come to the conclusion I should go for it. His eyes darted from mine, dropping to my mouth at the movement while a slow sexy smile ghosted across his face.

Kiss me.

The crazy thing was, I could almost feel it. Ever since I'd first laid eyes on him way back in high school, I'd imagined how it would be. I'd thought about it so much over the years that I could almost swear it was a memory instead of a fantasy—almost.

I was desperate to know what he felt like. I ran a hand up his chest. He brushed an errant curl from my forehead, letting the back of his hand trail down my cheek to rest gently on the side of my neck.

This is it.

Soft lips met my forehead, my temple, my cheek. I whimpered as his hand slid to the nape of my neck, pulling me infinitesimally closer to his body. My breasts brushed lightly against his hard chest, and he groaned softly like a whisper over the evening breeze.

We jumped apart at the sound of a car horn. Then turned in unison to watch as it pulled up next to us at the curb. An oddly nondescript man got out and approached us. "Sadie Lynn Hill-Daniels?" he addressed me.

Barrett stepped in front of me, quicker to come out of our—whatever we were doing—than I was. "Who wants to know?" he demanded.

The man smirked. "Here you go, *Mrs.* Daniels. You've been served." With a reach around Barrett, he handed me a manila envelope then turned on his heel to leave.

My heart sank in dread as I studied the envelope, almost too afraid to open it because deep down I knew what it was.

"Whatever is in there, you're going to be okay, Sadie," Barrett soothed.

I looked up at him with a slight nod. I would always be okay. I might get shaken up along the way, but I had never let anything keep me down for long. "I know," I whispered as I tore it open.

Divorce papers. I'd expected that. Heck, I *wanted* a divorce. I had wanted one for years, and this would make it easier. What I didn't want was any trouble from Stephen and as I scanned the document, I knew I was about to get some. It was the petition for joint custody of the boys that made my vision blur and turn white around the edges. "No . . ." Everything I'd ever done since getting pregnant was for them.

Everything.

I couldn't lose them—not for a holiday, not a weekend, not for a day, not even for a second. The thought was unfathomable. It was why I had put up with so much crap from Stephen over all these years.

"What is it?" I was in a momentary panic, so with no thought, I handed Barrett the papers. "Shit," he ground out. "You need an attorney. I'll call my father's first thing in the morning for recommendations."

"I—" *I can't afford an attorney.* A dusty old pickup pulled into the place the process server had just vacated. "Shoot. It's my mother." Thus proving when it rained, it poured, because what in the heck was she doing here?

She came barreling out of the truck headed in my direction. "A man showed up at the house looking for you. Pretty sure he was a process server. You need to hide until I can get you an attorney. Or am I too late?"

"Too late."

"Damn it, Sadie Lynn, I told you not to marry that horse's ass. And staying married to him after the miscarriage was just as foolish as getting pregnant in high school in the first damn place. Now what are you going to do?" I slammed my eyes shut. My will to defend myself against her words had been temporarily shaken by the envelope I held in my hand.

I had gotten pregnant and married Stephen during my senior year. It was not the proudest or smartest moment of my life, but it was what it was, and I had tried to make the best of it. I lost the baby and a few years later had Flynn and Rider, thereby disappointing my mother even more. However, she had managed to separate Flynn and Rider from my choices and loved them unreservedly with whatever was left in her shriveled-up heart, and the boys adored her right back. She was a different person around them and it both broke and touched my heart in equal measure.

Why couldn't my sisters and I have had that with her?

"Hey now," Barrett interjected in a voice dark with warning. He stepped close and slipped his arm around my shoulders in a protective gesture so foreign to me, I almost burst into tears at the feel of it. "Do not speak to her like that." Startled, my eyes shot up to meet his. He offered a reassuring smile.

I found myself relaxing against him, which was a shock, seeing as how my usual response to being in my mother's presence was to either shut down completely or get into a screaming match with her.

Momma suddenly seemed startled to see him as if her angry focus had been so intent on me, she'd overlooked him. "I'm just upset. Sadie knows I don't mean it." I glared at Momma, and she glared right back at me, both knowing she meant every word alongside a thousand more she wouldn't dare say now that she noticed Barrett was standing at my side.

"Maybe you should go home, Mrs. Hill. I'll take care of Sadie."

Her lips pursed in disgust as she looked us over. "I'll just bet you will." The assumptions she had just made about me and Barrett were written clear as day on her face. "Sadie, we'll talk about this some more at the farm. I expect to see you there with your sisters for dinner as usual." She spun, stormed off into her truck, and drove away.

After finally making it out of my stunned and horrified reverie, I looked around the street for witnesses. "Oh god, how loud was she? Did anyone hear? I am too mortified to judge correctly," I asked without meeting his eyes.

"Nobody heard, and if they did, they know better than to say anything," he ground out. "I actually—"

"Don't, please. I don't want to talk about this. I realize Everett probably told you a bunch of stuff. But Willa and I are different and I—"

"We don't have to talk about it. We don't ever have to talk about anything you don't want to." His earnest voice was a comfort.

"Thank you." His brother Everett was married to my sister Willa, and I knew for a fact Everett knew all about how horrible our mother was. "I—I have to go, it's the boys bedtime. I'll see you at work tomorrow. Thanks for, uh, the game and for . . ." I shook my head and gestured down the street to where my mother had driven off. The words to thank him for standing up for me were stuck in the back of my throat along with a lump that meant I was about to cry. I needed to get inside before this situation got any worse and he saw me break down.

No one was allowed to see that.

"Anytime, Sadie. Say the word and I'm there. Anytime at all." The stubborn tilt of his head told me he meant it. That, along with the look in his eyes—soft and sympathetic—also told me there had been a seismic shift in the way he now perceived me.

My feelings got the best of me and I reached out and squeezed his hand before grabbing the ball to head into the garage to close it and lock up for the night. My mood was sinking almost as fast as the sun in the sky. It was going to be a long night.

CHAPTER 5

BARRETT

Divorce papers and a petition for custody meant her ex was back in town, most likely to stay. I had no idea what had occurred during their marriage other than what I had gleaned from town gossip over the years, and none of what I'd ever heard was good. Much like when I knew him in school, Stephen was a philandering jackass.

After watching a defeated Sadie walk alone into her garage last night, I went back to my place. It was too soon to insert myself into her business directly, but that didn't mean I would keep out of it entirely.

And our almost-kiss? I shoved it out of my mind. I had to, or it would have tormented me all night just like the first one had.

Her ex and I had been in the same graduating class at Green Valley High and I'd never liked him. Stephen had been bad news from day one in kindergarten and had remained an asshole all throughout our time in school. He had always treated his girlfriends like property and I had no respect for a narcissistic man like that. There was no way I'd let Sadie deal with him on her own. Taking care of problems—and people—was what I was good at. The worry I held about saying the wrong thing to her started to dissipate as I considered how I could help her rather than what I would say to her.

"Lizzy, you ready to go?" I shouted as I finished preparing travel mugs of coffee for me and Sadie.

She slid onto a barstool with a grimace. "Morning." I grinned and slid a glass of orange juice and some toast across the counter to a harried looking Lizzy. "I'm running late. *Ugh*," she shoved the orange juice away. "I can't drink that. My stomach hurts."

"Still nervous about work?" I questioned.

Her eyes darted to the counter before meeting mine again. "Yeah, I'll be okay though. She smiled when she spotted the second travel mug. "Still making coffee for Sadie? I approve. And the street soccer last night? Niiicceee! Though, I would like to eventually try my hand at meddling so maybe dial it down a notch." I couldn't help but think she was deflecting.

"Are you sure you're okay?"

"Yeah, Dad. Hey, what will I tell Grandma if you land Sadie all on your own?"

My mother was a notorious matchmaker. I decided against telling Lizzy about her previous efforts to get me closer to Sadie.

"Don't go getting ideas from her," I warned. "I'm just being neighborly."

"No worries, I got sixty percent of my ideas all on my own. But the rest are from Grandma, so watch out."

"Great," I grumbled. The writing was on the wall. My mother had taken credit for all three of my brother's marriages and I was the only single one left. I let out a huge sigh and shoved the last half piece of toast into my mouth as I contemplated gentle ways to get her and Lizzy to butt out.

I headed outside. My heart skipped an involuntary beat when Sadie's garage door went up. She waved to me, smiling when she caught sight of the two travel mugs sitting on the hood of my truck. "You shouldn't keep spoiling me this way, but I can't help but be glad that you do." After crossing the sad little dirt patch, she grabbed her coffee from the hood. She took a sip and sighed. "This is perfect, thank you."

"Anytime," I answered, reiterating my promise from the night before. Her eyes darted to mine, lips parting on an exhale as she gave a slight nod. Her eyes dropped to my mouth before she forcefully turned away from me. She felt it too.

A black Cadillac SUV pulled up to the curb in front of Sadie's house. "Great, now what?" Stephen got out and headed our way, brandishing a legal sized manila envelope like a weapon pointed in her direction. Sadie took a few rapid steps back almost bumping into the wall near the garage door as she fled.

"Sadie, honey, I need to talk to you." She shook her head, eyes wide with alarm. That was all I needed to see. I stepped in front of her and with a lurch forward, she took my hand and held it in a death grip.

Stephen heaved out a sigh. "Fine, we'll do this here. Look, all I want to do is make this easy for you. These are signed—all you have to do is add your signature and you'll be free of me. I'm sorry for what I did. The way I left was terrible, it was weak . . . I was scared to face you and the boys, and I have no other excuse. But I'm back on my feet now and I want to make things right between me, you, and our boys. There's a check in this envelope that will hopefully make it up to you a little bit." I didn't believe for one second that he was capable of making anything easier for anyone other than himself.

Her hand dropped mine and reached out for the papers, but I snatched them before she could grab hold. "She's not signing anything without an attorney looking at it first. You should leave."

He glared at me. "I don't see how this is any of your business, Barrett."

"And I don't see why you think Sadie is your concern anymore. You left her months ago. Alone. With no money, no place to live, and two little boys to support."

"So, it's like that, is it?" He advanced on me, then backed off after a quick glance around the neighborhood.

"Like what?" I snapped. "I have no idea what you're talking about. This situation is going to end up however Sadie wants it to. I'm making it my business to see to that."

"You make a lot of things your business that you shouldn't, Barrett, and you always have. I'm warning you right now to stay out of mine. I won't let it slide like I did back in school. Do you hear me?"

"I hear you," I scoffed, squaring my shoulders as he attempted to threaten me by pointing a finger in my direction.

Clara, clad in her gym clothes, strode out of the garage and rushed Stephen, shoving him in the chest. "Get out of here, you prick—"

"Clara, no! Keep the boys inside. Go stay with them for me, please," Sadie frantically interrupted her.

"Don't you even think about messing with her, you asshole," she warned, and after a final glare at Stephen, Clara lifted her chin toward Sadie and stalked back inside.

"I can't deal with any of this right now. I've got to get the boys to school and go to work. Please do as Barrett asked and leave," her voice was barely a whisper, but that didn't matter. He clearly was not planning on listening to her.

"Can I see them?" With eager steps, he headed toward the open garage door.

"No, you may not," Sadie came back to life, shaking my hand off her shoulder and dashing to the side to block his path toward her house. "They have school today. It's been months with no word from you, Stephen. You can't just show up here and expect to get your way. That's not going to work anymore. I have to tell them you're back and prepare them to see you first. You can't spring yourself on them like this—it might freak them out. Plus, how do I know you aren't going to leave again? Do you have a place here? A job? How am I supposed to trust you? I refuse to let you hurt them ever again. They've been through enough because of you."

Stepping back, he grudgingly agreed. "You're right, I wasn't thinking. I'll call you and make arrangements for a visit. We'll talk everything through first and I'll answer all your questions. I'm not going anywhere, okay? I'm back in Green Valley to stay. I bought a house. I'm supposed to move in in two weeks. I'll check in with you then."

"A house? How wonderful for you. Fine. My cell number is the same, just in case you wondered. You know, since you never bothered to call to check on me or the boys while you were off doing whatever, or *whoever*."

"I guess I deserve that." He studied her face with wide eyes before turning to leave. She'd surprised him. We watched as he got into his SUV and drove off.

I made a decision. "Get the boys, I'm driving y'all on the school run today. And we'll carpool to work. In fact, maybe we should carpool every day. Think about it."

Her eyes snapped to mine. "What? No. That isn't necessary," she protested.

"I don't want you out there alone right now. I don't trust him one bit, and he's definitely up to something. And you won't be talking to him alone."

She started nodding before I finished talking. I could tell she was getting lost in her own thoughts again. "Yeah, I'll need an attorney. Internet divorce papers won't be good enough now that he's back. And he's not the one I have to worry about," she muttered without looking at me.

"What?" I hovered between my need to know exactly what she meant and the desire to respect her boundaries. Who did she have to worry about if not Stephen? I was fairly certain if I pushed her to tell me, I would probably only end up pushing her away.

"Nothing," she answered after a beat. "On second thought, we'll ride with you today. I'm too pissed to drive and I can't think straight. But it's a maybe about the whole carpool idea thing. Be right back." Absentmindedly, she handed me her travel mug. I stood there and watched her go into her house. She didn't seem angry; she seemed lost. Whether it was in thought or lost in fear, I couldn't tell. I didn't know her well enough—*yet.*

"I missed something, didn't I?" Lizzy joined me on the driveway. "The look on your face is intense."

"Sadie's husband is back. And I think I may have missed something, too," I answered without thinking.

"Oh no."

"Yeah, this isn't going to be good."

She shrugged and opened the truck's passenger door. "You'll fix it for her."

I focused on her in surprise. "What?"

"You'll take care of Sadie and her boys. I mean, it's what you do for everyone you care about—fix stuff, solve the unsolvable, give awesome advice, et cetera." Her utter faith in me touched my heart. "Plus, you like her."

I shook my head and winked at her. "I don't know what you're talking about."

She laughed. "Okay, Dad, sure."

As we loaded our things into the truck, I informed her about the potential carpool situation to which she graciously offered to drive Flynn and Rider to school herself if I bought her a car. I told her I'd consider paying for half after she'd been at work for a few months.

We chatted in the driveway and waited for Sadie and the boys.

And waited.

And waited some more.

After exchanging a concerned glance, we headed up Sadie's walkway. This time the ruckus was inside.

"I heard Daddy!"

Another shout joined the first. "Where is he?"

"Take my truck to work, Lizzy. Tell Grandpa and Garrett what's going on, so they'll know not to expect us anytime soon." I gave her my keys.

"Those poor boys," she whispered before looking me dead in the eye. "Fix it, Dad."

"I don't know if this is fixable, sugar. But I'll do my best." I rang the bell. They were sweet little boys and hearing them so upset broke my heart.

Almost immediately the door was flung open by a red-faced Flynn.

"Flynn!" Sadie came running after him. "What did I tell you about answering the door? Oh, thank god," she gasped when she saw it was me. "I thought it was—"

"You're not my dad." His tiny voice broke my heart. Tears filled his eyes before he roughly rubbed them away with his palms.

"I'm sorry, bud. I just came to check on you." I caught a glimpse of Clara holding a crying Rider on the couch. "What can I do?" I offered.

Sadie's shoulders rose and fell in a helpless shrug. "I—"

"I want my dad," Flynn answered. "Where did he go, Barrett? His voice squeaked out as he swiped under his eyes, struggling to fight his tears.

"Come here, baby." Sadie reached out for him, but he dodged her.

"No, I want my dad!" he shouted. "I heard him outside. He went to work, and he's been taking so long. Why didn't he come back? I want my daddy." His little body shuddered with a silent sob, but still no tears fell.

Sadie knelt and held her arms out. "I know you do sweetie, and it will happen soon, okay? I promise. Come here, please."

He dodged her. "No. I don't want you right now."

I stepped inside, closing the door behind myself. "It's okay to cry, Flynn. I know you're hurting."

"But Daddy said brave boys aren't 'sposed to cry."

I sat on an ottoman at the edge of the couch. "Yes, they are. Even grown-up men cry sometimes. I cried when my dad was in the hospital last month."

He stopped and stared at me; two fat teardrops hovered on his lower lids. "You did?"

"I sure did. And do you know who gave me a hug and helped me feel better?"

His eyes drifted to Sadie then back to me. "Was it your mom?" he murmured. He blinked and they fell.

"Yep. Mom hugs are the best. Why don't you let your mom take care of you, bud? You'll feel better."

Sadie knelt with her arms held wide open. He hurled himself into her body, knocking her onto her butt. "Sorry, Momma," he cried into her chest.

"It's okay, it's okay" she crooned. "And I promise. I will make everything all better for both of you."

"I promise too," I added.

"And so do I," Clara said.

"Me too, Flynnie," Rider finished.

CHAPTER 6

SADIE

How much more was I supposed to put up with from him? After Stephen left us, it was nothing but day after day of soothing the boys' tears and attempting to answer their questions, which was not easy considering he'd left me with zero answers and no way to contact him. They had missed him so much and were just now getting to the point where they could sleep without lavender baths, ten bazillion bedtime stories, and the lights on. Heck, it was just since we'd moved into this house that they didn't end up in bed with me at some point during the night. Stephen's surprise appearance this morning meant all that progress was gone now.

"Earth to Sadie." Clara's voice broke through my brain fog.

"Huh?" I came back to reality sitting on my butt on the floor with Flynn finally relaxed in my arms and Clara, Rider, and Barrett staring down at me.

"Are you okay?" Barrett asked. He stood in front of me with his hand held out to help me to my feet.

"Fine, yeah. Well, no. My head is pounding." I turned to Clara. "I think I'm getting a migraine."

Barrett hauled me to my feet from the floor, which was impressive since I still had Flynn wrapped around me. "You're taking the day off," he ordered. "With pay. Don't argue. I'm going to head to the office now, but I'll bring you lunch later. No worries, I know what you like." We watched him walk out the front door and I sat back on the couch with Flynn still held in my arms.

"He knows what you like, huh?" Clara snickered.

"I am too emotionally exhausted to have this talk with you right now, Clara," I shot back, forgetting about the little eavesdropper currently residing on my lap.

"Okay. So, boys, your momma isn't feeling good. How about we ditch school, get Daisy's doughnuts and hot cocoa, then sneak into Grandma's back forty and play on the swings or maybe have a game of tag, or do some teeter-tottering?"

Flynn perked up. "Can we bring the soccer ball?

"Absolutely."

He scrambled out of my arms and cupped my cheeks with his tiny palms. "I feel better now. You should take a nap for your head."

"I think I will." I hadn't had a nap since before giving birth. I pecked him on the forehead then followed it with my customary neck raspberry and a big squeezy hug. He laughed, proving he really did feel better.

"I'll take the boys for the entire day." Clara offered. "And you will take a nap and relax right here. We'll talk about everything tonight—together. I'll bring dinner home. The only thing on your to-do list of guilt-induced, wannabe type-A, bullshit insanity is to get some freaking rest today. Okay?" She tilted her head in the direction of the envelope on the coffee table.

"You said 'bullshit' Auntie Clara," Rider helpfully pointed out.

"Remember our talk," she hissed. "You're supposed to pretend not to hear it whenever I cuss. Earmuffs!" She tickled him on the side. "And why are you tattle-telling on me, little dude? We're about to party all day."

He laughed and ran off. "Sorry!"

I shrugged instead of answering Clara about not looking in the envelope. I couldn't guarantee something like that; it would only end up making me a liar. I watched from the couch as they collected things to play with at my mother's place then leave.

I meant to go to my room, take my migraine meds, and go to sleep, but instead I grabbed the envelope to read the papers Stephen had dropped off.

These documents were different than the ones from yesterday. Instead of a divorce, support, and joint custody, these asked for the divorce and full custody, with no offer of support of any kind.

Was he trying to trick me? Did he think I wouldn't read before signing?

What a foolish game he was attempting to play.

Of course, he thought I was stupid. A notion I had done nothing to disabuse him of over the course of our marriage. I tossed the offending papers and envelope to the coffee table and a check slid out. One quick glance confirmed the fact that he indeed thought I was an idiot—five thousand dollars? He had some nerve after his disappearing act. Plus, he'd not only left us without a word, but he had also run up our joint credit cards, opened up a few new ones in my name for good measure, and mortgaged our house into an oblivion so deep I had no hope of digging my way out of it. We'd had to move because it went into foreclosure. *Five thousand dollars, my ass.*

Fuming, I gathered all of it, shoved it into the envelope and stalked into the kitchen. I stuck it in a drawer and spun around wondering what to do next.

My head still pounded, but by some miracle—probably rage induced—the migraine had gone away. I opened the fridge and spotted the champagne Clara had bought weeks ago to celebrate our new place. We'd never had a chance to drink it because I was always busy with the boys. I gathered it, the orange juice, and one of her fancy glasses. I also stole her bubble bath from the shopping bag on the counter and headed into the bathroom to break in my new soaker tub. I never had any time for a bath either.

Panic started to creep around the edges of my thoughts, but I beat it back by rationalizing that I was fine for the moment and my boys were more than safe with Clara. Stephen wouldn't dare step foot on my mother's property. The last time he'd been there for one of our Sunday dinners Momma had waited until the boys went out to play, then threatened to castrate him with her rusty garden trowel if he showed up for dinner ever again, all because he'd dared to criticize her mashed potatoes. No one had ever criticized Momma's potatoes—or anything else she did, made, or said, for that matter. Except for my father, who had gone to town for milk and never coming back, and Stephen, who she had threatened to kill. And me, of course, who had bi-weekly nightmares and had lost the ability to relax.

I turned on the faucet, then poured a generous amount of the shimmering bubble bath under the flow. Clara was right; I had time to deal with this tonight. I fixed myself a mimosa—heavy on the champagne—and waited for the tub to fill.

After sinking into the bubbles, I sipped my drink and tried to prevent my mind from whirling out of control, but it was no use. My mind was made to whirl, and I had been stressing out hard lately. I eyed the pretty bottle of bubbly and made the choice to forgo the orange juice as I poured another glass. Everyone was entitled to a day of drunken leisure, right?

Hell yeah. I had earned this.

Deciding to see how pruney I could get, I settled my back against the gentle slope of the tub. I hollered at Alexa to play some Adele, and with my foot, I turned the faucet handle back on, so a tiny stream of hot water ran on a constant trickle. I attempted to relax and let my mind wander.

I had to force it away from my boys. What had I thought about before I had them? Dang, I could barely remember what my life had been like pre-motherhood. I had devoted myself to making their childhood the opposite of mine so completely that I forgot what used to drive me. I'd forgotten who I was.

Who am I?

That question hovered around in the near-drunken periphery of my thoughts and wouldn't leave until I acknowledged it fully.

Had I *ever* known who I was?

I swallowed the last of the champagne and set the bottle on the lip of the tub. I was willing to do anything to get rid of the sense of loss for who I had never been. Or even tried to be.

Barrett entered my mind. Beautiful, perfectly successful, brilliant Barrett, with his muscles and kindness, his extensive collection of travel mugs and endless supply of yummy morning coffee. I thought about our delightful bickering, our almost-kisses, and his adorably awkward attempts at conversation. I grew tempted to grab my showerhead and replace Rip Wheeler with Barrett for my mental pornspiration, but the doorbell rang before I could get my groove on, damn it.

"Alexa, stop," I bellowed. I toed the faucet off, sat up, and attempted to unplug the tub without face-planting in the water. I was the perfect amount of tipsy and feeling relaxed for the first time in at least four years.

After slipping into my bathrobe, I headed to the front door. I refused to start worrying again. If it were Stephen here to trick me into signing his second set of sneaky papers? I'd just ask him to kindly eff off so I could enjoy my day, or perhaps Karate kick him in the nuts. During all those years married to his useless ass, I'd never had a day to myself like this. What a turd he'd turned out to be. The lying, cheating, jerkface poop.

"Coming!" I hollered as a knock followed the bell. "Oh, Barrett." A wave of heat started at my feet, and I flushed red, top to toe. This reaction was ridiculous; there was no way he could know what I'd been about to do to myself in the tub.

"I brought breakfast."

"Oh!" I laughed as my stomach rumbled, the only thing in there the champagne bubbles.

"You look—"

"Drunk?" I leaned in with a hand on his chest and confessed. "Because I am just a little bit—oh my, you have a nice chest. Very muscley and firm." I patted it. "Good job working out and stuff."

"Thanks." He chuckled. "Maybe you should eat? How's the headache?"

"It's almost gone, thanks. Yay for food! Follow me." I started to head into the kitchen, then sensing his hesitation I turned back and stopped. "Come on, silly. I'm not a day-drinking lush. I want you to know that. I don't want you to think bad things about me. The last time I had anything to drink was at Aunt Genie's bar right after Willa came back to town." Willa had run away as a teenager. She'd been back for a while now, and I couldn't be happier she was finally home to stay. "Clara and I went there pretending to party when really we were scared that she wouldn't want to see us. Clara was the good cop, or the one who asked the questions, or something that made sense at the time, and I was the drunk cop, a distraction to throw her off our plan to make her talk to us. Dang it, I can't seem to concentrate on anything right now."

"You've had a lot on your mind lately," he observed, lips quirking up in a grin.

"Exactly! You're so smart." I watched as he placed a cooler bag on the table, my stomach growling in earnest as he began unearthing containers filled with what had to be a homemade breakfast. "Who made all that?"

"My mother. She told me to come feed you if you were hungry, make sure you had medicine for your headache, and check to see if you were alright. I hope biscuits and homemade strawberry jam are okay with you?"

"Always. That's my favorite breakfast treat. Would you like some orange juice?"

"Sounds good."

"'Kay, I'll be right back, it's in the bathroom."

"The bathroom, huh?" His eyes were sparkly and brown like a cup of coffee in the morning light, and they crinkled at the corners when he smiled. Why hadn't I ever noticed he was even more beautiful with a smile?

"I was drinking mimosas in the tub," I confessed in a loud stage whisper as I walked down the hall. I heard him laugh and was sorry I had missed the look on his face as he did it. I was also worried he would still be here after my Drunk Sadie Phase One happy buzz wore off. Drunk Sadie Phase Two always involved nostalgia and melancholy, and ain't nobody needs to see that. I'd just have to gulp the food down and get him to leave before my mood devolved into dramatic, heavy sighs and sloppy tears. "Good plan," I congratulated myself on my brilliance as I headed back into the kitchen with the orange juice.

He laughed again, woot! I saw it this time, all crinkly eye corners and a big white smile. "Planning something?" he asked with a chuckle.

I gestured grandly to the kitchen table. "Nope. Sit down, I'll pour you a glass." I stumbled—over air? Or the floor?—as I headed his way, but with a huge step forward, he caught me before I could fall. "You saved me," I murmured. "You're such a nice guy."

Memories crashed into my mind as tears formed. I widened my eyes to keep them from falling, then widened them some more and tilted my head back to keep them resting on my eyeballs instead of rolling down my cheeks. *Gah!* I knew it was hopeless, and the tears began to fall, like tiny crystalline balls of betrayal rolling down my freakin' face. Self-betrayal at that— the worst dang kind.

Phase Two was present and accounted for. I needed to get him out of here.

He took the orange juice and set it on the table behind him and grabbed a napkin from the holder to press it gently against each of my cheeks. "Tell me what's wrong."

"Do you remember your senior prom?" I blurted. Visions of my fourteen-year-old self in a frilly pink dress flashed in my mind. I slammed my eyes shut but the image did not go away. I had been there with Stephen, and Barrett had gone with Leeann, his now ex-wife. What a fool she was to leave him.

This is not how to get him out of here! Abort, abort!

I spun out of his hold and wandered into the living room in a panic.

Should I set something on fire? No! Then we'd both have to get out of here and Clara would be so pissed that I'd burned down our new house.

His footsteps trailed behind me. "Yes, I remember dancing with you. I remember everything. You were there with Stephen. You were only a freshman—way too young to handle a jerk like him."

"You tried to save me that night too," I said before I could think. My mouth kept running away from me—damn the champagne. And let's face it, the Adele music I had been listening to hadn't helped either. Between the alcohol, the all-too-relatable sad lyrics, and now the presence of beautiful Barrett, I was experiencing an overload of feels. "Never mind." That night had been wandering in and out of my memory banks since it had happened. It had been the start of my hopeless crush on him.

"Sadie," he whispered, "tell me what's going on, please. You can talk to me."

I stopped my restless pacing in front of the fireplace and faced him because I wanted him to know. I had always wanted him to know what his words that night had meant to me, how I'd clung to them throughout the years like a tiny beacon of hope.

On second thought, I turned back to the fireplace. I couldn't face him and get the words out without crying. "We were dancing, and you told me I deserved better than Stephen. You told me to be careful of him. You were so kind and respectful to me. You were the only man besides my father who had ever made me feel like

I was worth anything. But then my dad left, and it broke something inside of me. I never lived up to the hope you gave me that night."

"Oh, sweetheart. Damn him for making you feel worthless. Damn both of them. They were so wrong. You're worth everything."

"Barrett . . ." My voice was nothing but a breath of air between us, but he was close enough to hear it.

Silently, he stepped even closer, close enough I felt his warmth at my back. "Don't say my name like that unless you want me to hold you, because I will."

"Barrett," I repeated and turned around to find him standing so tall and strong, gazing down at me with fire in his eyes. He felt like safety. He looked like comfort. He was everything I hadn't had in my life for far too long to remember.

With a fingertip, he lifted my chin, our eyes met and held. "I shouldn't touch you right now, I should leave," he murmured. "You're drunk, and I want you too much. Lately you're the only thing on my mind."

Did he really say that?

"I'm not drunk anymore. I've moved into Phase Three."

His lips quirked up in a small smile. "What's 'Phase Three'?"

"It means I'll remember everything tomorrow and I'm capable of making decisions." Somehow, I had slipped into a dream; this didn't feel real. The dream Barrett of my past had collided with the one standing right here in front of me and my feelings exploded into my heart like a nuclear bomb.

"I'm not so sure about that." He brushed a tear from my cheek with a thumb, then bent to kiss my forehead. "Come here."

I took his outstretched hand and let him lead me to the couch where he sat and pulled me into his arms to sit at his side. My head came to rest on his shoulder, and I sighed. "Thank you."

"For what?" His deep voice rumbled into my ear, lulling me into a state of comfort so profound that I gave into it fully and went limp in his arms.

"For how I feel right now."

"Get closer," was all he said in reply.

Never in my life had I wanted anything more than to get closer to Barrett Monroe right now. I sat forward and he pulled me sideways onto his lap. We both laughed because at six feet, I was much too tall to be held this way. He opened his legs so my bottom could rest on the couch, and I snuggled back into him, resting my cheek on the broad wall of his chest and wrapping an arm around his waist. He undid my bun and stroked my hair, letting the strands fall through his fingers. Then he pressed a kiss to the top of my head.

"Tell me what you need and I'll do it. I'll do anything for you." One of his hands snaked around my waist to pull me closer and I became acutely aware of two things: one, I was clad only in a bath robe, and two, he was doing absolutely nothing to get beneath it. Barrett Monroe was a perfect gentleman. My heart filled with feelings I had no idea what to do with because I had never been lucky enough to feel them before. I decided I should get one hundred percent sober before I contemplated this any further.

"I don't know what I need," I finally answered, but it was a lie. I needed nothing more than this feeling to go on forever. But I couldn't ask for that; how does one ask for such a thing? Or even explain it? For now, I would take this moment of peace and carry it with me like the memory of that dance in his arms so long ago.

CHAPTER 7

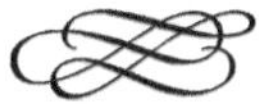

BARRETT

"I should go," I said, ruffling the top of her blond waves with my breath as I sighed. Holding Sadie this close had my mind spinning. I didn't want to let her go. But I had to, or she would soon find out exactly how much I wanted her. Fighting against getting hard was becoming near impossible with her in my lap like this. And no matter what she said about Phase Three, she had been drinking and she was upset. I could not let myself go any further with her today.

She had captivated me. Obviously, she was gorgeous; everywhere she went heads turned and jaws dropped. But working with her over the last few months, then especially after she'd become my neighbor, let me know what was beneath that beauty. The more I discovered, the more I respected her. As my admiration grew a hesitance about spending time with her, or possibly pursuing anything more with her, grew as well. Even though I wasn't in charge of Monroe & Sons, it was my family's business. Did I dare cross that line with a co-worker? I had a reputation to consider, and so did she, for that matter.

"Heading back to work?"

"Yeah . . ."

"Okay. And I should, I don't know, maybe sleep off the champagne and the rest of my headache." She moved out of my arms and stood.

The loss of her body against mine jolted me. We hadn't even kissed, so where was this coming from? "There's some ibuprofen in the bag on the table."

"You thought of everything," she murmured.

I stood. "I'll leave you to your nap." The awkwardness that had existed between us started creeping back and I hated it. It was as if the natural conclusion to what we just shared today had slipped away. "I meant what I said before—anything you need, Sadie. Just ask."

She nodded, eyes wide on mine. "Okay, Barrett."

"Get some rest, sweetheart. I'll see you in the morning."

"Tell your dad and Garrett I said thanks for the day off."

"Will do. Lock up behind me and eat your breakfast." She followed me to the door. Once I heard the lock turn, I left. Involuntarily, my hand went to my chest. Why did this hurt so much?

The drive to the office was odd. My heart raced out of control, pounding like it was trying to tell me something. The temptation to turn around and go back to her was strong, but I ignored it. Now wasn't the time.

Could such a time ever exist for us?

I pulled into my usual spot, frowning when I recognized Leeann's Mercedes parked in my mother's spot.

"Honey, get back in your car and go home. Leeann is here." My mother's voice from behind me stopped me in my tracks.

"Yeah, I know. That's her car."

She moved in front of me and put her hand on my arm. "Lizzy texted me. I just got here. They aren't getting along, and she's upset. I'll take care of it."

"What are you talking about? I'm going in." A world did not exist in which I would not go to my daughter when she needed me.

"There's no reason—"

Shocked, I cut her off. "Mom, I'm going in, and I can't believe you're trying to stop me."

"Fine. I knew you would. I just thought that maybe you could deal with the after-math rather than helping Lizzy and I get Leeann to leave. There's no sense in the both of you getting riled up by her nonsense."

I had no idea about any nonsense going on between Leeann and Lizzy, but I was damn sure going to find out. Grudgingly, she stepped aside, and I entered the house with her hot on my heels.

"Barrett, thank god." Leeann rushed up to me, then turned to face Lizzy who sat glaring at her from her perch behind the reception desk. Leeann's body language was such that she had to assume we were about to gang up on Lizzy. But I intended to do no such thing. Garrett and my father must have been out on a site. They wouldn't have left Lizzy out here upset and alone.

Lizzy rolled her eyes. "I'm at work, mother. We can talk about this on the phone later."

"No, we won't, little miss. We'll talk about it face to face so you can't hang up on me when I say something you don't like. And your daddy is here now so you're going to listen." She addressed me, like I was nothing more than a trump card to help her win an argument. "Help me talk some sense into our daughter."

"Why don't you back off a bit, Leeann? You're upsetting her."

"She's upset?! She's. Up. Set? What about me? I'm teetering on the brink here, Barrett! Will you help me convince our daughter to be in my wedding? Please? This is a big deal to me."

My heart lurched with shock. "First of all, a wedding? You're getting married? Again?" When she left us, she had sworn she needed her freedom. Her career was what she'd wanted—not me, not Lizzy, not our family. Being tied down in a small town was something she couldn't tolerate anymore, so she had left. But that hadn't stopped her from getting married again, repeatedly. The concept of holy matrimony to her was a joke. Yet each time, for some reason, felt like a knife in my gut.

"Yes." She rolled her eyes. "Didn't Lizzy tell you?"

"Apparently I'm going to be a big sister too," Lizzy grumbled. "Though, I never thought I'd have a step-father who I could practically be a sibling to. I'm sorry I didn't tell you, Dad." Her expression told me there may be more to this tension between them than either one was letting on.

"It's fine," I attempted to soothe her. "Let's all settle down and talk. Lizzy, it's not your job to tell me these things—"

"Taking her side, as usual. Letting her get away with everything, as usual. Putting her first before everything and everyone else, *as usual*. Some things never change, Barrett—"

"Leeann, honey, this is not about taking sides," my mother interjected. "And she's your daughter, she *should* be put first. You can't force her to be in your wedding if it makes her uncomfortable. Don't you think it's time to grow up and think of someone else for a change—"

"*Grow up*," Lizzy repeated with a mirthless laugh. "Grandma, you should tell that to Craig, my future stepfather who is practically my age."

"Eliza Kay Monroe!" Leeann's angry voice filled the room. "I've had it with your smart mouth. I've already apologized for what I said the other day, but you won't stop punishing me for it. Enough is enough! Craig is twenty-four and I have had enough ridicule from you. And excuse me, Becky Lee, do not even dare to tell me to grow up. I'm grown."

"Whatever you say," Lizzy snarked. "It's always about you and what you want. So, if you want to marry a dead-beat, gym-rat dude-bro and have him leech off you for the rest of your life, that's your business, not mine. It's disgusting and I don't want any part of it. I hope you and your idiot piece of man-candy have a happy life together."

"Do not speak to me that way! You don't mean that—"

"That's enough." I had to stop this before someone said something too ugly to take back. Regrets were hard to live with and I didn't want that for Lizzy. My mother opened her mouth to speak but I cut her off. "Mom, enough, please. Take Lizzy upstairs or out to lunch or something. I'll handle this."

"'*This?*' So, you're going to *handle me*, Barrett?" Leeann was good and angry now.

Damn it.

It was a fact: time dulled memories. Flashes of us fighting in the kitchen or having it out in the bedroom closet so Lizzy wouldn't hear flooded my mind, making me wonder why her latest impending wedding had me so upset. I didn't want to talk to her right now, or ever, let alone ever get back together with her like Lizzy had implied the other day. "That is not the way I meant it and you know it."

"Perfect Barrett Monroe being perfect. *As usual.*"

"We're not doing this." I gestured back in forth between us. "Lizzy is old enough to make her own choices and I'll stand by her decision."

She rolled her eyes. "Fine. Then she can stay with you forever, and you can reimburse me for her last—and failed—semester at UT. I'm leaving. Tell Lizzy goodbye and tell your mother to watch her mouth around me. I've had it with this entire family. God, no wonder why I left."

I watched her storm out without answering. I was not the type of guy who needed the last word. Not when I knew I was right, anyway.

"Damn, Barrett, what the hell happened? Leeann almost ran me over." Garrett breezed in through the garage entry carrying a Daisy's Nut House bag of takeout, my father following close behind with drinks. "Where's Lizzy? We brought lunch."

"With Mom, somewhere." I explained what happened and watched as Garrett shook his head the entire time and my father looked concerned.

"Man, you didn't quite dodge the initial bullets, but at least you're not getting shot at anymore on a regular basis. What a piece of work that one is. I can't believe you pined after her crazy ass for all those years." He dug out a turkey sandwich and took a huge bite.

"Garrett," My father said in his attempting-to-stop-an-argument dad tone.

"I did not pine." That was a lie. In the early years after the divorce, I *had* pined. In fact, I had pined my ass off.

"Bro, you pined. I'm glad that's over with."

"Can I ask y'all something?" I tilted my head to the office door.

Garrett answered, "Yup, let's go sit down." I followed them to the small table in the corner.

"Why am I—" I didn't know how to ask the question without sounding pathetic or like I'd lost my damn mind. "Why would her getting married again upset me? She told me and my heart dropped. I don't want her back—"

Garrett swallowed his bite before answering. "You can't accept the fact that you couldn't make it work with her. You're a control freak, a fixer, a type-A perfectionist—"

"Okay, okay, I get it."

"Look," he said, "it's not the wedding, it's the fact that she's marrying someone else when you tried so hard to fix your marriage. You don't really want her back and you know that. But the fact that she's moved on and doesn't want *you* and y'all's marriage back haunts you because you still see it as a failure."

"Some things aren't meant to work, Barrett," my father interrupted sagely. "You spend a lot of time taking care of people, son. Like Leeann, for instance. You took care of her because you wanted her love. You need to find someone who loves you back for you to care for, then you'll get it back. You hear?"

"Yeah, I hear you. But, what about Lizzy? About family? Marriage is supposed to be forever. I'd thought Leeann was the love of my life and when she left, I thought I'd be alone forever."

"Lizzy is our gift. She's your reward for trying so hard to make something last that was never meant to be. You're a good father, Barrett, and you were a good husband. You just didn't have the right wife. Leeann isn't a bad person, she's just not *your* person."

"What about now? Do you still think you'll be alone forever?" Garrett asked.

"I don't know—" Sadie crossed my mind. *Did I know?*

"I think you do know. Or at least you finally have some real hope this time, and it freaks you out," Garrett argued with a knowing smile.

"You got married too young, Barrett," my father added. "You got what you wanted at the time. But you're a grown man now. Life isn't about getting what you want anymore, it's about discovering what you need. There is a difference."

"I don't know if love is even real, and I sure as hell don't know what I need."

"That's fear talking," Garrett said.

"Okay, expert," I chuckled.

"I am, all right," he shot back with a smile. "Thanks to some good advice I got from you. Turnabout is fair play."

"Love is real, son. But some people can't let their hearts slide into those perfect little moments life sometimes presents us with. The ones that make us fall in love. The moments that make us feel alive. Don't be one of those people, Barrett. Open your heart again."

"I'll try." I thought back to playing soccer with Sadie on the street, her gorgeous face in the morning light, and her sweet curves in my lap earlier this morning. My heart stirred in my chest.

"Take the rest of the day off with Lizzy. Take her to lunch and relax. Get her to talk to you. Leeann's not a bad person, not really, but she ain't no picnic either." Dad said with a laugh.

"Will do. Thanks, y'all."

"We'll see you and Sadie here bright and early tomorrow. We need to wrap up the Bandit Lake site for good. It's time to get that mess out of our hair."

"It's cursed," Garrett said.

"It's not cursed. It's just a bit of a challenge is all." I looked at their skeptical faces and laughed. "Okay, you're right, it's cursed. But we'll get it done."

CHAPTER 8

SADIE

My buzz was gone. And the wave of sentimental, nostalgic bullcrap I had been riding had also disappeared. Now I was alone in the house and a little embarrassed. After putting the remaining biscuits and jam away for later, I sat on the couch and contemplated my next move. It had been years since I'd had a day to myself, and I felt like I should make the most out of it. I would allow myself this one worry-free day before all the crap hit the fan and I had to deal with Stephen, his dueling divorce papers, how I would afford an attorney, and whatever it was Stephen really wanted from me. And let's not forget Dana, the stupid scheming cow.

So, I'd already done the bubble bath-with-alcohol thing, and I preferred to service my undercarriage while in the tub or shower, so unfortunately the mood for a Rip Wheeler and/or Barrett Monroe ménage à moi was gone. I sank back into the cushions of the couch with a heavy sigh and picked up the remote. I should do lunch with someone, or get a mani-pedi, or go on a hike. My van needed an oil change and the yard needing mowing. I could get those chores out of the way . . . I wrinkled my nose. None of that sounded appealing. My cell vibrated from the coffee table, and the screen showed it was my little sister, Gracie. "Yo."

"Me and Weston are at Daisy's. Meet us for brunch."

"Aren't y'all supposed to be in school right now?"

"Aren't you supposed to be at work right now?" she shot back. "You don't hear me asking you any judgy questions about your life choices, do you? I do school when I feel like it and Weston was just at the dentist. He's got a mouth full of cotton and is doped as all hell. Come keep me company while I feed him a smoothie."

"Okay, sure. Why not?"

"Wicked. I'll see you soon. Want me to order something for you?"

"Yeah, coffee. Black. And some toast. My stomach is full of champagne. I'm going to walk to Daisy's. I might still be legally drunk."

"Eff that. I'll have Ruby swing by and get you on her way. And drunk? For real, you? Miss Mother of the Year? This should be interesting. Expect questions when you get here."

"Whatever. Isn't Ruby supposed to be in school too?" Who was I to mom-bomb her with questions when my own kids were off at the farm ditching with Clara? *Gah! What kind of mother was I?*

"Ruby does school when she feels like it too. She's got so much extra credit she could blow off the rest of the school year and still get straight A's."

"Must be nice." I had barely managed to graduate. Between cutting with Clara and our friends to get drunk behind the library and dating Stephen off and on throughout high school, I never bothered to study or do homework. Plus, my reputation had been horrible. I'd been a freshman when I started dating him, which was apparently enough to be labeled a slut, even though he was my first and only. Scarred for life, I tell you. Half the town thought I'd slept with half the town and nothing I ever said made a dent in my crappy rep, so I quit caring long ago.

"Right? I'm smart, but school bores me. I'm happy with C's and maybe junior college. Most of my interests don't require a degree anyway. *Boom!* I just texted her. Ruby will be there in five."

"But—" She hung up. I was not dressed or made-up. I needed way more than five minutes. My jaw dropped when the doorbell rang. It couldn't be . . .

But it was. Ruby stood there, smiling ear to ear. "Hey, Sadie. Lucky for us I was already on your street when Ruby texted. We're ditching for doughnuts, among other things." She looked me up and down with a critical eye. "I'll wait."

I grinned. "Thanks. I just had a bath."

"A bath? Interesting. I know about the champagne. And I heard Barrett was here not that long ago bringing you breakfast and Advil. Husband him, Sadie. He's a Monroe boy, and I've witnessed what they're all like. Trust me when I say you should jump all over the opportunity. You're almost divorced. Just ask him if he's free next week for marriage. Also, expect questions at Daisy's."

"You girls are too much," I muttered as I headed down the hall.

"Better than being too little," she shouted after me.

"You got that right," I yelled in answer. I rushed through a basic face, messy bun, and a sundress and heeled sandals, and met Ruby back in the living room.

"That was fast, and you look hot! Someday you'll have to teach me your speedy ways."

"Become a mother to twin boys, you'll learn to do everything in a hurry real quick," I deadpanned.

"Yeah, just one baby is a lot. Aunt Sabrina is barely hanging on. Between the baby, Harry, the girls, and her and Wyatt's work schedules, she was a mess. Wyatt too. You know him, he's hands on. Pop hired a nanny for them. She was pissed at first but the need for sleep outweighed her objections. And Wyatt does whatever makes Sabrina happy so . . ." She finished with a shrug.

"A nanny would have been nice, at least at night. Flynn and Rider would never sleep at the same time and Stephen was no help since he had to work."

She scoffed. "I'm sorry, what? Like, having two infants and zero sleep wasn't work? If I ever get married, my husband had better help raise his dang kids. Otherwise, what do I need him for?"

"Hmm, yeah. It was worth it though. They were the cutest little guys." Stephen was useless when they were babies but when the boys got older, he became a great dad—until he left us, that is. Plus, I had a huge fear of letting my boys down. All I cared about was giving them a better childhood than I'd had with a mom and a dad who stayed together and gave them a beautiful home. But after

Stephen disappeared, I discovered I could do it on my own. This big house with Clara was nice, but I could afford to support my little family in a smaller place if I had to and still give my boys all the love they needed. It made me feel good.

"I'm glad, Sadie. They're sweet little boys, and I think you're a great mom."

I turned to her and smiled. "Thank you, Ruby."

Thoughts of Stephen filled my mind on the drive to Daisy's even though I had decided to forget about him for today. I sighed, sick of him and the fact that he had dominated my life for so long. I used to think I needed him so I could be the mother I wanted to be. He was a liar and a cheat, but he'd taken care of me and the boys. He put me through design school, and I never wanted for anything. Well, except for fidelity and real love, but apparently that had been too much to ask of him, so I kept quiet, played dumb, and settled.

The time he had been gone had been a revelation and I wanted to keep the empowered feeling I'd developed in his absence. Stephen had forced me to make a change in my life. Through his leaving I'd finally found out what I was capable of. However, I refused to be grateful to the likes of him. I had earned what I was about to get—my freedom. I mean, I was still a mother so I would never be completely free, nor did I want to be. But to no longer have Stephen dragging my life down was a huge weight lifted off my shoulders, and that was the kind of freedom that meant everything.

"We're here. You got lost in your brain, Sadie. I've never seen someone stare out of a window so hard."

I snapped out of my reverie, startled to see we had arrived. Daisy's Nut House was a Green Valley staple. With delicious diner food and doughnuts, coffee and pie, everyone in town loved this place. "I'm sorry. I guess I have a lot going on."

"I know you do. Just holler if you need anything. I mean it. Babysitting, hacking social media accounts, grocery shopping, making a mockery of him on my podcast—"

"Wait, what?" I asked, regretting that I'd been only half tuned in to what she had offered.

She winked. "You heard correctly. Let me know."

"Y'all girls are something else." I followed her into Daisy's, marveling at the difference between me as a teenager versus Gracie and Ruby.

"Better than being something average," she countered with a grin, grabbing my hand and tugging me along with her.

"You got that right, honey. Don't ever change."

"I don't plan on it."

"I'm so happy you and Gracie are friends. She needs someone like you."

"I need her too. I used to be pretty lonely. It isn't easy being—"

"A semi-evil genius, or maybe even a superhero in disguise?" I teased.

She grinned at me. "Yeah, something like that."

"Yo!" Gracie waved us to her table, we sped over and sat down.

"Is he okay?" I pointed at Weston sitting in the corner of the booth with his head propped up against the wall.

He smiled at me as I approached. "I'm fine, I'm just sleepy from the meds." His head dropped to Gracie's shoulder and she wrapped her arm around him with a soft look that only crossed her face when she was playing with Flynn and Rider. "Order my smoothie for me, Blondie. Please?" he asked.

I gasped. "I didn't know he called you Blondie. Gosh, y'all are so adorable, I can hardly stand it." I pretty much squealed. Gracie and Weston were precious together. He was the only person aside from our sister, Willa, who could crack through the hard exterior she had built around herself since our father left. They gave me hope that I could end up with something sweet like they had.

"Yeah, well he's not supposed to do it in public, dang it. And I can't even get mad because his brain is not fully functional yet. And don't get out of control with the *oohs* and *ahhs* and 'how cutes,' Sadie. I can't stand that stuff and you know it," Gracie grumbled.

"You need to see that love can be real," Ruby argued with Gracie. "Embrace the sentimental dorkitude that is my brother. The poor fool adores you."

Gracie blushed in answer and ducked her face.

"She loves him too, Ruby. She's just allergic to the word like most of us Hill girls. Usually, whenever we dare to say it, it turns out ugly and bites us in the ass."

"Aright! Y'all, enough. I love him, obviously. He's drooling on his shirt and tipped over in the corner of the booth like a drunkard, and I still think he's hot. He wanted to get a smoothie instead of going home, and here we are, jeez. Speaking of love, Sadie . . . look who just came in. Isn't he your—I don't know what to call him? What are we calling their thing, Ruby?"

"A crush? Do old people even have crushes?" She laughed and I fought the urge to stick my tongue out at her. *Old, my ass.* "They're still at level one. Not even a date yet, and Becky Lee nick named them Badie. I preferred Sarrett, but what are you gonna do? She is the master matchmaker, not us."

"Do not even get this crap started." I sipped the coffee Gracie had ordered for me, then shot them both a glare that hopefully provided sufficient warning that I was not about to be match-made, messed with, or manipulated. Hell, I wasn't even divorced yet. It was a fact that I would do well to remember considering the dangerous level of my Barrett Monroe crush status—which, after this morning, had gone bonkers.

"Okay, we totally won't start anything," Gracie and Ruby exchanged side-eyed glances full of lies while Weston laughed softly to himself in the corner of the booth.

"They're gonna mess with y'all so hard," he said, sounding totally stoned, the poor thing.

"I'm just going to slip into denial and ignore everything, including Barrett, and y'all, and all of your"—I waved my hand around the table—"crazy shenanigan plans. If Barrett sees me, he can say hi. And don't either one of you wave him over or point me out to him. Things should happen naturally, you get me? I'm gonna go get a stress doughnut. Be right back." I grabbed my handbag and made my way to the line at the counter for something chocolate and hopefully gooey and covered with sprinkles.

"Sadie?" A voice I hadn't heard since high school spoke over my shoulder and it was all I could do not to swing my purse at her stupid—and most likely smug—face. Oh, how I was going to enjoy bursting her bubble.

I turned. "Dana." We had briefly gone to high school together. She was Stephen's age, his ex-girlfriend, and the source for all the "Sadie is a slut" gossip that had gone around about me back then. And probably now too, come to think of it. This was one woman who couldn't let stuff go.

She had also slept with Stephen when I was in the hospital giving birth to Flynn and Rider. This was a fact they did not know that I knew. I had figured it would be less humiliating to play dumb rather than admit I knew my husband had cheated on me, so I had ignored it to suit my own purposes.

I thought I'd had two good reasons to stay with Stephen, but that was over now. I'd proven to myself I didn't need him anymore and nothing could humiliate me because I no longer gave a crap what anyone thought about me. I was not the one in the wrong and putting up with their brand of bullcrap was in the past.

CHAPTER 9

SADIE

"I need to talk to you, Sadie. Can we go someplace quiet, please? What I have to say to you might come as a shock."

"Nothing you can say will shock me. Go ahead. Talk."

"Not here." She crossed her arms, then ran a hand through her hair. She was fidgety and nervous, and she was oh-so-right to be scared of me right now. "We should really go somewhere more discreet," she insisted.

"Oh, right. So everyone within earshot won't find out you screwed my husband when I was in the hospital giving birth to our children? That's the kind of discretion you want?"

"Sadie! Please." Her eyes darted around the restaurant, probably meeting many of the eyes that were now avidly watching us, and listening, and maybe even recording on a cell phone. "Y'all have kids together. Let's take the high road for their sake."

"High road?" I scoffed. "You know me. I come from the back road, and you're about to become part of something called making a scene. You don't get to come in here with your veiled threats, trying to intimidate me with some sort of shocking news. Now, what do you want to say? Just spill it because I'm not going anywhere with you. This line is long, and I want a doughnut."

"You want to do this here, that's just fine with me. I was going to let you know that I'm dating Stephen now, officially. We're in love and we're getting married." She flashed her hand at me, her finger fully bedecked in a fat diamond ring. "And I was also going to mention Flynn and Rider and doing what's best for them. I think you should let Stephen see them."

"Really? *You* think so?" I laughed at her audacity and refrained from slapping her stupid face.

"He misses them. And I feel like it's important that I—as their future stepmother—get to know them, don't you think?"

"Who the hell do you think you are? Stephen hasn't been gone on a business trip, genius. I had no way to contact him. He left us alone for months, with our home in foreclosure, no money, a mountain of credit card bills he ran up in my name, and nowhere to go but to my mother's place. He knew perfectly well how that would go for me. How *he feels* is not my problem. And you? You have no business or right to make demands where my children are concerned, stepmother or not. It's up to Stephen, me, and our attorneys to iron this out."

She tried to course correct. "I think we got off on the wrong foot today."

"There is no right foot for you and what you have done, and for the sake of clarity, I know everything. I mentioned that y'all slept together when I was in the hospital. But I also know you've been begging him to leave me ever since. I do not understand why you're here attempting to fight Stephen's battles for him when he has been busy rejecting you for the last almost eight years."

She blanched and took a step back. But I wasn't done, I advanced on her. "Stephen, I know she's in the hospital," I recited in a high-pitched whine, "but I need you so bad. Is there any chance you could get away? Even for a little half hour?" I finished with a glare. "The problem with text messages is they can so easily find their way to the wrong pair of eyes when the intended pair belongs to a dumbass who doesn't know how to lock his phone with an adequate password. I was giving birth, you cow. You begged my husband to leave me in my hospital bed and screw you when I was birthing his children. Who the hell does that?"

"Oh, snap! Ruby, take Weston. I've got to stop this or she's gonna end up in jail." A glance at my table told me Gracie was about to intervene. I shook my head indicating she should stay put, but she pulled a face and extricated herself from the booth anyway. Weston shot me a dopey thumbs up and Ruby shouted an encouraging, "get her, girl!" These kids were nuts.

I had spent my life dealing with the crap others had continuously piled my way. From my father leaving me, from mother and her constant barrage of cruelty, from my entire high school slut-shaming me, from my oblivious, cheating husband, and now this witch right here trying to get me to do their bidding. All of them thought I was a dumb blonde idiot, too stupid to know what was going on right beneath my nose.

I am not stupid.

And now I was done.

With all of it.

There was no longer a need for me to hide who I am.

"Okay, look, I'm sorry. About—"

"About what? Finally getting him to leave me? Don't forget that I know you, Dana. You're the kind of woman who likes to have her cake and eat it too. But this time you're trying to take my cake. I don't give a crap about Stephen, but Flynn and Rider are none of your damn business. What you need to realize real quick is I'll make you choke on that cake if you mess with me. Don't you dare attempt to use my boys against me. You have zero input on this situation. And if you think Stephen has any loyalty to you, you're kidding yourself. We both know how many years you've waited in the wings begging him to leave me. I was just a mother trying to keep her kids' father around. *For them*, not me. Everything I do is for my boys. I would move an entire fucking mountain for them if I had to, and I have and will put up with anything to give them what they need. *Anything.*"

"Okay, okay, fine, but Stephen and I are in love, Sadie. You were hanging onto something that was never really yours. He has always loved me, he was mine first back in school, everyone knows that—"

"Oh my gosh, you dumped him, stupid, and then he asked me out. Everyone knows *that.*" She opened her mouth to interrupt me, but I was beyond fed up with her crap. "Quiet. Hush. You like to take, to win, to beat somebody else to get what you want. You didn't want him back until he was with me. And you like married men too, don't you? What a challenge, right? I suspect that you won't like this one as much when he's married to you. But you're welcome to him. I'm done, I'm letting you win. You did not beat me."

"He left you. For me."

"Yeah, he did, after nine years of your whining and pining and pathetic text messages. And now I'm happier than ever and my boys will be too. I hope you have fun with my leftovers." Turning my back on her, I got in line for my doughnut.

"Bye now." Gracie snickered.

"But—"

"She said she was done, Dana. Move along." I whirled to come face to face with Barrett. I didn't give the first poop if Dana left or not—I was done with her. I had said what I needed to say.

"Can I buy you a doughnut?" he asked.

Gracie answered for me. "Oh, snap! Now that's a pickup line I can get behind! She likes all things chocolate and I'm going back to my table now." Dana was still standing there when Gracie turned around to leave. "Dang, Dana, go home, girl. You're attracting stares, and not the good kind."

"Chocolate, got it." Barrett confirmed as we watched Gracie, then finally Dana, walk away.

The line moved slowly; Daisy's was crowded with people and the ones who caught my eye so far had seemed supportive. I'd returned a couple of waves and a chin lift. One or two gave me 'call me' hand signals and a few mouthed *Go, girl.* This town was something else; the word nosy didn't cut it. It was like Green Valley had its own personality. It wouldn't surprise me if Daisy's patrons burst into song like something out of a musical or busted into some synchronized dance moves. Today's theme would be cheaters and all the ways in which they sucked.

"I made a scene, Barrett. And this isn't my first time. With a scene, I mean. It's kind of my thing." I smoothed my hand down my dress and adjusted the bracelets on my wrist. My nerves, and the realization of what I had just done, got the better of me for a moment and I blushed. "Are you sure you want to be seen with me right now?"

"You did what you had to do and that deserves a doughnut and maybe even dinner tonight?" My eyes shot to his and he winked. "Or perhaps some more champagne?" He winked. "Do you like The Front Porch?" Good god, that was Green Valley's fanciest, most visible place to stake your claim on someone.

Holy moly, he was asking me out. Beautiful Barrett Monroe wants to date me. For real. Not just steal a kiss somewhere.

"Are you sure you know what you're asking for, Barrett?" My lips turned up at the corner in a smile that I tried to fight. This day had just taken an epic turn for the better.

One side of his mouth tipped up to match mine. "I sure do. I'm asking you, Sadie Lynn Hill, out to dinner. Will you say yes?"

Hell to the yes. "Yes." I managed to play it cool even though my heart was pounding at a frantic beat and I was already trying on outfits in my head.

"Good. Does six o'clock work for you?"

Crap! I was supposed to talk stuff over with Clara tonight and she'd been keeping the boys all day. Could I ask her for more time? "Actually, I have to make sure Clara can watch the boys before I say yes. I'm so sorry. I jumped the gun when I said I could go."

"I completely understand. Talk to Clara, let me know. It doesn't have to be tonight. I promise I know better than to ask for a last-minute date, but I couldn't help myself. We can make an actual plan."

"I really am sorry, Barrett."

"Sadie, I'm a parent too. I know how it goes—"

"Yeah, you do get it, don't you?" We made it to the front of the line where he bought my doughnut and ordered takeout for him and Lizzy.

I walked back to my table and tried to rejoin the world after having my head launched into the clouds by beautiful Barrett and our future date.

"He asked you out, didn't he? Y'all got quiet for that part and I couldn't hear." Ruby guessed correctly as I sat down.

"Yeah, he did. For dinner tonight. But I have to make sure Clara can keep the boys—"

"I'll do it," Gracie immediately volunteered. "Tell me what time."

"He said six."

"If Clara doesn't feel like it, I'll be there. Or maybe I'll hang with her tonight so I can get the scoop when you get home. Or should I say *if* you get home . . ." She waggled her eyebrows at me. "Oh! Can Weston come too?"

"Yeah, sure. Clara will be home regardless 'cause it's her DVR binge watch night. And I'm not talking about this with a bunch of teenagers, jeez."

"But we're not like other teenage girls," Gracie snarked with a grin.

"Well, that's true. But we're still not talking about it."

"Fine, I'll just wait until spaghetti night and listen in when you talk about it then." My sisters and I had started having weekly dinners together prepared by Willa's hunkalicious sweetheart hubby, Barrett's brother, Everett. He cooked a mean spaghetti dinner and found it delightful instead of annoying when we sat around his table laughing like loons and gabbing about all our secrets. Willa and Everett had taken Gracie in soon after Willa returned to Green Valley and they were now her legal guardians. I was shocked when Momma had allowed it. She had always refused to let Clara or me take Gracie for more than an overnight.

"So, I guess I'm going out on a date with Barrett tonight. It's really happening." My inner teenage girl was twirling in my brain, making my outer grouchy old lady get dizzy with possibilities. *Would I finally get to kiss him? Ahhh!*

"Hell yeah, you are!" Gracie grinned at me and squeezed my hand across the table. "This is so cool. Good things are finally happening for you, and I'm stoked."

"We are both so stoked," Ruby confirmed. "And Becky Lee is going to pee herself with glee."

"Please, don't tell her. I don't need that kind of pressure yet." I had witnessed first-hand how excited Becky Lee Monroe got when one of her sons was involved with a woman she liked. And I knew she liked me; we chatted every day and often had lunch together. My boys adored her, and she adored them right back. And if I took my brain out of denial for a minute, I could recall the things she'd already done to push me and Barrett closer.

"Wear your red dress, the one that wraps around and shows off your boobs. He'll lose his mind. And I hate to break it to you, but Becky Lee probably already knows. You know how this town is." Gracie pointed out. "There are eyes and ears everywhere."

"*Ahh!* You're probably right. I'm going home. Ruby, catch you later. Gracie, see you at the house tonight."

"Do you want a ride?" Ruby offered.

"Nah, I need to walk the rest of the champagne out of my system." I wanted to be completely sober for dinner—or more importantly, *after* dinner where I was determined to get a real kiss. Or not? *Gah!* Why are decisions so hard?

* * *

I finished applying my make-up and took a minute to contemplate my face in the mirror. I wondered if I had made a mistake by agreeing to go out with Barrett tonight. So many things could go wrong if we dated and it didn't work out. But the smile involuntarily lifting the corners of my mouth told me that I should do what I wanted for a change. I should take what I needed instead of sacrificing my desires for everyone else.

It's my time.

After smoothing my blond waves over my shoulder, I took a step back, taking in the red hue of my dress. It was as red as my cheeks. I hadn't even needed to apply blush tonight. I laughed at myself and my mushy thoughts. I was already getting carried away by the idea of being with him. But I knew I needed to slow my roll.

I slid my feet into my gold sandals, bent to fasten the straps, and tied the delicate bows with a smile. My heels clicked across the dark oak floor as I headed into the living room. "Clara? Boys?"

"We're outside on the driveway! Come see what Auntie Clara bought for us today. The guy just finished delivering it and it's awesome." Rider was at the fridge gathering an arm full of juice boxes.

"What did she get you guys?"

"A basketball hoop! We're playing a game called HORSE. It's so fun!"

"Wow! I'm coming." I followed him out.

Gracie and Clara were chatting on the porch while Weston showed Flynn how to shoot the ball.

"I did it!" he shouted, turning to smack Weston's hand in a high five.

"I told you! I knew you could do it." Weston turned to address Gracie. "Come on, Blondie, get over here and show us what you got!"

"*Gah!* Weston!" Her annoyed voice was belied by the fact that she had rushed into his arms the second he called her over.

"I like that. Can I call you Blondie instead of Aunt Gracie?" Flynn asked.

"Nah, little man. That's my special name for her. You need to make up your own." Weston winked at Gracie who promptly buried her face in his neck with a groan.

"Okay, I'll call her Blueberry Pancakes because whenever we go to Daisy's for breakfast, we both always get that. It's our thing, right, Aunt Gracie?"

I could see the laughter light up her eyes from here. "Yeah, Flynnie. It is." She ruffled his hair. The smile on her face was huge and I was so happy for her.

Rider had his thinking face on. This should be interesting. "Good one, Flynn. I know! I'll call her Fart Girl because every time we go to Taco Bell after school, we have farting contests in the car on the way home and she always wins." Rider announced. "That's *our* special thing!" Laughter burst out of me before I could stop it.

"Rider! Oh my god!" Gracie cried.

"Okay, Rider. Maybe you should think of something else to call Gracie." He opened his mouth to speak but I cut him off. "And ask her privately before you say it out loud. Okay?"

"Okay, Momma."

Weston kissed the top of her head. "No worries, Fart Girl, I love you no matter what comes out of you after a Taco Bell run."

She covered her face with her hands. "Oh god. Please send some aliens down to abduct me."

"I love that boy. They are just so stinkin' cute together," Clara said under her breath as I slid into Gracie's former seat next to her on the porch. "And you look hot, girl. I approve."

"He's here," I hissed at Clara as Barrett pulled into his driveway.

She laughed and poked me in the side. "You're giddy. I have literally never seen you this happy."

The truck door slammed, and Lizzy stepped out. "Weston?" Clara and I exchanged worried glances as Lizzy stood at the passenger side of Barrett's truck gaping as Gracie stood in Weston's arms. They both stared back, wide-eyed at a clearly mortified Lizzy.

Did she still have feelings for Weston?

Lizzy and Weston used to date, and from what I'd heard it was pretty serious. But she broke things off when she left Green Valley to go to college.

My heart broke for poor Lizzy, whose face crumpled as she burst into tears and ran into the garage.

"Fuck," Clara whispered.

"You've got that right."

Dinner with Barrett was not happening tonight, that was for sure.

CHAPTER 10

BARRETT

Shit. I hadn't told Lizzy about Weston and Gracie because I didn't think she cared anymore. I had figured if she still had feelings for him, she would have stayed in Green Valley. Guess I was wrong about that.

"Barrett," Sadie called as she made her way over here while the kids and Clara hurried into the house.

All I could do was stare and try not to drool. To my shame, the sight of Sadie in that dress temporarily shoved Lizzy out of my mind. "Stunner," I addressed her, grinning when her cheeks turned almost as red as her dress.

"I think we have a problem."

Guilt struck me hard as I answered. "Yeah, I think I made a mistake by not telling her about Weston and your sister."

"Why didn't you tell her?"

"One, it never came up. And two, I thought she was over it. Partially because it never came up, but also because she was the one who broke up with him and left town."

"That is some sound reasoning," she agreed.

"Really? I didn't just colossally screw up my daughter by not giving her a warning?"

"No, but I think you're going to have to spend the evening with her. Talking, bringing her copious amounts of ice cream, or at least just keeping an eye on her."

"You're probably right. But damn, you in that dress . . ."

"It isn't going anywhere. I can wear it again. And I have more where this came from, don't you worry."

"I can't even imagine what you own that could top this. Rain check?"

"Of course."

"I'm so sorry." I turned to go inside, but quickly turned back. "Damn, this sucks."

"I'm a parent, too. I know how it goes." I grinned as she handed my words from Daisy's back to me.

"Can I call you later?"

"Absolutely. Take care of your girl."

"I will."

When I got inside, I found Lizzy standing in the kitchen with tears running down her face. "I'm so stupid, Dad. I never should have left. I missed finishing my last year of high school with my friends only to flunk out of my first year of college. Mom is—you saw her! I left things with Weston so horrible. I hurt him, but I'd hoped that we could at least be friends. Never mind, I can't talk about this. I have literally ruined my entire life!"

I rushed to her and gathered her into my arms. "Shh. You're so young, sugar. Your life is nowhere near being ruined, but I understand why it feels that way right now. Changes like this are hard. And I'm so sorry. I would have told you about Weston and Gracie if I had known it would upset you."

Her eyes shifted to the side. "It's not your fault."

"I wish you would have asked for my help."

"I couldn't. I felt bad for leaving you and moving in with Mom."

"Why?" I pulled away to watch her face as she answered. "She's your mother. I missed you, but I was happy you were going to college and following your dreams."

"But I wasn't. Turns out she wanted me to follow hers. She got so pissed when she found out I flunked out. She wanted me to go to law school and join her firm. She wanted, like, another version of herself. She doesn't give a shit about what I want. Dad, I don't want to be a lawyer. I can't talk to her anymore, about anything."

"You don't have to be a lawyer. All you have to do is follow your heart and be happy."

"Is that what you did with your life?"

"No. You're almost grown so I'll be honest with you. I wasted a lot of years waiting around for your mother to come back to us. I thought we belonged together, for a lot of reasons that turned out to be pretty stupid. But listen, the point is your first love isn't always your true love. Keep that in mind whenever Weston crosses your thoughts." If only I had given myself this advice after Leeann left me, I could have moved on right away rather than keeping my heart in the past for those first few years, then being a gun-shy fool for the rest.

"Most kids want their parents back together. But I like it like this. I can't live with her, but I love her. I'm glad I can always come back to you. Thanks, Daddy."

"You always have a home with me, Lizzy. No matter how old you are."

"Um, speaking of how old I am . . . Now that I'm back home, Grandma wants to throw me an eighteenth birthday party—" *Shit.* "Uncle Wyatt is married to Sabrina now and she's Weston's aunt . . ."

"Yeah, I see what you're getting at. And Everett and Willa have Gracie living with them now. They're her legal guardians, practically her parents—"

"They do? I didn't know that. Crap, Dad. How am I supposed to even exist in this family anymore? This is so awkward. I missed so much while I was gone. Thank God you haven't asked Sadie out yet. I know you like her, but it looked like she had a date tonight. Her dress sure was pretty. I'm so sorry, Dad. But I'm relieved, too."

My heart dropped. I didn't know what to say. "Uh, yeah, it was pretty. But we're talking about you. You're going to be okay, Lizzy. I promise. I'll make sure of it."

"I know you will. You always make everything better. I'm going to go fall into a Netflix coma and stop thinking about all of this. Can we have pizza for dinner?"

"Whatever you want, sugar. I'll order it." She beamed and darted off to the living room.

Shit. What am I supposed to do now?

My only choice was to take this one day at a time. Lizzy would eventually realize she was over Weston, then I could ask Sadie out again.

I grabbed a beer out of the fridge then shut it with a slam. Nothing was ever that simple.

We spent the evening together eating pizza and catching up on the Marvel shows we'd missed watching together while she'd been at her mother's place. After ice cream sundaes for dessert, she headed off to bed with no more tears and feeling much better.

I wished I could say the same.

I grabbed a second beer and headed upstairs to my bedroom. The sight of Sadie in that red dress still burned at the back of my mind. She was gorgeous—quite literally the most beautiful woman I had ever laid my eyes on—and she was driving me insane. Tonight was supposed to be ours. A chance to shove the awkwardness away for good. A chance to talk about something besides work. A chance to show her I wasn't a total tool who could never say the right thing.

Just a fucking chance at something good for once in my life.

I wanted something more for myself for the first time in years.

I wanted to know her. I already knew her face, her wide blue eyes and the adorable freckles that covered her skin. Her full pink lips and the delicate arch of her eyebrows that would adorably lower in annoyance whenever she glared at me for saying something dumb. I knew she was a gifted designer and great at her job. She was a perfectionist like me, but I knew she would never admit it. I knew her surface—the things she let me see. But I saw a little bit more today, and it made me want it all.

Ever since she'd fallen asleep in my truck, she had been in my dreams, and every day I woke up with the memory of her smile. I wanted her dream smiles for me to be real. I wanted her eyes on me, lit up and happy, wide awake, in the light of the day.

I was a person made up of lists and rules, my work, and making sure I was the best father I could be for Lizzy. I went through the motions of life convinced my chance at happiness had come and gone.

Sadie made me feel like—well, I wasn't quite sure yet. All I knew was that she made me feel alive for the first time in a very long while.

With a shove, I slid the door to my balcony open and stepped outside feeling the soft breeze from the mountains cool my heated skin. I could see up into the Smokies from here and I loved it. Green Valley was beautiful at any time of the year, but fall was spectacular. I sat with my feet propped on the railing to look out over the trees, colored from gold to red to deep brown, but then my eye caught on something below and I froze.

Sadie, dressed in pink, surrounded by flowers, covered with a white blanket, and reading a book. I didn't even think before I spoke. "Sadie," I called, unable to resist temptation. "Good book?"

CHAPTER 11

SADIE

Damn, this sucked.

Everyone was getting settled in the living room when I got back inside the house.

"Is she okay?" Gracie asked.

"She will be. Barrett is going to stay with her tonight, to talk it out with her and stuff."

"I'm sorry, I should have stayed home. I had no idea she, uh, still cared." Weston stumbled over his words. "But, Gracie, I'm all about you. I promise."

"I know you are. I believe you. Let's get out of here though. Want to hang at Willa's?" Weston took her outstretched hand, they said their goodbyes, and left.

I hovered in the doorway, for some reason unsure of what to do. Clara waved me into the kitchen. "What happened?"

"Dinner is off for tonight. It seems like maybe Lizzy wanted Weston back. She's a mess. Barrett is going to take care of her, obviously."

"Shit."

"Exactly."

"This complicates things for y'all."

"I know. There is just too much between us, Clara. It's never going to work. I knew better but I just—"

"You want him. And you'll get him. We'll figure it out. Go change and relax. I'll feed the boys and do bedtime for you."

"Are you sure?"

"Yup, we'll watch *Captain Underpants* on Netflix and come up with cool nicknames for each other. "Auntie Clara" is boring now that we have a Blueberry Pancake Fartgirl in the family."

"Oh god, those boys." I sighed. "Okay, I'm going to finish some work then maybe go read before bed." I could get used to this. I almost never had a night to myself.

A few hours later, the boys were tucked in for the night, Clara was absorbed in her DVR binge, and I had relocated my evening to the covered patio through the French doors of my bedroom. A book and mug of hot tea sat on the glass-topped white iron table next to my padded outdoor sofa of the same material. I had decorated this space to be my own little private oasis. This would be the first time I got to use it, so it didn't matter that it was cold outside because I had a perfect little firepit to keep me warm. This space encompassed everything I loved; it was feminine, simple, and elegant in shades of cream and pink. I had planted potted peonies, white climbing hydrangea, and pink roses I was training to grow on a trellis. It would be gorgeous out here when it all bloomed.

I pulled the white afghan Clara had knitted for me over my legs and settled in with my book.

"Sadie." Barrett was sitting on an Adirondack chair with his long legs stretched out to rest on the railing of the balcony of what I assumed was his bedroom. "Good book?" he asked before taking a sip from a bottle of beer.

I smiled up at him, trying to play it cool as my heart skipped a beat. "Yeah. How's Lizzy doing?" I didn't know whether to run inside and grab a robe, or pretend I wasn't dressed in only a thin little sleep tank and pair of shorty pajama bottoms.

"She's asleep. Can I come down and sit with you? We should talk."

"Of course." Through all the time living here, I'd never seen him on his balcony, and I'd spent almost every evening in the backyard playing with the boys. This had to be a sign.

"Would you like a beer?"

I held my mug aloft. "I have tea."

I watched as he stood and went inside. Soon enough, there he was at my garden gate, dressed in grey sweatpants and a white T-shirt, a pair of black Chucks on his feet. That T-shirt did nothing to hide all that Barrett goodness—pecs, abs, and biceps galore, plus his big shoulders. Had I mentioned those? I could barely resist a swoon. As it was, I was tempted to fan myself with my book. It was not fair that he seemed to be perfect in every way.

"This is a beautiful space." His eyes warmed as he took a seat across from me on the matching chair to my sofa.

"Thanks, I wish I had more time to spend out here."

"I'm sorry about dinner," he said.

"It's totally fine. Please don't worry. How is she?"

"She came back to town with plans. Apparently, she thought they would pick up where they left off. I can't help but wonder if there's more to it, though."

"Oh no. I hate to be the bearer of bad news for her. But it really won't happen. Weston is into Gracie. I've been spending time with them, and it would shock me if they broke up. I heard the L-word with my own ears tonight."

"I thought as much. I've seen how they are together at family gatherings."

"Damn," I murmured. "This complicates things for us even more."

His eyes shot to mine. "I have hope that it doesn't have to. Eventually she'll realize she's over him. She left town—she had to know on some level he would move on, right?"

"I don't know about that, Barrett. Feelings are complicated sometimes. And the deck seems to be stacked against whatever it is we're trying to do. We already work together, which made our dinner date sort of a questionable idea to begin with. And our siblings are married—imagine if we dated and it didn't work out? We're going to end up sharing nieces and nephews someday. And now we have this whole teen drama thing in the middle of us. Plus, there's always the fact that I'm still married, albeit only by a technicality because I'm so done with that asshat and it's just a matter of time before I'm free."

A frown crossed his face as he sat forward to protest. "I—"

I held up a hand. "I'm nowhere near finished. I'm about to go through what is shaping up to be a nasty divorce. Plus, I have serious trust issues. Sure, I manage to maintain a rockin' bod and I have a nice face, but that means nothing when you consider the emotional trauma I've managed to acquire over the years—you've met exhibit A, my mother—and I'll be brutally honest. I can be a huge handful sometimes, Barrett." I wasn't ashamed to be confident about my looks, especially since according to some people, it was all I was good for. And I felt honesty was always the best policy. He should know what he was getting into with me.

"I already know all of that, except I do not think you're a handful—" he protested.

I shook my head and took a sip of tea. "Don't underestimate me, Barrett. I'm a hot mess—you have to know that. And I'm in for some real trouble, unless Stephen can manage to rid himself of the evil witch who's attached herself to his side like a demented little barnacle. And you? You're, like, immaculate perfection. The complete and utter opposite of me. I have a big mouth and I'm not afraid to make a scene. And lately I've been dealing with a major addiction to my snooze button. Oh, and no matter how hard I try to hide it from you, we both know I'm a disaster in the morning, a full-on train wreck. You should probably forget about me and go for someone more like you. And final confession, I know on the outside I can sometimes look hot—the red dress, the pencil skirts, and high heels—but almost one hundred percent of the time what lies beneath the surface is a comfortable, reliable pair of basic granny panties."

He burst out laughing. "First thing's first, I don't care about what your panties look like, Sadie. It's what's in them that matters," he teased.

"You did not just say that!" My laughter joined his, breaking the brief tension that had risen between us.

"Hey, I never could say the right thing to you, remember?"

"It wasn't just you," I confessed. "When I want something I can't have I get very testy. Basically, my crush on you made me a huge grump."

"Ah, and mine on you made me stick my foot in my mouth on a regular basis. But more importantly and back to the topic at hand, I was married to someone like me. Now she's in Knoxville about to marry her boy toy, living it up, and driving our daughter insane. So please don't tell me what I need."

"Oh."

"Yeah, 'oh.' I don't want to be with someone like me ever again. I had that before, and it didn't work for far too many reasons to count."

"We shouldn't do this. God, we both know we should quit while we're ahead, so nobody gets hurt because of us."

"You may be right about that, but that doesn't negate the fact that I want to try."

I looked away. "I do too, so much."

"You and me could work. Opposites attract, right?" A devastating grin crossed his face, and for the moment, I lost my will to argue with him.

"Barrett," I breathed.

"Don't say my name like that unless you want me to kiss you. Because I will."

I grinned and tossed my book to the side. Who needed a romance novel when I had a walking, talking, smoking-hot hero right here on my patio? "Barrett," I repeated. I wanted to be kissed by him. I wanted him to hold me again, to feel him hard and strong and solid against me. He made me feel good, but more importantly, my heart felt comfortable with him, like he would be careful with it.

He stood, towering over me as I sat up, swinging my legs around to put my feet on the ground. Gentle hands grasped mine and tugged until I was standing in front of him in my tiny pink silk pajamas.

"What are you wearing, baby? Look at you," he breathed as his eyes roved over my body. "You're gorgeous."

"Thank you, Mr. lady-killer sweatpants and sexy white T. You're hot as hell, Barrett and I am so into you right now." I reached out and felt up his biceps so he would know I meant what I'd said.

I grinned as his cheeks grew pink above his beard.

He blushed!

Could he be more adorable?

He framed my face with his hand, then ran them into my hair, tunneling through the strands to rest them at my nape and pull me into him.

"So soft," he murmured before placing his lips on mine in a gentle kiss. It was just a brush. Mouth to mouth, barely a whisper of a touch. But I felt it down to the tip of my toes which were now curled on the pink paisley patio rug we were standing on.

Electric tingles spread throughout my body, and I sighed in contented pleasure as I ran my hands up the hard planes of his chest. "You're not soft, not at all," I whispered as I wrapped my arms around his neck and pressed myself against the solid wall of his body. "Kiss me some more."

"Anything you say," he murmured against my mouth before his hands tightened gently in my hair to tip my face back. His eyes drifted to my parted lips for a beat before he surged forward. His tongue moved with mine as his hands slid down the silk of my pajama top to grip me around my waist with his big palms. What had started out sweet grew carnal real fast as his hands lowered to my ass and he pressed our hips together.

It was essential, it was exquisite, it was everything I had fantasized about and more, and I never wanted to stop.

But I had to stop.

I wasn't ready for more than this, not yet.

Pulling back, I informed him, "I'm not having sex with you tonight." Again, honesty, the best policy, yadda yadda yadda.

His eyes crinkled in a smile. "I didn't come over here to pressure you into anything, Sadie." He drew the back of his hand down the side of my neck. "We can stop, and I'll go back home, or we could talk out here."

"Or maybe we could just make out for a little while? We could go inside?" I inhaled a sharp breath after the words came out.

"Deal." He reached out a hand and I took it with a bemused smile. "Am I correct in assuming your room is through those French doors?"

"Yes, the boys are asleep for the night and Clara is occupied. No one will question it if I put on music." We switched positions, like a dance; then I was the one tugging him through the entrance to my bedroom.

Once inside, he pressed me against the wall and kissed me like I'd unleashed him. "You drive me crazy," he growled against my lips. "I forget about everything else when I'm with you."

"Likewise," I pulled back to whisper in his ear before taking a nibble of his neck.

He was a great kisser. How could his lips be so soft and firm at the same time? He slid his tongue into my mouth while his hands ran up my back and drifted into my hair, using them to tilt my face and kiss me deep, to draw it back and place sucking kisses to my neck and upper chest, and just generally make me regret my decision to not have sex with him tonight. But it had been so long I had almost forgotten what it felt like, and I was nervous. Plus, this thing between us was new and I didn't want to add more pressure to it with sex.

"Sadie," he murmured against my neck. I could swear that Barrett was into *me*, not just what he could get out of me, and I loved it. Goosebumps rose over my skin as he placed gentle kisses along my jaw, my cheeks, then my lips, once, twice . . . "Tell me where to touch you. Show me what you want." He stepped back, holding out his hands for me to take.

"What?" I breathed.

Quite suddenly, I felt like crying.

I blinked. Without meaning to, he'd touched my heart.

Tears pricked at the corners of my eyes, and I blinked some more to make them go away. This was not a moment for crying; this was a moment to savor.

"I won't make assumptions about how far you want to go. Put my hands on you," he said as his eyes grew soft on mine.

I took his hands and led him to my bed. "Sit with me?"

Wordlessly, he joined me to sit on the edge of my bed, grinning when I ducked under his arm and placed his hand on my waist. I leaned in, pressing my lips to his. "I love this," I whispered, and he smiled against my mouth.

"I want to make you feel good. About being with me, about everything," was his simple reply.

"I've never felt like this. It's beyond good, Barrett." I studied his face. I wanted to memorize the expression he wore: gentle and so, so sweet. Just like our long-ago dance together, I wanted to embed it in my mind.

I could fall for him so easily. This moment was just one more thing that brought me closer to the brink.

I sighed and slid my palm along his cheek, running my hand into his dark brown hair to bring him back to my lips.

We sat there and kissed with his arm around my shoulder and his hand sifting through my hair, the other at my waist unmoving except for a gentle squeeze now and then. I had never *just kissed* before, and it turned me on more than anything I'd ever felt in my life. I burned, the flames of desire shooting through my body making me want all of him with nothing held back.

Strangely, I felt both shy and bold at the same time, but most of all I felt safe with him. "Are you okay?" he asked between kisses.

I was more than okay. I was perfect. "Yes. It never crossed my mind before that I could ever be with someone like you. This feels like a dream," I confessed before I could think.

"What do you mean, someone like me? You're the dream."

"I'm far from a dream. A girl like me never ends up with someone like you—"

"Stop that talk. You've always been larger than life, brave and beautiful. You've been in my head, Sadie Hill. For years I've thought about you. I'd see you around town and wonder what it would be like to be with you just like this."

"You're joking."

"I am not. Every time you've ever smiled at me, I've felt it. Right here." He placed my hand on his chest. "Every single time."

I sank back into my pillows and reached for him. He kicked off his shoes and moved to lie beside me, gathering me close so I could rest my head on his chest. "I've made so many mistakes in my life, Barrett. But I know deep down that this isn't one of them, no matter what stands between us."

"You're not the only one with regrets, Sadie." He placed a kiss to the top of my head.

"Oh, I don't have regrets. I would make every mistake again and again into infinity because all of them led to me having my boys, and I wouldn't trade them for anything in the world."

"I love that you feel that way," he said. "I wish I felt like that. I wish I could have had Lizzy without ever meeting Leeann."

"You're a good father, Barrett."

"And you're a good mother."

"Lizzy will be okay. We'll both make sure of it." I sighed and cuddled into the warm shelter of his body.

"You're right. And eventually she'll come around."

"But what should we do about, well, everything else?" About Monroe & Sons and us being co-workers, my impending divorce and possible custody fight, Willa and Everett . . . all of it crossed through my mind. It turned me cold, and I shivered in his arms.

He held me tighter and tipped my face back to meet his eyes. "We have right now. And Sadie, we will always have *right now*. Living in the moment is all we can do. Life is too unpredictable. One thing I've learned lately is the more you try to control it, the more everything just flies out of your grasp."

Right now.

Could it be enough?

We spent the next few hours with very few words passing between us. We kissed and he held me. Occasionally he would whisper something sweet to make me swoon further into his arms.

Lying here with him, I felt like the girl I never got to be. I had grown up too fast, never having the chance to go slow with a man. Stephen had been full of pressure and false promises, and I had been empty inside and too young to know better, so I had eaten it all up. Barrett took his time, giving me something I never knew I needed.

We held each other and kissed almost all night, drifting off to sleep together every now and then. He slipped out my back door to go home right before dawn with goodbye kisses and a promise that we'd talk soon.

CHAPTER 12

BARRETT

I decided to work from home today. Lizzy was currently at the office for the day. And if she caught sight of me and Sadie together at work, she would undoubtedly notice the chemistry between us. I didn't want her to worry or hurt more than she already was.

I worked steadily through lunch, organizing timelines for projects and assigning crew members to each one. Garrett had taken my father's advice and had started delegating tasks so he could spend more time out at work sites, like he preferred. The first thing he did was exploit my organizational skills and dump a ton of office work on me, but I was more than happy to take it on. It was easy and mind numbing—a great distraction from my life.

From my position on my living room couch, I could watch the neighborhood comings and goings through my front window. So I knew Sadie was also working from home and it took everything in me not to blow off my tasks and go to her.

Ever since my father's heart attack I had felt a sense of restlessness. Like I was wasting my time. It wasn't work; I loved my job. It was the entire rest of my life, except for Lizzy, that felt like a waste. All I had was a job that I loved and this huge and mostly empty house. I had planned to fill it with kids but obviously my ex-wife had been harboring all kinds of other ideas she had conveniently neglected to tell me about. I had been so bitter, but now I could finally admit to myself I had been afraid to try again.

"Shit," I muttered as I watched my mother's car pull into the driveway. I loved her to death, but I was not in the mood. Especially since I had a pretty good guess about why she was here—to get into my business, meddle, matchmake, and push me into doing her bidding, as she was so prone to do. "Shit," I repeated as my brother Wyatt, ever the gentleman, got out of the driver's seat to run around and let her out. I was tempted to dive behind the couch to hide, but it wouldn't do any good. My curtains were wide open.

"Yoo-hoo!" She called as she waved at me and rang the bell. "I see you, my handsome boy. I brought cookies!"

"It's open," I yelled. And even if it wasn't, she had her own key. I heaved out a sigh and dug my palms into my eyes.

"Hey," Wyatt greeted tiredly as he sank into a seat by the window, reclined it, and immediately shut his eyes.

"Cora still not sleeping?" My new niece was not fond of sleep, or being put down, or anything that didn't involve being lavished with attention. Wyatt and his wife had four kids between them. I could only wish to have such problems.

"Not so much," he replied. "We have that nanny for the nights, but I work so often, whenever I'm home I want to take care of her myself. I don't want to miss anything, you know?"

"Yeah, I do."

"You're both such good daddies and I'm so proud of both of y'all. But enough about that. We have to talk, and this is serious. We have a potential problem brewing and it's threatening a project I've been working on."

"A project?" I chuckled. "Is that what you're calling it these days?" Matchmaking and meddling were the fuel that had fired her up for the last year as my brothers got married one by one.

"I'm sure I don't know what you're talking about," she huffed daintily.

"If I wasn't so tired, I'd laugh," Wyatt said through a yawn. "We both know why I'm here, Mom. You want me to talk to Weston about Lizzy, right? Or have me get Sabrina to do it."

"The thought had crossed my mind," she answered. "I just think if we can get them to sit down and talk it out then Lizzy will move on. She just thinks she wants him back because he's familiar and comfortable and she is convinced her life is a mess."

"I agree with you, but—"

"Oh! Shh! Who is that?" She pointed to the street, and we watched as a brand-new Cadillac Escalade pulled up to the curb in front of Sadie's house. "Sadie is home right now," she informed me.

"I know," I answered before thinking.

"Well, of course you do." She was smug. I shook my head. "After we leave, you should take these cookies over there and finish the workday with her."

I shrugged. It wasn't a bad idea. But I kept my response noncommittal. Her hopes were already sky-high when it came to me and Sadie and there was too much currently standing in our way.

Wyatt opened his eyes long enough to tell us the Escalade belonged to a prominent divorce attorney from Knoxville.

"Good for her, getting that mess out of the way!" she exclaimed. "You're about to be all clear to make your move." She added a wink in my direction.

"Look, this match might not work, and you have to accept it," I warned.

"Nonsense. I will accept no such thing. She's perfect for you, Barrett."

"I won't hurt Lizzy. And I also won't hurt Sadie by leading her on—"

"Hush. You are my most stubborn boy, Barrett William Monroe. This shruggy and grumbly badditude you have going on right now is telling me you're not going to take my help and that is not okay with me, mister. Nope." Her tone was sulky. Her arms were crossed, and her eyes were narrowed on mine. I was going to get her help, whether I wanted it or not.

"Just let her help, man. Make it easier on all of us."

"You're a good boy, Wyatt, thank you. You two are perfect for each other, Barrett, everyone says so. And look, I know Sadie has had her difficulties over the years where her reputation is concerned, but don't you pay any mind to it, none of it is the truth."

"I don't listen to crap like that—"

She patted my arm. "Good boy. I raised you right. But even still, I've been sick over it because she's such a sweet girl and a wonderful momma." She leaned in with a conspiratorial grin. "I finally found out who's been spreading the lies."

"Who?" I asked, now fully invested

"Remember Dana Miller? Everett took her out once or twice a few years ago, if I remember correctly. That pretty face can only do so much to hide her rotten personality. She was so mean to him about his Trek Wars, the comic books, and that Firefly Galactica show he likes so much. No one tells my boy he needs to stop collecting toys and grow up when he's already perfect and handsome and sweet and—"

"Yeah, Sadie had a run in with her at Daisy's. It got pretty ugly."

"That's horrible! Poor Sadie. You make sure to be there for her, Barrett. Now, back to why I'm here—Lizzy's birthday party. She was out of town when she turned eighteen and we missed it. I want to throw her a late party. Wyatt will bring Weston. Gracie will be there with Everett and Willa, of course. And Barrett, you make sure Lizzy shows up. Don't let her fake sick and skip it. We're going to iron this all out once and—"

"That is a terrible idea. I'm not doing it." Wyatt interrupted without opening his eyes. "They're almost grown. Let them sort it."

"It is not—oh, look! Sadie is coming over here. Wyatt, wake up! We have to go so they can be alone. Move it, mister!"

He huffed out a beleaguered sigh. "I'm up. Later, Barrett."

They took off just as Sadie made it up my walkway. "Hey, did you send that attorney to my house?" I already called Clara and Willa, neither one of them did it. Was it you?" She asked without preamble.

"No, it wasn't me."

"Well, who else could it be? Your mother? Not Gracie . . . she's too young, right?"

"My mother was just here doing her thing. That's the kind of secret she wouldn't be able to keep so I doubt it was her."

"Good point. Well, it couldn't be my mother, could it? Oh dang, maybe it *was* her. She loves the boys and hates Stephen. She won't want me to get screwed over and lose them."

"What did he have to say? Are you okay?"

"Yeah, I'm great, except for becoming an anonymous charity case. He brought my own petition for divorce. It's reasonable and fair and would be perfect if he can get Stephen to agree to it. The only thing I hate is the idea of sharing the boys. It's why I—" She paused.

"You can tell me."

"I'm sure you heard most of it at Daisy's, right? The classic tale of the cheated upon wife in her birthing bed, starring that cow, Dana, and my dipshit soon-to-be-ex-husband."

I hid my smile. She was cracking jokes, but clearly it was a painful subject. I had noticed that she often used sarcastic jokes to cover her feelings. "Yeah, I heard. But if you want to talk about how you feel about it now that they're together out in the open and whether or not it bothers or hurts you, that's an entirely different thing, right?"

"I get your point and I appreciate you for being kind about this. He cheated on me. He slept with Dana when I was having the boys. I pretended I didn't know and stayed with him. I figured they would need their father around and I couldn't bear the thought of ever having to be away from them, like for the weekend or whatever custody deal we would have ended up with. But I'm over him and I have been for a very long time. Dana had no right to butt in. And if he tries to mess with me, it will get ugly. I'm through with taking his crap, Barrett."

"My mother said we should keep an eye on her."

"Really? Why?"

"She didn't have a reason. Just a gut feeling."

"I'll watch my back."

"I'll watch it too."

"Thanks. Okay, I'm done talking about Stephen. He's ruined enough of my days. And even though I feel bad about being a charity case, I'm also relieved, because there is no way he will be able to screw me over. Whoever hired that attorney knew what they were doing. He's mean as a snake."

"Would you like to come inside with me?"

"Are you sure it's a good time? When do you expect Lizzy to be home?"

"Huh? What?" Had she just asked me a question? I had gotten caught up in what I would do to her if I got her inside with me. She was beautiful in black yoga pants and a red tank top, her hair piled up high in a bun. It was a new look this time. A surprise cross between the morning pajama-and-wet-hair chaos and the fancy attire I usually saw her in.

She took my outstretched hand with a laugh. "Lizzy. When will she be home? I assume we have time to maybe make out a little bit or something."

"We have time." I tugged her inside.

"*Right now . . .*"

"Exactly." I pulled her into me and kissed the soft skin between her neck and shoulder, bared by the thin straps of her tank. I was gentle as I held her close, but what I wanted was to leave a mark on her, to sink inside of her, to make her mine and never let her go. Frustrated, I set her back and apologized. "I'm sorry, Sadie." Turning away, I stalked into the living room. I had no business kissing her.

"Talk to me." Her rapid footsteps across the hard wood trailed behind me.

"We shouldn't do this. I mean, I can't do this to you."

"What do you mean?"

"I feel like I'm going to end up leading you down a path to a broken heart. It has nothing to do with work or Everett and Willa. They're adult enough to handle it if—"

"I get it. They'll survive if we don't work out. This is about Lizzy."

"Yeah. What am I supposed to do? Tell me what to do, Sadie."

"Like you said last night, we have right now. Nothing exists beyond the moment you're in anyway. Think about it, Barrett. Plans get unmade all the time, expectations remain unmet. And tell me, when do dreams ever come true? They don't, we both know that. Take what you want when it's right there in front of you. That's what I intend to do from now on."

"Will that be enough for you? Me being selfish, taking up your time in secret, and possibly putting my daughter ahead of you and what you deserve from a man?"

"You're what I want. And I say it's enough."

"I don't think you're right about dreams not coming true, Sadie."

"Don't say my name like that unless you plan on kissing me again, Barrett."

"Sadie." I couldn't resist her no matter how hard I tried. The only thing I could do was my damnedest to make her happy and keep her from regretting her choice to be with me.

We moved to the couch where I pulled her down, shifted her beneath me, and kissed her lips with the passion and conviction I wanted to display out in the open. This was untenable and inevitable at the same time. I was torn between the right thing to do and the only thing I wanted. I should let her go . . .

But I couldn't.

We should have waited to be together for so many reasons, but her mouth was perfect and she tasted like heaven. I wanted more than kissing; I wanted all of her. My cock hadn't been this hard in who knows how long, and I knew she felt it when she shifted her hips, positioning herself against me until I was cradled by her soft heat. I ground myself against her and we both groaned at the friction.

"You feel so good." I was never one to act without thinking everything through first. This thing with Sadie defied everything I had ever known about myself. I was out of control and living in the moment for the first time in my life. She had freed something inside of me and I didn't want it to stop. Everything in my life felt better when I was with her. No matter what she said about expectations and plans, she was my dream, and I would do whatever it took to make it come true.

"Don't stop." Her hands drifted down my back and lower to cup my ass in her hands. She shifted her hips up as she pulled me tighter.

"I can't stop. I don't want to stop. Tell me what you want." She slipped the thin straps of her tank top off her shoulders and pushed my head down. I grinned against her soft skin and kissed a trail down the gorgeous column of her neck as she shoved the cups of her bra down, baring her gorgeous full breasts to my gaze. "You're fucking beautiful." I sucked a perfect pink nipple into my mouth, and she arched up with a mewl of pleasure, telling me without words that she was sensitive here. Gently, I kissed my way to the other breast, licking up the underside and over her nipple with the flat of my tongue before pulling my mouth away to blow on it—warming then cooling the tight little peak with my breath.

"Oh god," she hissed. Goosebumps covered her skin as she panted beneath me.

The more I tasted of her skin, the further under her spell I fell. She smelled like peaches and cream, sunshine, and spice, and if her pussy tasted this good, I'd never come up for air. I'd be happy to die with my face buried between her thighs, making her come for the rest of eternity.

"Dad! I'm home early! Do you want to get burgers at Daisy's for dinner tonight?" The interior garage door slammed shut and I shot to my feet. I had never moved so fast in my life.

"Fuck," I hissed. My eyes drifted to Sadie on the couch, legs spread, tits bared, lips swollen and red from my kisses, and her long hair a wild mess of waves spilling over the couch cushions from my hands being in it. "Fuck!" I repeated. "Goddamn it. Shit!" I added for good measure. My brain had turned to mush. I felt like I was in slow motion.

She scrambled up, tugging her tank top to cover herself as she rose.

"Your bra," I murmured.

She tugged up the cups with haste and looked wildly around the room as she smoothed her hands through her hair.

"Work." I gestured to the coffee table, spread with papers and plans from Monroe & Sons. I sat and gathered a bunch, shoving them into her hands before getting my own stack to hide the hard on she'd given me.

A startled giggle burst from her mouth, and I touched my forehead to hers. "Holy crap, Barrett," she whispered before straightening the sheaf of papers I'd shoved at her and choosing a colored pen from the pile we'd apparently knocked to the floor.

Footsteps clicked across the kitchen, through the dining room, and family room. Lizzy appeared in the arched living room entrance with a smile. "Oh, hey, Sadie," she greeted. "They said you were working at home today." Thank god for the teenage obsession with texting because Lizzy had barely looked up from her phone.

"Yeah, I needed, uh, this." She held her papers out. "Thanks, Barrett. I'll get it back to you—"

"In the morning will be fine. I'll walk you home. Come on." I reached for her hand to help her, but she dropped it like a hot potato the second she was up.

"I'll see you tomorrow, Lizzy."

"Bye, Sadie." Without looking, she sank into the recliner by the window, throwing her legs over the side to continue her text conversation.

We walked to Sadie's porch in silence, each lost in our own thoughts until she broke the silence with another giggle "I haven't had something like that happen to me since I was like, fifteen years old. My mother had a sixth sense about when to bust me with Stephen in the barn out back."

"Something like that has never, ever happened to me. Ever," I confessed. "I was kind of a planner back then."

She huffed out a laugh. "Yeah, I bet you were. Perfect Barrett Monroe, always fully stocked with a wallet full of condoms and the ironclad knowledge of the work schedule of the parents of whatever girl you were dating. I'm honored that I was the one to shake that up for you." She tugged my face to hers by the collar of my T-shirt. "How does it feel?"

I reached around her to open her door and push her inside, slamming my lips to hers. "Like I've been missing out," I growled against her lips.

"Damn straight you were." She thrust her tongue into my mouth and grabbed my ass. "I wish you could stay."

"Not more than I do." I pressed our hips together, grinding my erection into her.

"God, what a waste," she murmured. "Make some plans and stock that wallet, Barrett. If all we have is *right now*, we'll need to be prepared for it."

"Yes, ma'am." I kissed the tip of her nose before palming my dick into submission and leaving as she blew me a kiss in her doorway.

CHAPTER 13

SADIE

By now, I'd forgotten all about Rip Wheeler. My showerhead, vibrator, and that weird little fingertip thingie that looked like a banana Clara had bought me as a birthday joke, all of it was now dedicated to Barrett Monroe with his magic hands, gorgeous lips, and huge dick. I made my way to my bedroom in a daze. My body was on fire and I needed to get off in the worst way.

"Sadie," Clara called. "I'm home."

"Crap, frick, damn." I slammed my top drawer shut in a fit of horny rage. I was throbbing in all my good spots. I literally needed just one flipping minute to myself and I'd erupt like a freakin' volcano. "Yeah, give me a second." After inhaling a deep cleansing breath, I reentered reality and headed to the kitchen to find her dressed in workout clothes and chugging a bottle of water at the fridge. "Good workout?"

"Huh? Oh, yeah."

"What is up with you and the gym? You're there every day lately."

"Nothing. I'm just burning off stress. You look . . . disheveled." One nosy eyebrow popped up as she looked me over. "Your tank top straps are stretched out. You should probably change into a fresh shirt. First base?"

"Second. And it's none of your business. Chris? Or Jordan?" I snapped back with a nosy eyebrow of my own.

"Jordan is just a friend," she replied.

"Ahh, I see choices have been made. Monroe adjacent. Good man. Approved."

"Not that I need it, but thanks." Her lips lifted in a small smile, but the sparkle in her eyes let me know how happy she was with her decision.

Chris Barrett was a cousin to the Monroe brothers on Becky Lee's side and worked as a supervisor for the company. Of note, Becky Lee had named Barrett after her maiden name. Of further note, I now knew who Clara midnight texted with every night. Her phone's *bing* notifications could get out of control.

I resisted the urge to steeple my fingers, make plans to meddle in her business, and *muah-ha-ha-ha* at her. After all, I still had meddle-worthy business of my own I wanted her to keep her nosy nose out of.

"Don't even think about sticking your nose in," she warned. She knew me well.

"Shut up." I grinned and shoved her shoulder. "Don't even think about it."

Her smirk made me suspicious, but I let it slide. "Do not mention Chris tonight and I won't bring up you and Barrett." Tonight was spaghetti dinner night at Willa and Everett's house.

"Thank you for reminding me. I promised to bring Everett my cherry cheese-cake. Don't worry, I'll make one for us too."

"You could probably get that man to do anything for the recipe. Huh . . ."

"No '*huh.*' I see your mind working. You're planning something, Clara. Knock that crap off. And that recipe is my secret. Don't you dare give it to him. It's how I make people like me."

"You don't need cheesecake to make friends, dude. And my mind is not working or planning. It's full of revenge plots against Dr. Dickhead and Henry Cavill *Witcher* memes, like usual. Quit worrying." Dr. Dickhead was her old boss. Let's just say her lawsuit against him was still pending and I was curious to see what would take him down first. The law, or her bad temper?

"Whatever, nosy pants." I opened the fridge, gathering my ingredients. No-bake cheesecakes had to chill for a few hours before you could eat them. A stab of jealousy hit me. I wished I could chill for a few hours then get eaten. *Gah!* Barrett had me all worked up. I needed some alone time, and I knew I wasn't going to get it. I had way too much to do.

It was a minimum day, which meant the boys would be off the school bus within the hour. They always came to spaghetti night with me. They would watch movies or play with Everett's toy collection, and he always ate with them and kept them entertained so we could have our sister time. Willa was lucky to land him. He was amazing, and so good for her—and for the rest of us too, I had to admit. He was like the brother we all secretly wished we had grown up with. They were expecting their first child and were so far beyond excited it was ridiculous. Everett was setting himself up to be the ultimate dad. He had already built a nursery and a playroom and was working on a custom backyard playscape.

What would it be like to have a baby with Barrett?

Stop it. I immediately shoved that thought way out of my mind. I mean, I couldn't even go to his house for a spontaneous visit if I felt like it. Not yet, anyway. Baby thoughts should be put on the back burner, but in reality, I should not have them anywhere near the stove since I wasn't divorced yet.

"How's the Barrett situation going?" She had taken a seat at one of the barstools at the kitchen island with her water and a bag of Cheetos. Her words knocked me out of my insane maternal reverie, and I refocused on her smirky face. "You're lost in thought over there. It's either very good or . . .?" Her shoulders and eyebrows shot up at the same time, indicating I should finish the thought.

"Lizzy wants Weston back, as you know. So, the situation is fraught and awkward. And potentially impossible," I informed her as I started rage-smashing graham crackers for my crust.

"Alexa, play Adele!" she shrieked. "We need tragic background music. And nothing is impossible."

"If she stays hurt and never gets over him then I can't see how it will get any better."

"She's eighteen! For frick's sake."

"And?"

"Ninety percent of eighteen-year-olds are total fucking morons. Remember how dumb you were? And me? And, like, everybody we hung out with back then?"

"Yeah, but unlike us, she has a father who gives a crap and will absolutely put her first."

"Okay, but she's a child, Sadie. She'll get over Weston. She's probably over him now. She's just back in town all butt-hurt over something and he's like an old comfy pair of jeans she wants to slip back into. She doesn't love him. If she did, she wouldn't have dumped his ass and gone off to college. Am I right?"

"You have a valid point. But that won't stop Barrett from protecting her. And honestly, I wouldn't want him to set her feelings aside for mine. He's a good dad, Clara."

"Gracie told me Lizzy wasn't even going to tell Weston she was leaving. She was just going to go off on her merry way to college in Knoxville. He found out at the last minute from Wyatt who ran into him at the Piggly Wiggly and accidentally spilled the beans by mentioning, and I quote, 'the good news about Lizzy' and then it all came out. Keeping huge, life-altering secrets like that is not a nice thing to do to your boyfriend. And it's also not the behavior of a girl in love with a boy." She stuffed a Cheeto in her mouth with a smug look.

"Really? Wow, I didn't know that. I wonder if Barrett does?"

She shrugged. "I have no idea. I doubt Wyatt said anything to him. Men don't talk about that stuff."

"Right? I highly doubt they discuss Lizzy's love life."

"So basically, y'all are sneaking around then?"

"Seems like it. But nothing is official. We don't have a label on whatever we're doing. I kind of don't even fully understand what it is we're doing. One minute we're fighting over aliens and the next he's saving me from falling tiles and we almost kiss. Then last night we made out for hours in my bed." I paused to contemplate, scrunching my face in thought. "I should probably give up on him for now. There are so many reasons why me and Barrett will never work. And now we have to keep it a secret from Lizzy? And I probably shouldn't let Stephen or that troll-faced witch Dana find out. She'll use it against me somehow, for sure."

"God, Sadie, we both know forbidden love is the hottest kind. You have no chance. The more you fight it, the hornier you'll get for each other. Y'all are like Green Valley's *Romeo and Juliet* without the death. Well, maybe not *Romeo and Juliet* since you're both hella old and our families get along, so never mind. *Ahhhh*! This is so hot. I'm excited for you. I would give anything to be in a sexy forbidden relationship!"

"No problem," I replied, deadpan. "Quit texting Chris or I'll disown your looney ass."

"Gee, thanks. Somehow that didn't feel like a true threat."

"I'll try harder next time," I joked, but she didn't laugh. "Did you change the subject in your mind without telling me? You're supposed to laugh at my jokes," I joked again.

Guilty eyes met mine. "I have to tell you something. I worked at the farm stand before the gym today." Sometimes my sisters and I helped our mother out by working the shop counter at Lavender Hills. "Momma is the one who hired your mystery attorney, and a private detective to boot. She may have even put a hit out on Stephen too, for all I know. She was beyond pissed at the thought of him going for full custody of the boys. She ranted about it all morning. I'm sorry I didn't tell you immediately. I couldn't figure out how to tell you without making your head blow up. I don't want your head to blow up. You have enough going on, and I don't want to clean up that kind of mess. I'm sure brain goo stains."

My heart fell from the heights it had been soaring in while I was telling Clara about Barrett to the knowledge that I was going to be indebted to my mother even more than I already was. "Holy crap. I had the thought it might be her, then I rejected it. Really?" I studied the swirling granite pattern in the countertop. I couldn't meet Clara's eyes. My mother had always made me feel small; I could never meet anyone's eyes whenever I talked about her. "I don't want to be grateful to her. I really don't. And I don't want to owe her."

"You don't owe her shit. You didn't ask her for this."

"But you know how she is. She'll use it to lord over me. Like, one more mess of mine she had to clean up. Damn it, I really didn't want it to be her."

"Aren't you sorry you didn't accept when I offered?" she teased, trying to lighten the mood.

"I won't take your money, Clara."

"Damn your stubborn ass, Sadie." She laughed. "We can go see her in the morning." She held out a hand and I took it with a squeeze. "We'll find out what's going on together. She wouldn't tell me any details. She wants to talk to you about it herself. I only know it was her who did it because she's such a shit liar. I could read the truth on her face when I asked her flat-out."

"I can go to the farm on my own. Don't worry about it."

"Are you sure? I don't mind going with you."

I nodded. "I'm sure." It was a lie; I wasn't sure. I was never sure what would happen around my mother. Her moods were mercurial, ranging from bad, to worse, to mean as hell. But this was something I had to do alone.

Curiosity, dread, and the ever-present sliver of stubborn hope I still held in my heart to one day have a relationship with my mother is what kept me going back to her, over and over. Sometimes I wondered what it would take to finally set me free.

"Don't let this ruin dinner tonight, Sadie. I'll go with you if you change your mind."

CHAPTER 14

SADIE

Everett had inherited a huge old house from his grandfather along with a building in town he'd turned into a gamer shop. He had been renovating for months. Willa had been helping him, but since she got pregnant, he hadn't let her lift a finger. It was finally finished now and gorgeous. We pulled up to the stately old colonial and parked at the curb.

I turned back to address the boys. "I want y'all to be on your best behavior for Uncle Everett."

"We always are. He's the kind of grown up we like. He's not boring." Flynn answered as he gathered the new model cars I had bought him. "He's going to help me put these together."

"Yeah, and tonight we're 'sposed to learn all about the magic of—what did he say, Flynn? I forgot."

"The magic that is *The Empire Strikes Back*, and all the reasons why it's the best movie ever made. It sounded like a school project when he said it last week, but it's *Star Wars* stuff and Uncle Everett is cool, so we're going to give it a chance."

"Well, if he tries to make me write about it, then I can't make any promises," Rider said. "I don't even write when my teacher tells me to."

"I don't think he's going to have you write an essay, Rider. You should be good," Clara said with a laugh before getting out and sliding the back door open for the boys.

"Yo!" Gracie ran down the front walkway. "Hey, y'all." She hugged each of us in turn before taking the boys' hands and running inside with them.

"Being here with Willa has changed that girl so much," Clara marveled. Gracie had been sullen, quiet, full of rage. No matter how much Clara and I had tried to help her and be there for her over the years, she couldn't seem to deal with Willa running away from home, or our father leaving us.

"I think having Willa back in the family, and her being with Everett, the baby on the way, and our dinners together, and just everything that has happened lately has done all of us a world of good. Like, as a family, we have hope for the future or something. Good things are finally happening," I mused, tilting my head in concern as I watched tears fill Clara's eyes. "Oh, honey."

"*Gah!* I'm sentimental tonight. I hate that shit," she grumbled as she brushed a tear away. "Don't look at me."

I pulled her close for a quick hug before turning to grab my pie carrier from the rear of the van. "Are you doing okay?"

"I'm just emotional lately," she answered. "Plus, every time Momma does something halfway decent it gives me hope that someday we'll get along with her. But as you know . . ." When it came to our mother, we were constantly hovering between wishing for something more and resignation to the fact we would probably never have it.

"Yeah, I don't have a lot of hope for tomorrow," I admitted.

"Hey y'all, come on! Y'all are the first to get here. Everett's almost done cooking." Willa's smiling face in the doorway shoved our blossoming negativity aside and we exchanged a smile before heading up the walkway. "Is it wrong that all I want to eat right now is that cheesecake?" She grinned and pulled me into a side hug.

I patted the carrier with a grin. "Who says you can't eat dessert first?"

"You do, Momma! Every night. Remember?" Rider yelled from his perch on the living room couch.

"Well, that's going to make things difficult tomorrow at dinner," I deadpanned. Once we were inside, I stopped to inhale deeply as the smell of garlic and tomatoes, Italian spices, and fresh baked bread greeted us. My mouth watered. Everett appeared behind Willa, and I handed the cheesecakes to him with a smile. "It smells so good in here."

"Thanks." He handed them back to me. "Put them in the fridge for me?"

"Sure." How strange. Usually when he was cooking, he wanted us nowhere near the kitchen, or his "domain of husbandly duty." Did I mention Everett was adorable? I passed through the dining room into his huge kitchen. Before I could rein it in, a massive smile split my face in half, and I blushed. "Barrett," I breathed. "Hello." I refused to acknowledge the heart palpitations, or the stomach swirl, or the delicious tingles that arose in my southern hemisphere.

He stood at Everett's kitchen, looking sexy in a pair of jeans that hugged his booty just right and a black T-shirt that fit snug around his chest and biceps. The same Chucks from the other night were on his feet. I stood back for a second to take it all in. He was at the stove stirring the sauce with a wooden spoon. "Everett invited me. Lizzy is out to dinner with my parents. They are attempting to cheer her up."

"How fortuitous." I dialed my ridiculously huge smile down a notch as I attempted to regain my composure.

His soft laughter met my ears. "Right? I'm sure there was no scheming whatsoever to get us in the same place at the same time."

"Oh, not at all. This totally *does not* have your mother written all over it." I put the cheesecakes in the fridge and turned to find him watching me with a ghost of a smile decorating his features.

"Come closer, baby. No one's around, so I get to kiss you hello." I slipped into his waiting arms and he tugged us to the side, out the door leading to Everett's back porch. "I don't want to steal your sister time, but I couldn't let you go back in there without stealing a kiss from you first."

My happy eyes met his. "I would expect nothing less of my sort-of, kind-of, almost-man."

"There's nothing *almost* about what's happening between us, Sadie."

Our lips met in a soft kiss, and for the first time ever, I wanted to blow off dinner with my sisters to run off with him somewhere.

I wanted more slow, sweet kisses in my bed, but this time I didn't want to stop. My heart took a leap, bounding out of control as I wrapped my arms around his neck and settled into his warmth, kissing him with abandon while he pressed my back against the wall of Everett's screened porch. "I want you," I confessed.

"You have me." His lips moved over mine, drifting across my cheek to my neck. "Call me your man again. Tell me you want to be mine." His soft growl tickled my ear before he gently bit the lobe, then darted his tongue out to soothe it. I was only slightly embarrassed when my knees went weak because he absolutely knew what he was doing to me; it was deliberate. With a soft chuckle, he took hold of my waist to keep me steady and I melted against him, giving myself over in a way I had never done with anyone but him.

My body was moving too fast for my brain to catch up. I was nothing but a swirling mass of electric feels, lost in his arms, breathless, unable to speak. He pressed me harder against the wall with his hips against mine as his fingers drifted low into my waistband, caressing the skin he'd bared at the small of my back. I pulled him close with both arms, feeling the soft hair at the back of his neck as I threaded my fingers through it, tugging his mouth back to mine for more kisses. Deeper this time, our tongues tangled together as we neared the threshold of our control. I felt him hard against me and I wanted nothing more than to be able to finish what we were starting.

"God, Sadie, what you do to me . . ." He pulled back and nudged my forehead with his as his eyes smiled into mine. I smiled back. He was soft and tender now. Gentleman Barrett was back, yet somehow this small moment was more intense than the wild clinch we'd started out in. His whiskers scraped against my cheek, and I sighed, letting my eyes flutter closed as his head dropped to my shoulder.

"I wish—" I paused. "Never mind."

"Tell me." He whispered against my skin.

"Not tonight. This is a wish for another day. When we're alone."

"Okay, baby." He stepped back but I held on. I was stuck in a dream half come true. I felt lost, like I'd forgotten how to breathe, or even think. My head spun as

I clutched his forearms. For a second, we stood staring at each other. Then he pulled me into his chest.

"I've never felt like this. I don't know how to believe in it," I confessed. "What do we do?"

"Hold on to me."

"I am." I let out a soft laugh and squeezed him tighter. "That's it?"

"Yeah. We don't let each other get away, Sadie. If we hold on, this will never end."

"Okay, Barrett. I won't let go."

A knock on the inside of the door forced us to separate. "Sadie, quit canoodling with Barrett and come on." It was Clara. I looked up to find her nose pressed against the window of the door. She stuck her tongue out and waved me inside.

"Call me tonight? Maybe come over again?" I asked.

"Count on it." He dropped a kiss to my forehead, then we went inside.

"Since Barrett is here, we'll allow boys at the table for dinner," Clara magnanimously offered with a wave of her arm. "Sit down, Barrett. Right there." He sat. My eyebrows lifted as she pushed me toward the chair next to him. Clara was usually all about "sisters before misters," so this was a change.

"Ugh, not us." Rider scoffed. "We're eating in the giant TV room with all the toys, not with a bunch of boring girls."

"You guys can stay here if you want," Flynn told Everett and Barrett. "We're out of here."

"Yeah, who wants to eat with a bunch of yucky girls," I teased them. "Is that okay with you Everett?" They adored Everett and had never once acted out around him or got rowdy with his toy collectibles. Probably because he was like a big kid. He loved my sister to pieces and was instrumental in keeping her here in Green Valley with us, where she belonged. So yeah, I adored him too, as did Clara and Gracie. The fact that he hosted our spaghetti sister fest every week was just an added bonus to his appeal.

"Of course, my dudes. Let's get y'all set up."

"I can do it." I said the same thing every week and he always shushed me and took care of them himself.

"Barrett, I love your brother," I declared, making him laugh.

"Who doesn't?"

"No one. He's one hundred percent loveable," Clara stated, elbows on the table, fingers steepled as she eyed Barrett. "So, what's your deal? You're the quiet Monroe boy, aren't you? Kinda nerdy, a little bit of a control freak? Intriguingly hot and mysterious."

"What?" he chuckled nervously. Clara could have that effect on people. She was not afraid to be nosy.

"Hey, y'all!" Molly entered, followed by Sabrina. This was shaping up to be a party of sorts.

"I forgot to tell you I invited our bonus sisters." Willa maneuvered her baby bump between the table and the wall and took a seat.

"The more the merrier." Clara waved them over. "Okay, so Barrett is the quiet one . . ."

Molly laughed and slid into a seat at the table. "Oh! Are we boy-banding them? Garrett is definitely the bad boy."

"Okay, that's my cue to leave," Barrett announced as he got up. "I'll catch up with you later, Sadie."

"Goodbye, shy, quiet heartthrob!" Molly hollered after him. She laughed when he mock-shuddered.

Before he could exit the dining room, Everett appeared in the entrance carrying a huge platter filled with the spaghetti and meatballs. The table already held a green salad, a cloth covered basket of garlic bread, and several bottles of red wine. "Nah, man. Let's eat with the boys in front of the TV. We do not want to be in here." Barrett took the platter from Everett's hands, set it in the center of the table, and left the room.

"I never intended to eat in here. They always end up talking about stuff that freaks me out," he called to Barrett's retreating back. "What is it this time?" Everett directed his question to Willa, but Molly answered instead.

"We're sorting you and your brothers according to boy band classification." She wrinkled her cute little nose as she studied him. "You can't be the sensitive boy next door because that's Wyatt, obvi." She looked over at Sabrina. "Am I right?"

"Oh, totally." Sabrina giggled as she poured a glass of wine and passed it to me.

Everett took a seat. Unlike Barrett, he was unembarrassed—probably because he had grown used to our antics. Maybe he was immune to it by now. "*Obvi*, I'm the cute, nerdy one. Right, Willa?" He winked at her and, from our spots around the table, we all semi-swooned.

"Yeah, babe. That's you in a nutshell." She blew him a kiss. He caught it and put it in the pocket of his Henley.

"You're the one who's always shirtless with the puppy dog eyes," Clara confirmed as she looked him up and down with a smirk. "Isn't that right, Evvie? I've heard the stories. Fixing this place up, chopping wood outside, flaunting that shirtless bod at Willa every chance you got." He winked at Willa and shrugged a shoulder while she turned bright red.

"Y'all are a bunch of nuts," Gracie said, eyes big as she reached for a bottle of wine, hoping we wouldn't notice.

"No," Willa and I told her in unison.

She rolled her eyes and grabbed a can of Coke instead. "Whatever."

"This is a lot of meatballs," Sabrina said as she attempted to scoop a serving of spaghetti with the normal noodle to meatball ratio onto her plate without launching a poor meatball right out the door.

"This is why we love Everett," Clara informed her with an emphatic slap to the table. "Restaurants don't give you enough meatballs. Everett doesn't believe in meatball shaming us because we're girls. Like, pile it up, fifty-fifty, noodles to meat." She turned to an amused Everett and continued. "We like meat. You understand that, and I love you for it, broseph."

"I do what I can." He laughed as he started filling plates for himself and the other males in the house.

"When I have a spaghetti craving, I need to become one with the pasta, and he does not scrimp," I added. "But what I respect most of all is you don't judge our gluttonous behavior, Everett."

"Every week I leave this house a pound heavier, and my body is at least one percent parmesan cheese," Clara confirmed. "Sometimes I have regrets when I can't button my jeans the next morning, but I don't see myself changing anything." She shrugged and lifted her glass. "Cheers to you, Everett, the best brother-in-law ever!"

"Heck yes." I lifted my glass in agreement. "To Everett!"

Gracie and Willa exchanged glances and grinned as Everett turned red and shook his head before leaving the room. I guess we'd found his limit.

"Is it like this every week?" Sabrina asked with a laugh.

"Are you asking if we make Everett blush and eat our weight in pasta every week? Yes." I confirmed. I finished twirling noodles onto my fork and pointed it at her for emphasis.

"I can't miss this," Molly announced. "I'll bring pie next time. Or whatever y'all want."

"You got it, Molls," Willa said. "Just bring yourself. You too, Sabrina. And bring Ruby next week. We're all sisters now."

"I love this. Here's to our new sisterhood." Molly raised her glass for another toast.

"Here, here, to found family and family by blood. And to finding the people you belong with. Love them hard. Make it awkward," I added. Clara wasn't the only one in a sentimental mood tonight.

"Cheers!" We *clinked,* then dug in.

"That was beautiful, Sadie. Where did it come from?" Clara asked me after chugging back her entire glass of wine.

I sipped mine to make it last, one of us had to stay sober. "Ask Sabrina who's been checking out the entire inspirational self-help section of the library for the last few months. I didn't become this evolved on my own."

"Can confirm," Sabrina answered with her quiet little giggle. "We have a self-help-slash-inspirational book party of two at the library almost every week over coffee and doughnuts."

"I love that," Clara said. "I need lots of help. Can I come next time?"

"Of course you can." Sabrina beamed at her. She had always been so shy, but once you were lucky enough to get to know her, you'd have a friend for life. Clara and I had known her as kids when she would occasionally come to the farm with Willa, but back then she was so painfully shy I had only spoke to her a handful of times.

They were all about to become regular fixtures at spaghetti night, and I was here for it.

I couldn't help but think of Lizzy. She belonged here with us, just as much as Gracie and Ruby did. And if I wanted a future with Barrett, I had to think of something to help her get over Weston.

After dinner I pulled Gracie aside to have a chat about the situation. It felt very juvenile, like I'd time traveled back high school, but I had to know what was going on.

"Have you talked to Weston about Lizzy?"

She rolled her eyes. "He's over her. I would feel bad for her if she hadn't like, smashed his heart into tiny pieces when she left. It wasn't nice, Sadie. He'd be her friend if she was into that though. So would I, for that matter. I don't have anything against her—not yet, anyway. If she pulls anything we'll have problems for sure though."

"I totally get that. I don't think she's that type, is she?"

"Not so far. She's always been a cool girl as far as I know, but having a broken heart changes people."

"It can, yeah." I grew quiet as I pondered what she said.

She eyed me, a knowing look on her face. "I don't keep secrets, Sadie. We're all grown up enough to handle the truth."

"It's much easier to think that way when you're the one who has what you want. Isn't it?"

She considered what I said for a second. "Point taken. If she hears anything about you and Barrett, it won't be from me or Weston. I promise."

CHAPTER 15

SADIE

After dropping the boys at school and arranging to have another work at home day, I made my way to see my mother. Lavender Hills loomed gorgeous as ever as I drove up through the rolling foothills leading out of Green Valley proper and into the mountains above town. Gradually, the green hills turned purple as I grew nearer to my childhood home. I lowered my windows to inhale the rich scent, letting the breeze from the window blow my trepidations away. I was an adult. I could leave whenever I wanted now that I had a better place to be.

God, how I hated it here growing up.

After I came back home with my boys, I had discovered an odd sense of peace on this land, as if my childhood had somehow blended into theirs, distorting the memories of my mother's cruel words that had always caused me such pain. I watched my mother love my sons and hope began to bloom along with a burgeoning sense of anticipation that would not die no matter how many times I told myself to forget about it, that nothing here would ever change, that *she* could never change.

I pulled my van into a space in front of the store. Momma would be pissed I was taking one of the good spots for customers, but I was in a hurry to get this over with. Truth be told, I was also in the mood to provoke her. My heart was divided in half, filled with a mixture of resigned indifference and foolish hope. The hope hurt too much. A good fight with her would surely chase it away for a while.

The farm stand was designed to look like a small stable. Bushels and baskets of both freshly cut and dried lavender decorated the front of the store beneath the wide windows and like everything else on the farm, it was flawless. The beauty of this place was astounding, the contrast to the ugliness that had always existed inside the walls of our childhood home stark. I could see Momma working with a couple of her new employees behind the counter. I heaved out a sigh, flinching when the *ding* of the door announced my presence.

"Give me a minute, Sadie." She held up a finger as she finished helping a customer.

"Okay." I wandered around as I waited for her, my eyes drifting over the perfectly packaged handmade soaps and perfumes, the sachets, lavender wands, and wreaths. Momma also sold fresh and dried herbs, and teas. And let us not forget the reputation she sold—Mother Earth incarnate, hocking all-natural, organic bullshit to the largely unsuspecting citizens of Green Valley.

My stress levels had been high before I even got here. They would likely be through the roof by the time she finished behind the counter. I snuck a honey stick from the display and cracked it open. Momma also raised bees and harvested the honey. I rolled my eyes as I sucked the honey from the plastic tube.

"I'm done. Let's go to the house," she said in an unreadable tone. I followed her through the parking lot and up to the white picket fence that lined the homestead. I hung back as she led the way. When we reached the white-washed, wrap-around porch, she pointed to a rocking chair. "Sit down, Sadie. I'll bring out some lemonade."

Once we were settled with our frosty glasses of lavender lemonade, she turned to me with an expression I'd never seen on her face. My heart pounded hard as that stupid anticipatory feeling flooded through my veins. Nothing good ever happened here; I needed that hope to die.

"Why?" I finally managed to ask. "I don't want you helping me. I don't need to be beholden to you any more than I already am after staying here with you—"

Her face was near expressionless, as usual. "Stop. Please listen. You're a good mother. The boys belong with you, at least fifty-fifty. And I know Stephen is a good father—the boys talk about him all the time. But I will not allow you to be taken advantage of."

"I'm not stupid. I won't let him take advantage of me. What do you expect me to do? Do you want me to work off the cost—"

"No, you don't owe me a thing. Nothing, I promise. I don't want anything except for you to let me help you—"

"You want to help me? No strings? No verbal cut-downs? I married him, Momma, and you told me not to do it, remember? Who are you right now?"

She laughed, the sound bitter and brittle. Tears filled her eyes as she looked toward the trees dotting the horizon beyond the lavender fields. "Sadie, I never wanted to have children and I didn't want to get married. I wanted to go to college. I wanted to see the world and have adventures. I wanted to write, to be creative, and dream and—"

My eyes narrowed as I caught hers. "You're telling me who you were. Aren't you?"

"Yes," she whispered. "It's the only way you'll understand. It's the only way you'll let me help you keep your babies and set you free. And I want you to let me help you, Sadie. I know it's selfish, but I need to do it."

I nodded. I was ready for her to go on, to get this over with, but unsure if I was ready to hear what she had to say.

"Since the moment I first met him, all your father wanted was me. He did everything to keep me with him, including messing with my birth control pills after promising he'd follow me to college, after saying that we could live together while I followed my dreams. But he lied to me, and he trapped me in Green Valley. He trapped me with you, Sadie, and I resented it. I was angry and stuck and I had nowhere to go. He controlled everything—the money, the bills—and after you'd grown, he wouldn't even let me have the car keys to take y'all to school. Y'all girls hated riding the bus, but he didn't care. He didn't trust me to come back to him if he let me leave the house alone. And when he finally left me, I had four of you. What was I supposed to do? Where could I go?"

"Why didn't you tell Aunt Genie? Or ask your parents for help?"

"My own damn stupid pride. They warned me, just like I warned you about Stephen, and I warned Willa about that bastard, Tommy. And look at what happened with Clara, my god—"

"Yeah, maybe we should have listened to you. Or at least to each other."

"My family hated your father. They all warned me against him. But I was a foolish girl with stars in her eyes and I refused to listen to anyone. At first, I thought I could have it all, but I soon learned different.

"I was stuck here, so, I stayed. And I used every spare cent he gave me and every dollar I could pilfer from his wallet behind his back to create this farm. I built the most beautiful cage in the world, right here on Lavender Hill. I wanted to be able to provide a way out for you and your sisters. I wanted to make my own money so you could have a life, go to college, or art school, or beauty school, anything other than being trapped by some no-good, selfish asshole. I wanted so much more for you girls, and I regret so much that I didn't give it to you or show you the right way to get it for yourselves."

"Momma . . ." I breathed.

Her eyes were haunted, full of pain. It hurt to look at her. "And I'm sorry, but if I had to do it all again, I wouldn't. I would run from your father and Green Valley, fast and far, and never look back. For all those years, raising you and your sisters, I was beyond angry. I couldn't see a way around the rage that filled every fiber of my being. But most of all, I didn't want any of my daughters to end up being trapped like me."

"Oh my god." I reached out to grab her hand. I never thought I would ever relate to her.

Her fingers gripped mine back as our eyes briefly met. "Soon after you moved back to the house, something changed in me. I watched how you were with Flynn and Rider, and it took some of the darkness out of my soul. Then I started getting to know them. I let them into my heart in a way I never could manage to allow myself to be with you and your sisters and I saw every mistake I had made with you girls as clear as day. It made me sick how wrong I had been. I should have taught you and your sisters to be strong with love instead of trying to make you hard and cold like I was. Strength doesn't have to be borne from cruelty. I could have taught you a different way."

"But you were broken, Momma. Daddy stole your whole life away from you." Tears flowed from my eyes as I imagined how she had felt. Was it like how I had felt lying in my hospital bed after finding out Stephen had slept with someone else?

She shook her head. "There is no excuse for what I've done. Sadie, look at me. Then have a look at yourself. Where I failed, you thrived. You're a good mother. Your boys are lucky to have you. The only way I can think of to make up for what I've done to you and your sisters is to love your babies. I'm a better grand-mother than I ever was a mother. I will never ask for your forgiveness, because I don't deserve it. How could I? I've caused you and your sisters far too much damage to ever be forgiven for it. But I will be here, in the background of your lives, where I belong. And when I see fit, I will move heaven and earth to keep you and your sisters safe."

I brushed tears from my cheeks as I allowed her words to sink in. "Is this why you let Willa and Everett have custody of Gracie?"

"Yes."

"Is this why you hired my attorney and the private detective?"

She sighed. "Yes."

"Thank you."

"I don't deserve your thanks."

"Well, I'm giving it anyway, Momma. Take it."

"Typical. You never were much good at listening." The wink accompanying her grumbling voice startled me.

Shocked laughter burst out of my mouth. "Neither are you! Let us tell you what you deserve. You don't get to make that call."

She considered my words before answering. "Point taken. I'll let y'all lead the way."

"Maybe Sunday dinners can be different from now on?"

Her surprised eyes met mine. "Maybe. I will promise to try. And I promise to get my temper under control. I snapped at you about the process server the other day and I have no excuse other than I was worried. I couldn't stand the thought of Stephen taking the boys from you."

"Gracie has your temper. Her therapist is helping her work through it. So, okay, you promise to work on your temper, and I promise to keep coming to dinner. Every single Sunday. Pot roast and perfect mashed potatoes." I nodded decisively "And the boys can visit you whenever they want. They love you, you know."

"I know. And I love them too. With all of my heart. Those boys are precious, and it's all because of you."

Hearing a compliment from her was like listening to a foreign language. I stared at her for a few seconds before answering. I wasn't quite sure I understood her correctly, but I wanted so much to believe she was sincere. "We'll work up to it," I finally declared.

"Work up to what?"

"To loving each other."

Tears filled her eyes. "Sadie, I don't deserve your love."

"But you will. You're the most stubborn person I know. If you want to deserve it, then someday you will."

"Okay," she whispered. "I don't deserve a chance like this, but I want to take it. I want to do right by you and your sisters even if it means I have to walk away if we try and it hurts y'all too much."

"Why do you think we kept coming back to you all these years, Momma?" I whispered back. "We want to try."

Her eyes filled with tears. "I love you girls, I do. Sadie, I love you. I just don't know how to—I'm so sorry."

"We'll work up to that too."

"To what?"

"Forgiveness."

"Alright, Sadie. I promise I won't give up."

The more I pushed her, the more she seemed to go along with it. I decided for one more shove. "I want you to make an appointment with Clara and Gracie's therapist. He gave us a family discount since Willa and I and the boys started seeing him too. He's nice, you'll like him. You just dump everything messing up your head on him and he'll help you sort it out. It's amazing."

She smiled at me. It was weird to see her smile and I immediately wanted to see it more. "I'll give him a call. Lord knows I need help sorting through all the feelings I've shoved down over all these years. And I'm sorry for what I insinuated about you and Barrett the other day. He isn't a horse's ass like Stephen. The Monroes are good folk, all of them, especially their momma. And he will be the lucky one if you choose to give him your time."

I stared at her for a minute, in disbelief this was happening. "Holy crap. I never thought a day like this would ever be possible."

"Neither did I." She stood. "I need to get back to the store. Take care of those boys. I'll see y'all on Sunday. Bring Barrett and his girl along if you like."

"Holy crap," I repeated.

She patted my hand with a laugh before heading down the path toward the store. "We'll talk more at dinner on Sunday."

Clara would not believe any of this. I hardly believed it myself.

* * *

I was back at home.

Clara had driven the boys to school for me today. She must be at the gym since she wasn't here.

I needed to get to work. Well, first I needed to peel my eyes away from the kitchen window. I was in a daze, standing there with the hazy sunlight beaming its rays of light on my face as I leaned with my hips propped on the inside corner of the counter staring into a hope-filled oblivion.

The indifference about my mother that had been edging out the hope I'd held onto over the years had blown away in the lavender breeze as I'd driven home from the farm, and it freaked me way out. I wanted her to try; I wanted to have a real mother. It's what I'd always wanted from her since I was a little girl. But the thought of actually getting it someday was almost too much for me. My heart was no longer divided in half. It was teetering on the edge, about to fall.

My nose tingled and stung. My eyes pricked and I closed them against the tears and the bright light from the window. I wanted to go back and hide in the dark. Hope was scary. Had I just driven home out of a dream?

Dang it. What I really needed was Barrett. I wanted so badly to run to his house, straight into his arms, and tell him all about my mother, and my hope, and my worry, but I couldn't do that. I was overwhelmed by my feelings. I was desperate to believe in my mother and aching to tell Barrett all about it. I knew he was working from home today. His garage door had been open when I got back, and his truck was inside. Forcing myself to stay here was nearly impossible.

I had told him I was okay with *right now*.

But how long would I have to wait to have him all the time? Whenever I needed him?

Argh! My little crush on him had blown the heck up. That tiny burning torch I had carried for him over the years was now a raging inferno about to burn me alive. Realistically, I could no longer refer to it as a crush without being a big, dumb liar.

This morning had been something else. I had so much to do for work, but I was frozen.

I came out of it at the sound of our garage door going up. Clara was home.

She entered the kitchen slowly, eyeing my tear-streaked face with careful perusal. "How did it go?" Her side-eyed question made me laugh. "Are you okay? What are we working with? Do we need to run out for more alcohol? Chocolate? A litter of puppies?"

"Clara, I don't even know where to begin. I don't know if my heart can take all of these changes."

"Was it that bad?"

"No, it was so, so good. It was unlike anything I'd ever seen from her. We might have a real shot at a relationship with her—and it scares the hell out of me." I told her everything I'd discussed with Momma, and she agreed to start going to Sunday dinners again with me. We also agreed to hold off on having Willa and Gracie come to dinner until we felt more certain about everything. They'd been hurt enough. We had too, but we were already used to bearing the brunt of it.

"I can't believe it, but I want to, so bad, Sadie."

"I know, I do too. It's what we always wanted—" My cell rang. It was Barrett. "I have to take this. It could be about work. Speaking of, I haven't even started today."

"Get the phone. We'll talk later. I think I'll need at least two business days to process this information anyway." Back to joking, she headed off down the hall.

CHAPTER 16

BARRETT

Rain pattered against my front window. Clouds had chased the morning sun away, turning the day as gloomy as my thoughts. Working from home had become my new normal over the last few days. Unfortunately, I couldn't concentrate worth a damn right now.

Lizzy was in bed with what she had claimed was a headache. Day by day she seemed sadder, and she wouldn't talk about it. I'd actually called Leeann to see if Lizzy had opened up to her, but I should have known better. Finally, I asked my mother to give talking to her a go, but she hadn't been able to get Lizzy to confide in her yet. It had me worried, but what could I do? She was an adult. I couldn't force her to talk to me.

Sadie was back home, working like I was. Mere feet separated us, but it felt like a chasm that would take an eternity to bridge.

The Bandit Lake site was still a nightmare, but I knew Garrett had plans for Sadie to start another project soon—a small bungalow that one of the crews had just finished remodeling across town. I found myself plotting ways to get myself added to that project even though my further involvement there was unnecessary.

Stolen moments. Hidden gestures. *Right now.*

It was not enough. Not when I had finally discovered what I needed in my life.

My phone taunted me from the coffee table. I shouldn't call her when there was no way to be with her today. Lizzy was sick. What if she needed me when she woke up?

Selfish.

I picked it up anyway, tapped the screen, tapped her name.

"Hello?" Her sweet voice in my ear was still *not enough.*

"Can you meet me at the Bandit Lake site?"

"Is something wrong?"

"Yes. I'll tell you about it when we get there."

"I'll ask Clara to meet the boys when they get off the bus, okay? Just in case we run long."

"Perfect." I left a note for Lizzy about where I'd be and let her know I'd made her favorite vegetable soup and it was in the fridge ready to be heated up for dinner. I didn't want to wake her with a text.

"We'll be working on that blasted house forever, won't we?" She laughed before ending the call. There was nothing wrong at the site that I knew of. But the odds were in my favor; I was sure I could find something after we arrived.

I made a stop at the Piggly Wiggly for a few things before heading to the site. Halfway there, I found her at the side of the road examining what looked like a flat tire. I pulled in behind her. "Are you okay?" She was shaken up, eyes huge in her face. I took her hand. "Come with me. We'll call the Winston's garage for a tow."

"One of my tires blew out." Fear filled her eyes. I opened the truck door and helped her inside. She shivered against the cold so I reached across her to turn the heat up.

"You probably drove over something in the road. If it's something else, I'm sure Cletus or Beau will find it." The Winston Brother's garage was the best in the area.

"You're right. That has to be it. I'm being silly, freaking out like this." She inhaled a huge breath and pulled her wet hair out of her face as she settled in the cab of my truck. "I shouldn't have stood outside like I did. I'm soaking wet. I don't know what I was trying to find. It's just a flat. But I was so scared, Barrett. I almost went off the road. This has been such a strange day." I had the sense it was more than fear from the blown tire feeding her emotions.

"You're not being silly, baby. A blowout would shake anyone up. I'll get you all taken care of, don't worry." I gripped her thigh, holding onto her as I scrolled to the Winston Brother's Auto Shop contact entry on my phone to arrange the tow. I nodded to her when they picked up, shutting the door to go around and get back in the truck. "All set. They have a driver in the area, so it will only be a few minutes."

"I'm glad you showed up. I don't know why I have the creeps right now. Flat tires happen all the time. Right?" A nervous giggle escaped, and I took her hand.

"Of course. All the time."

It was only a few minutes before the bright lights of a tow truck filled my windshield. After handing the keys off to the driver, we took off.

She switched the radio on. "I need a distraction. I don't like how I feel right now."

"Keith Urban. A quality distraction, I'd say." I glanced in her direction, smiling as she started singing along.

"I have to be honest." She grinned at me. "I sing along to everything, not just Adele." I reached across the console with an open palm, hoping she'd take hold of my hand. When she did, I felt it in my heart, and when she sang directly to me, laughing, off-key, and making funny faces, I swear I fell halfway in love with her.

The rainfall steadily increased to a relentless tempo as we drove and by the time we got to the Bandit Lake house it was pouring buckets. The garage was full of supplies, so I was forced to park in the driveway.

"Are you ready?" I asked. "We're going to have to make a run for it."

She hopped out of the truck. "I'm already soaked!" she shouted as she dashed to the middle of the lawn and spun in a circle with her head thrown back like something out of a movie. "You can run for it if you want."

I was damp, not wet, so I ran to the covered porch to unlock the door. "You all right out there, Sadie?" I chuckled as I watched her twirl again.

"Clara and I used to do this all the time when we were kids. We called it making rain circles. We would run out to the fields and spin around and around until we were so dizzy, we'd fall over in the lavender and lie on our backs to watch the dark clouds swirl above our heads. Have you ever smelled lavender in the rain, Barrett?"

I shook my head as I stood on the porch watching her. "I can't say that I have, sweetheart."

A small smile traced across her features before the driving rain washed it away. "You should. Next time it rains we'll go up there and I'll show you. Anyway, we'd go back to the house soaking wet and covered in mud. Gosh, Momma would get so angry, yelling and screaming about how we'd messed up her lavender and tracked mud all over her clean floors." She stilled her movements as the memory seemed to fade away. Her face twisted painfully as she walked to the porch. "My mother is—my mother told me she loved me for the first time ever this morning."

"Oh, Sadie." I couldn't tell if her cheeks were wet from tears or the rain and I got the feeling she'd run out to the lawn to hide the emotions the storm and the blown-out tires and her time with her mother had evoked for her today. But instead of escaping then, she had stirred them up by getting lost in the past. "Come here, baby." I offered her my hand as I threw the door open for us to go inside.

Thunder rolled and crashed in the distance as she placed her hand in mine. I felt it rumble in my chest, echoing the wild beat of my heart as I led her into the house, letting go of her hand to wrap my arm around her waist so she wouldn't slip on the tiled floor of the foyer.

"I'm okay, you know," she informed me as she stepped out of my arms. "I'm always okay."

I caught her eyes and watched as they flashed defiantly in the low light that filtered through the windows between the slats of the wooden blinds. "I know you are. You're a strong woman, Sadie. But you don't have to be strong all the time. Not right now, not with me."

"I know that." She smiled; it was almost indecipherable, but I knew her well enough by now to know she wasn't the type to dwell in a bad mood if she could help it. "I feel what I feel, and I don't want to be sad anymore."

"I love that about you," I confessed.

"What?" Her curious gaze met mine as she went still, waiting for my answer.

I tugged on the wet sleeve of her blouse. "Your heart. It's usually right there. You don't hide it."

"I like that you see me that way," she murmured.

"I like everything I see when I look at you," I returned, gratified when her body swayed closer to mine and her hands slid up my chest.

She shivered. She was soaked, probably freezing, so I gathered her close to warm her up, not caring that my clothes were now getting wet from the contact. Our mouths met in an inevitable kiss. She opened her lips, inviting my tongue to slip between, and I let out a low groan. The feel of her soft curves in my arms was like heaven and I wished I could stop time and hold her forever.

I was about to pick her up and carry her to the nearest bed when both of our phones went off, blasting out an emergency warning signal. Startled, we jumped apart. I pulled mine from my pocket while Sadie bent to retrieve her purse from the floor to get hers.

It was a weather alert. The rivers in the area were rising due to the rain and the road leading to Bandit Lake was in danger of washing out. The smart choice would be to stay here until the rain died down.

Wordlessly we locked eyes as we each began dialing family to take care of our respective children. Sadie connected with Clara, who agreed she should stay here and said she'd keep the boys tonight. Relief suffused her features; the boys would be safe at home. I called my mother who agreed to bring my father to my house and stay in the guest room. Lizzy was grown, but I knew she would hate to be alone if the power went out.

"It's this house. Cursed, I tell you." I chuckled.

"I don't think so. I think we've stumbled into a romance novel, just like the one I was reading the other night on my patio," she joked, lightening the mood.

"How so? Because we're stuck here for the night in a cursed house?" I laughed.

"Yep, forced proximity." She nodded sagely, eyebrows raised in amusement.

"Ahh, I see. What else?"

"I know for a fact there's only one bed in this place. It's gorgeous and comfy. I picked it out myself."

"Nice." I laughed before getting serious. "We should get out of these wet clothes before we catch colds. We could use the unused drop cloths to dry off with and put our stuff in the dryer. Garrett installed all the laundry room appliances a few days ago."

She burst into laughter. "Classic let's-get-out-of-these-wet-clothes, indeed. And we don't need drop cloths. The master suite bathroom is fully stocked with linens and towels and everything we could ever need."

I whipped my shirt off and tossed it at her. "You know I didn't mean anything by that," I insisted.

"Okay, now you're shirtless and you look just like the hero in my book. Hellooooo, six-pack abs, I bet you have the 'V' too, don't you? Let me see it!" she teased and poked my stomach.

"If you're lucky," I teased back with a wink and kicked off my shoes.

"Oh, ho ho. I'm gonna get so lucky tonight." She whipped her own shirt off and tossed it at my face. It was sopping wet and clingy and by the time I'd removed it from my head, she'd taken off her pants and shoes too.

She was wearing granny panties like she'd said the other day—that was no lie. But they were wet from the rain, made of skimpy white silk and lace, sexy as hell, and she may as well have been naked because I could see *everything*.

Her body was gorgeous, from the rosy tips of her rounded breasts peeking through her matching silk and lace bra to the flat plane of her stomach to the delicate flare of her narrow waist, and her long, long legs.

The power went out and we exploded in laugther. "At least I got a good look at you first," she said with giggles in her voice.

"I did what you said," I blurted.

"What did I say, baby?" She had stepped close to me when it got dark. I felt her hands at my belt tugging me even closer, her fingertips trailing along my waist. I shivered as her touch caused goosebumps to raise over my skin.

"I'll show you. Come to the window." She followed me over. I had left my brief-case on the sill last time I was here. "Open it." She popped it open, smiling as she pulled strip after strip of condoms from the interior pocket on top of my work files. "I also have food and wine in my truck," I mentioned sheepishly. My need to be prepared and plan ahead hadn't always been appreciated. Some, like my ex-wife for one, found my lack of spontaneity annoying.

"Gosh, you're brilliant. Perfect Barrett, being perfect again. I love it." She reached up, took my face in her hands, and planted a wet, smacking kiss to my lips. "Was there anything actually wrong here tonight? Or did you summon me here for you to have your wicked way with me?" Her sweet giggle was infectious. I traced her smile with a fingertip, then brushed a kiss to her lips.

"I was hoping *you* would have your wicked way with *me*," I joked.

"Oh yeah? How many of these things do you think we can use tonight?" I saw the white flash of her grin in the dim light of the window as she draped a strip of condoms around my neck.

"There's only one way to find out. But first, I have to make sure—are you okay? It didn't escape my attention that this was an emotional day for you. We don't have to do anything. I'm happy just to spend time with you, however you want. I need you to be sure."

Her hands softened on my face, then she wound her arms around my neck, pressing her silk and lace-covered breasts to my chest. "I'm sure that I want you. I'm sure that I'm falling for you. And I'm sure that I've been dying to know what you'll feel like inside of me for a long time now. Don't you want me too?"

I gripped her waist, hauling her tight against my body. "More than anything."

"Okay, then." She breathed, tilting her head back. Her eyes softly closed, while black lashes fanned out over the high freckled arches of her cheekbones. "Let's start with another kiss."

CHAPTER 17

BARRETT

"A kiss," I whispered in her ear. I pressed our mouths together, thrusting my tongue between her full pink lips to tangle it with hers. She dug her fingers into the nape of my neck, holding me tight, kissing me back until I was left with only one thought: once I had her, I would never be able to let her go. "Like this?" My voice was a low groan as I held myself back. We had all night; it made no sense to rush.

She broke away for a second. "Exactly like that. I love how you kiss me."

"I love how I am with you. You've unlocked something inside me, Sadie. I've wanted you for so long. But I couldn't let myself feel it."

"Because I was married?"

"Yeah."

"God, you're such a good man."

"And you're everything. Everything that's beautiful in the world? I can see it in your eyes." She slammed her mouth to mine. It was needy, greedy. She wanted me, and she was not shy about showing how much.

She reached between us, delicate fingers unbuckling my belt and undoing my pants. I kicked them aside and pressed my hips into hers. I was as hard as stone, I needed her, I was desperate for her, and I too, was unashamed about showing her how I felt.

If our first kiss was a beginning, this one was a turning point. Her body melted into mine as our lips and bodies moved together. Like a dance, we were in sync. She was made for me. She knew what I wanted before I knew it myself.

I could smell her, her wet arousal, the heat between her thighs I'd never let myself think about until now. It mixed with the sweet floral notes of her perfume and the scent of the rain that still clung to her skin, earthy and primal. Heady, lush, and about to be all over me.

I found the lace edge of her panties. My hands skirted the waistband, tugging them lower, down over the graceful curve of her hips until she grinned and, with a shimmy, they slipped down her legs. "Touch me, Barrett," she murmured as she kissed and sucked on my neck, my collarbone, my shoulders, placing biting kisses on my skin while trailing her fingertips up and down my chest, raising goosebumps in the wake of her soft lips and seeking hands. "Or should I touch you?" She reached inside my boxer briefs and wrapped her hand around my cock with a moan. Her other hand clutched at my bicep, fingers digging into the flesh of my arm as she stroked me up and down.

"I need to get inside you." It was all I could do not to lift her to the windowsill, spread her legs wide, and take her right there. I knew she was ready for me, that she would probably love it, even get off on it, but if I wanted to show her both sides of my feelings—the mindless desire that currently battled with how much I cared for her—I had to get her into bed. I had to make this last beyond a quick fuck in a window.

She meant more to me than that.

She meant the world.

I wanted to go slow, but I had to get a taste of her right now or I'd lose my mind. With my eyes locked to hers I pressed two fingers high inside of her. She was hot and slick, so much like the white silk I'd removed from her body only moments before.

But she wasn't the one to moan. I was. "Beautiful Sadie, I want you so much. You have no idea how hard you make me. How desperate I am for you."

She inhaled a sharp breath of pleasure and I felt her tighten around my fingers. "I love the things you say to me . . ."

This was exactly what I needed. Just a little hint of what was coming to get me off the edge. I found my way to that spot inside her, the one I knew would drive her wild.

I wanted to earn all her pleasure, needed to work for it to make it mine. I was thrilled when she clutched my shoulders with both hands and dug her nails in to hold on with her eyes wide on mine in surprise.

"God, Barrett." Her knees went weak as she gasped my name and those big blue eyes of hers fluttered closed. With my hand against her stomach, I backed her into the wall near the stairs before finding her clit with my thumb to swirl it in soft circles. I wanted her legs to shake. I wanted her to fall apart in my arms.

"I want you to come right here in the foyer before I fuck you," I growled into her ear. "Every time we come here to work, you're going to remember what I did to you and you're going to want me to do it again."

One of her hands gripped the balustrade while the other drove into my hair, pulling it as she panted out my name between gasping breaths. Her tits pressed to my chest. Her ass pressed against the wall for balance. I didn't stop until I felt her pussy pulsing hard and fast around my fingers, until I saw those gorgeous thighs shake, until my name on her lips went from breathless to moaning to a scream. Her hand in my hair became painful right before she fell apart completely. She arched back and I followed, gripping her waist with one hand as I carefully slid my fingers out of her and licked them clean. Then I swept her into my arms like a bride.

Her head dropped to my shoulder. "Good lord. What just happened?"

I nuzzled my nose into her hair and kissed her temple before whispering an answer in her ear. "I gave you a memory. You'll never look at a bifurcated staircase the same way ever again."

Her hazy eyes widened on mine, and I winked. Her laughter trailed behind us as I began to make my way to the ground floor master suite.

"Oh! Turn around! Grab the condoms." Luckily, she remembered. I had only one thing burning in my thoughts and that was to bury myself inside of her snug, wet heat and stay there for the rest of the night. The one she'd put on my neck had fallen to the floor somewhere. I turned and dipped to the side so she could rustle around in my briefcase and grab a strip. "Okay, got it. Hurry."

The bed was sumptuously decorated in satins, silks, and a gorgeous made-to-her-specifications white velvet coverlet that had taken months to get here from the manufacturer. The entire room was pure elegance, a showstopper. The centerpiece was this massive hand-carved, custom-made sleigh bed.

"We're about to destroy this bedding, you know."

"I don't care. I'll pay for it. I'll redo it. I wanted it all for myself, anyway." I let her slide down my body once we'd reached the bed. She reached behind her back to unhook her bra, tossed it to the side, then fell back to the bed, spreading her arms and legs wide and squirming against the soft velvet. "Isn't it dreamy?"

"Dreamy? You're the dream. You're every fantasy I've ever had, spread out for me like that. You are so fucking beautiful right now I don't know where to even begin." The sight of her naked on that bed would be permanently etched in the back of my mind. But right now, it was at the forefront, inhibiting my normal thought process. I stood there staring, dying for her, while she smiled at me, wicked and knowing.

With a sudden surge, she sat up, dug her hands into my hips to pull my underwear down. I barely had time to process what was happening before she sucked me into her mouth with a groan. Her tongue traced a circle around the crown of my cock and my eyes rolled back while all the remaining rational thoughts left my head. It took a solid minute before I was able to regain any sort of brain function.

"Not yet." I finally said through a groan. "I want to be inside you the first time you make me come." I pushed her back by the shoulders, exiting her magic mouth with a *pop*.

"God, yes, I want that," she whispered, reaching for the condoms that had landed on the bed. I took one and rolled it on before crawling up her body. Her legs gripped my hips, then wrapped around my back as I found her hands to raise them above her head, holding them down with my elbows planted in the bed.

Our eyes met, I nudged her opening with my sheathed cock and her neck arched back on an inhale as I slid inside, inch by inch. "Damn," I groaned as her hands tightened in mine.

"Slower. Go slow." She exhaled as her eyes shut tight.

"Am I hurting you?" The idea of causing her pain tore at my heart. I stopped.

"No, you're just so big and it's been a long time since I—" I eased out. She was wet for me, but I could do better. "No, don't stop, come back—"

I sat back on my knees. "Hush, baby, and let me do what I have to do. I won't hurt you. I can't stand the thought of it." I grinned as her back arched at my words and her legs shifted restlessly before opening wider for me. "Good girl."

"Holy crap," she moaned. "I knew you were bossy, but this is—" I bent low to glide my tongue from her opening to her clit, laughing against her soft folds when her words stopped making sense. *"Guuuuuuuuh. Barrrrret . . ."*

I pressed my hands against her writhing hips. "Relax. You're mine to take care of. I need to make you feel good."

"I'm about to do whatever you tell me to do," she mewled as her heels dug into my shoulder blades and she slowed her movements.

"Good girl," I repeated with a chuckle. I darted my tongue out to flick it against her clitoris while I pressed lightly against her lower stomach and thrust my fingers back into her.

While shoving her hips up to get more, she cried out, "What are you doing to me?"

I didn't answer. What words could be adequate for this?

"Now. Barrett. I want you. I need it. Get up here," she demanded, letting her legs drop to the sides while reaching low to grab me by the hair and tug me up her body.

I slid inside with one tortuously slow, smooth stroke and she opened to me, like a flower to the sun. We both sighed as our hips met and I was finally seated deep inside her.

Nothing would ever be the same for us again. Our foreheads pressed together, followed by our lips, and I knew this was it for me. No one else could ever make me feel this way. It felt like peace. It felt like love. It felt like time had not existed before right now; we were finally together as we should be.

"More," she said against my lips. "Give me more."

Faster. Harder. More, more, *more*.

I never knew it could be like this with a woman. All these years, existing on nothing when she had been right here, mistreated, cheated on, living without the love she deserved. I mourned the time we could have had together while at the same rejoicing that we'd finally found what we needed in each other.

Her hips rose as I surged into her. She wrapped one leg around my back and held on.

Faster, harder, *more*.

"Sadie." I gripped her hip hard as I took her, made her mine, left my mark on her as I sucked at the soft skin of her neck and ground my pelvis into hers, making sure she felt me on her clit after each thrust inside her gorgeous body.

More.

She cried out, hands sliding down my back, arms wrapping me up, legs holding me close as she came in pulsing waves around me.

I had to see it, I pulled away as I kept driving inside the slick, wet heat of her, holding myself up on one arm above her as I watched her let go for me. Her face was beautiful in the moonlight shining through the window above the bed. Eyes closed, lips parted, head thrown back.

Stunning.

The base of my spine tingled as I got closer and closer to the edge then finally went over it with a roar.

"Nothing will ever feel this right," she murmured as she reached up for me.

I moved to my back, gathering her in my arms to tuck her against my side with her head over my heart. "We're not going back to the way we were. Not now."

"I know, Barrett. I don't want to go anywhere but where you go."

"Good."

She shivered in my arms. The chill from outside had gradually crept in since the power went out, and the heater had stopped.

"There are logs in the garage. I can build us a fire."

"Of course you can, my perfect Barrett," she said with affection, not knowing how much it meant that she appreciated that part of me. "We should stay in bed after, or we'll freeze our asses off."

"Sounds good to me. I'll be right back, and I'll bring the food too." I tugged on my boxer briefs and left to gather what we'd need for the night.

I came back to find her wrapped in a throw blanket. The bed had been remade for sleeping. Most of the many pillows were now on the floor and the covers had been thrown back on one side for me to join her.

"I can't believe how many pillows were on that bed." I set the food and wine I'd purchased earlier at the Piggly Wiggly on an end table, then placed the logs on the rack in the fireplace and lit it.

"Pillows are an essential part of master suite décor, Barrett. Don't fuss at me."

"I'll never fuss at you about your designs. Working with you has proved that I can build a house. But it wouldn't be beautiful without you."

"Oh, wow." She placed her hand on her chest. "I love the things you say." She looked up through her lashes. "Pillows are multifunctional too. They're pretty, but we can also put them in front of the fireplace and use them to get comfy if we decide to make love in front of the fire later."

"That's sweet, baby." I tipped her chin up and kissed her.

"Yeah, sure, but I meant you can shove a few of them under my hips and really have a go at me." She winked and blew me a kiss from her perch near the headboard.

I got hard. It was almost instantaneous. I held out my hand, she took it, and we had a go at each other in front of the fire.

CHAPTER 18

SADIE

Sunlight streamed through the window. It had chased away the gloom from the night before, providing me with enough illumination to realize I was sprawled buck naked in the awesome sleigh bed in the Bandit Lake house.

I stirred and the big arm wrapped snug around my waist also stirred, squeezing me tighter, pulling me closer into the hard wall of warm, naked Barrett tucked up against my back. My eyes opened with a pop as I stretched in place, encountering something huge and hard at my backside.

Oh.

My goodness.

I hadn't slept this well in ages. I had briefly forgotten where I was and who I was with. I covered my mouth with a hand as the memory of the night before played like a movie in my mind and a huge smile unfurled across my face.

It happened. I'd finally had sex with Barrett, and it was amazing. Better than a dream come true for way too many reasons to count. I had no idea his bossy, perfectionist, type-A personality would become so freaking hot when he focused it all over my naked body.

But I should have.

All the clues were there. He took care of everybody; it seemed to be one of his driving forces. He was detail-oriented, for sure. The way he memorized everything I liked when he touched me had paid off huge the second—and third, and fourth—time we'd had sex last night to the point where he could get me off in under three minutes. I couldn't even get myself off like that and I'd been flicking the bean regularly since I had discovered it was there.

I was in huge trouble. I had become addicted to his dick last night, I just knew it. In fact, I wanted it inside me right now and I didn't care how sore I was. He could break me in half and I'd smile and thank him for doing it.

Not only that . . . I was absolutely certain now that I was falling in love with him. The thought of leaving this house and the little bubble we'd found ourselves in last night was inconceivable. It hurt to think about.

I wiggled against him. He groaned in my ear but didn't wake up. "Barrett," I whispered. "It's morning."

"Sadie?" He kissed the top of my head. "Baby, come here."

"I can't get more 'here' than I already am, darlin'." I laughed and wiggled my ass against him once more.

"Open your legs, sweetheart. Let me inside that gorgeous pussy again." I threw my leg back over his hip and he entered me with one smooth movement. "I could stay here forever," he murmured. "You feel like paradise." One hand slid up my stomach to cup my breast, pinching and pulling on the hard pebbled flesh of my nipple as he glided in and out.

"You feel so good," I moaned as he stroked light circles between my legs with his other hand.

"You want to come for me, don't you?"

"So bad," I panted.

"I love it when you need me like this, Sadie. Say please. Let me give you what you need." His voice was gruff in my ear, a low rumbly groan, his breath hot on my skin as he whispered against me.

"Oh god, please, Barrett." My clit pulsed in time with his hard thrusts. My body tensed, spiraling out of control as he worked me higher and higher. My heart soared as he whispered how much he wanted me in my ear.

He was like two different men: the sweet one I'd known forever, whose foot went into his mouth whenever we spoke, and this beast at my back who demanded I say please before he would let me come. Gentleman Barrett disappeared when we were in bed, and I wasn't mad about it. I pondered the fact that he seemed to be obsessed with giving me orgasms and decided it *was* gentlemanly behavior, at least as far as I was concerned. And I wasn't above begging for it if the results were my soul leaving my body each time he gave me what I asked for.

"Please . . ." I said again, because it seemed to drive him insane whenever he heard that word.

Big hands flipped me to my stomach, and I spread my legs wide in anticipation because I knew what I was about to get.

"That's my good girl." His voice, like gravel in my ear, sent sparks up and down my spine as he thrust wildly into me. I shivered as his big arms bracketed my body, and his chest rose and fell against my back. Then he moved a hand between my legs, trapping it between my body and the mattress and I went off the split second he touched my clit.

A dark chuckle filled my ear and I arched up, giving him better access so he could finish. And he did after four more hard drives into my body. He gave me his weight for a second before rolling us back to where we started, so we were spooning once more. "You were made for me." His words drifted into the room, tying us together, wrapping us in the truth of their meaning. *We were made for each other.* I shivered at the thought of it, my future unwinding in front of me like a map full of happy places.

"I wish we didn't have to go home," I confessed, slightly ashamed because while I had missed my boys, I'd rather be here with him having my mind and other parts of my body blown all day long.

"I feel the same way."

"We always have *right now* . . ." I murmured. "Yes?"

"Yeah, baby." He pulled me tight. "I'm giving every moment I can steal to you."

"I want all of them. Promise me."

"I swear it."

* * *

I was home sitting on my couch mindlessly watching TV, but really plotting ways I could be alone with Barrett.

He'd dropped me off about an hour ago. We promised each other we'd find moments to share, a text, a call, maybe a moment on my patio. We came up with the idea to have a "neighbor movie night" with us and our kids. He thought it would be a good idea for us to all be together as friends before we told them we were dating. I found myself hoping for another weather event, but that was hardly something I could count on.

It turned out the road to Bandit Lake hadn't washed out last night and we could have actually gone home, but I was glad we didn't. I wouldn't trade the time we had spent together for anything. Was this what love was supposed to feel like? A desperate craving to be with someone even though you knew that no amount of time would ever be enough? And I had faith that even though so much was against us, we'd pull through at the end.

A knock at the door broke me out of the stupor I had become stuck in since arriving back home. "Coming," I called, hoping it was Barrett on the other side with a stolen moment we could share.

Stupidly, I threw the door open without looking through the peephole. "Oh. Stephen, hello."

"I came to talk about the boys," he said, diving in with no small talk or warning.

"Come in." I stepped aside, gesturing for him to enter. It was best to get this settled, and if I didn't like what he had to say I could always call my attorney or sic my mother on him. Or Barrett, for that matter. Or since he was no longer the weak spot in my life, I could handle it teenage Sadie's way and drop kick his balls up to his throat.

"Have a seat," I offered. He'd always been a handsome man. We were the same height. He was fair like I was, blonde and blue-eyed. The boys took after him as much as they resembled me.

He smiled hesitantly at me. "First thing. I'm not here to argue or fight with you, Sadie. I don't want to hurt you any more than I already have, and I don't want either one of us to get upset. Okay?" He had a lot of nerve trying to dictate how this conversation would go.

"Sure, fine." I took a seat in the corner of the couch, across from his place on the chair by the window.

Year after year since the boys were born, I had gradually been falling out of love with him. But now I knew what we'd had together was never really love. What he had given me was not even a shadow of how Barrett had made me feel last night. How he'd had been making me feel ever since I'd started working with him.

When Stephen left, I'd felt nothing but anger at the horrible position he'd left me in. Now that I was in a better place, I felt nothing at all except the selfish dread of having to share the boys with him.

"I did so many things wrong and I'm sorry. I had a long talk with Dana. She told me you knew about us. That you've known since—"

"Since I was in the hospital giving birth to your children? You broke my heart that day, Stephen. I didn't know what else to do and I had the boys to take care of, so I stayed—"

"I'm so sorry, I—"

"I'm talking now." I glared at him until he leaned back in his chair and shut his mouth. I was not in the mood to be lied to or gaslit or have my feelings minimized. He was going to hear me out whether he liked it or not. I had a few things to get off my chest. "I think I was in shock. Probably because I'd just had the boys and was in so much pain, but you wouldn't know about that, would you? You weren't there. I pretended I didn't know what you'd done, and I stayed with you. I hoped that I could forget about it, that it was a one-time thing, and everything would go back to normal. I almost talked to you about it but then I found your stash of love notes from her, and I realized you would never tell me the truth. And we both know she kept texting and you kept answering. I read everything you sent each other over the years, the texts, the notes you never threw away, and sometimes I could hear you on the phone with her at night when you were hiding in the bathroom or the back yard. You may not have been having sex with her the whole time, but you were still cheating on me. You get that, don't you?"

He looked out the window, unable to meet my eyes. "Yeah. I get it. I was selfish, Sadie. I regret the way I took you for granted. Dana fed my ego. I thought I needed it. She—"

"Stop. The reason I looked the other way—the grace I gave you all those years—was for the boys. Not for you. I couldn't stand the thought of being separated from them. Honestly, I still can't stand it, but I'm not willing to put up with you anymore. I deserve better and I'm so mad at myself that it took you leaving for me to realize that."

"I never meant to hurt you—"

"Are you crazy? You never meant to hurt me? You left us with no warning, Stephen. We were totally broke with nowhere to go but to my mother's house. I will never forgive you for that, not ever. So don't bother apologizing. You had to know what it would do to me to go back to her."

He leaned forward, pinching the bridge of his nose. "Yeah, I understand and I can't apologize enough. I couldn't take care of you and the boys. I lost every-thing, Sadie, and I knew they would be fine with you. You're a great mother. I know you don't want to hear it, but I'm sorry all the same," he insisted.

Ignoring his apology, I continued. "I won't keep the boys from you because ultimately, your relationship with them will have nothing to do with me. They love you, they want to see you, and I know you love them too. And as long as you treat them right and never, ever hurt them again, I won't stand in your way."

"Can I at least finish explaining everything? I want you to understand."

"No, I'm not interested in your explanation. Have your attorney tell mine about it when they figure out how you're going to fill up the financial hole you dropped me in. I don't want to hear it. What I'm interested in is you under-standing where I'm coming from, okay?" He nodded. "You have no idea how badly you've hurt them, the damage you caused them."

"I wish I didn't—"

"Uh-uh, be quiet. The bottom line is, if you hurt them again, it will be done with your last breath because it will be the last thing you ever do. Does that make you understand how serious I am right now?" His eyes flashed to mine and widened. He was used to something different from me. He'd been used to a faux-happy little wifey and homemaker, but I was no longer that woman. He'd hurt my children and I was not about to let it happen again.

"Yes. I understand. I won't hurt them, I swear it, Sadie. I can see my word means shit to you and I get that. But for them I'll make it right. I'll never let y'all down again. I never wanted to in the first place. I had nowhere else to go—"

"Good, fine, whatever. And Dana is to be nowhere near them. Not until after we're divorced, and you're married to her. And then we're going to have a serious discussion about it before it happens. I do not like that woman, Stephen."

"I agree with all of that, okay? Look, I'm not happy about her confronting you at Daisy's. We had words about it, and I broke off the engagement. She could have cost me my sons with that stunt. And the stunt with the second set of papers, and the wine bottles in your bin—"

My eyes shot to his. "What? Explain everything. Now."

He drew in a long breath before explaining. "When y'all moved in here she filled your recycling tote with wine bottles to make you look bad so I would have a better chance with the boys. She confessed everything to me after our talk about what happened at Daisy's."

"That was her? *Ugh.* What a psycho."

"I—yeah, kind of."

I rolled my eyes instead of responding. *'Kind of,' my ass.* I'd be keeping an eye out for her deranged, butt-hurt, stalker self from now on, and I made a mental note to call my attorney. No one messes with me and my boys.

He continued. "Remember the envelope I brought over here for you with the check inside?" I nodded curtly. "Those weren't the papers I had my attorney draw up and I'm sorry about that. I discovered it yesterday when I asked my lawyer if you'd cashed the check and he mentioned the changes I supposedly emailed him about. I never emailed him. It was Dana. She logged into my account and sent it. I wanted things to be fair between us, because of the boys. She accused you of not being reasonable because of what you said at Daisy's when she mentioned being their stepmother, and you said she wouldn't have a say in what happens between us regarding the boys. She was wrong and I told her so. I will not tolerate that. Flynn and Rider mean everything to me. And I won't let her say anything against you as a mother. She was beyond out of line."

"And none of this worries you? What else has she stuck her nose into?"

"No, no, no. She thought she was helping me. Look, I had nothing when I left you. I had no place to go. She took me to her beach house in California. She helped me get my life back together—"

Becky Lee's warning about Dana flashed through my mind. "Are you sure she's not the one who wrecked your life in the first place to get you to leave me?"

"She wouldn't do that," he scoffed. "She's in love with me. Always has been. I—"

"You are way too blasé about this. This is very concerning behavior."

"Don't worry. She knows how I feel about what she did. She won't want to make me angry. She's begging for me to take her back." A smug smile flashed across his face reminding me how he so obviously felt about women, the misogynistic jerk.

"Okay. Fine, believe what you want. But what about me? Is she planning anything to do with me? Didn't think about that, did you?" His arrogance and the overconfidence in his own appeal bordered on foolish. But it was typical when I considered what a big ego he'd always had.

"No, I won't let her hurt you. I told her to leave you alone, Sadie. She's done playing games 'cause she knows it will upset me. Trust me. When I said she wants me back, I meant it. She won't go after you, promise. I told her not to." My eyes couldn't roll back far enough at his answer. "All I could think about when I was getting my shit together was the boys. And you, my beautiful Sadie. I want our family back. I love you. I've always loved you, no matter what I've done that says otherwise. I'm working again, right here in Green Valley, making plenty of money to give you everything you need. You don't have to work anymore, not if you don't want to. And I have a house for us too. There has to be a way—"

"You have got to be joking. You were engaged to someone else a few days ago! You kept her dangling on a string for years while we were married. And think about what you did to me, Stephen. You're unbelievable! Don't forget what I know. The illusion of the happy little wife I let you see all those years is gone."

"But I stayed with you. I never slept with her, except for that one time. And that was only because it had been so long for us, Sadie. I got weak and I needed it.

You were pregnant and uncomfortable. The boys made you so huge, remember? But I love you, and it's over with her. She was just—"

"*You* got weak? *You* needed it? I was pregnant with your children, you ass! That's your excuse? Never mind. Don't answer that, you'll just piss me off more and this is supposed to be about the boys. You have no idea how to love a woman, Stephen. If you loved me like you say you did, why did you leave me? Why didn't you come to me with whatever was going on? I couldn't find you. Then all of a sudden, the bank started calling about the house and your stores going under. Overnight, everything was gone and I had nothing. Do you understand how scary that was? For the boys? For your parents? They didn't even know where you'd disappeared to. Your mother was beside herself. You are unbelievable."

"I had to be able to take care of you! Why can't you see that?" he shouted. "I only left you so I could come back better. Can't you understand that?"

"No. I can't. When you love someone, you don't leave them. You don't cheat on them."

"So it's over for good then? Aren't you sad about it? You're so cold right now."

"Yes! It's over! And I was sad for years and you didn't see it. Think about someone other than yourself for a change. And listen, the boys want to see you. If they didn't, I'd do whatever it took to keep you away. They seem to be the only exception to your selfishness. I used to wonder how you could be such a great dad while being an absolute shit of a husband. But I don't care anymore. As long as you're good to them, you can see them."

"Take me back and I'll prove I can be a good husband too. I'll change, Sadie. I'll do anything."

I stared at him. So clueless. So selfish. "Stephen, if you loved me at all, you would have asked me how I had managed while you were gone. You haven't tried to ask me anything about myself the entire time you've been here. It's all about you. It's *always* all about you. You never cared to know me when we were together."

"I did. I swear I did."

"Oh really? What's your favorite thing about me besides how I look? Do you even know how I like my coffee in the morning? Or what my favorite color is?

And that's just surface stuff. *I love you* is so much more than words that you say. Love is what you do before and after you say it. I hope one day you'll understand that."

He turned away again, defeated for the moment. He got up to leave. "For what it's worth, I really am sorry. I never would have left you if—well, I guess you don't care anymore."

"You never would have left me if I had been able to take care of you like Dana could? If I wasn't just a pretty face you liked to look at and was loaded with money like her? If I had a house for you to hide out in after your business went under like she did? Is all of that correct?" I sighed. "Look, Stephen, I don't wish you ill. I want you to be happy. It will be good for the boys to see you happy. But I will never take you back."

His face fell. "Fine. How about next weekend? Can I take them then? You can come look my place over first if you like. I have everything they need. They'll each have their own room. My mother will be there because I have to work, and I figured it might make the boys more comfortable to have her with us. And you trust her still, right? I know you don't trust me, and I guess I can't blame you."

I did trust his mom. She was a good woman and a wonderful grandmother. She had offered us a place to stay after Stephen left, but being in Nashville would have been too far away from Clara and Gracie and the boys' friends. I figured we all needed that support, so I'd chosen my mother's place. And I'd be fooling myself if I didn't admit that small thread of hope to finally win my mother's love had nudged me in her direction as well.

"Text me your address and I'll drop by. And I will be calling your mother."

"Will do." He ran a hand through his hair, wrapping his palm around the back of his neck. That was his tell he was nervous. "Maybe one day we can be at least friends?" Hopeful eyes met mine and I nodded.

"We can work up to that. We'll probably be grandparents together one day, after all."

He let out a sad laugh. "I really fucked up."

"Yeah, you did. Look, I'm going to text you the number of the therapist me and the boys go to. You need it. Call him. He might even give you the family discount." My laugh was sad too. But not for the loss of my marriage. I was sad I had wasted so much of my life with him. And I was also sad that I came from a family who needed so much freaking therapy. That crap was not cheap.

He hesitated, then turned around to face me once he reached the doorway. "My attorney thinks the papers yours drew up are fine. I'll sign them. Promise me I won't lose the boys. I'll do anything to prevent that from happening. Even call your therapist."

I softened a tiny bit because he really did love them—which was why him leaving us the way he did had been so weird. "I don't want to keep them from you. They missed you."

"Thank you. Once the papers are signed then it will be just a matter of time. Goodbye, Sadie. I'll be in touch."

"Goodbye, Stephen. The boys will be so excited to see you."

I was happy for the boys. They'd get their father back. And after the outburst from the other day, I knew they needed him. But that didn't mean my heart wasn't breaking at the thought of being away from them. It's what I'd spent the last almost nine years trying to prevent.

I shut the door behind him and found my book. Too many thoughts were racing through my mind and I needed to settle down. I read the words on the pages, but they didn't sink in. Finally, I tossed it aside and got up to pace.

I was almost divorced. It was happening. And Flynn and Rider would be with Stephen in a few days. That was going to happen too. I stopped at the window in the kitchen, remembering how I'd stood here watching Barrett jog around the cul-de-sac back when we'd first moved in. So much had happened since then. It felt like a lifetime had gone by.

"Yo! Sadie, I'm home!" Clara entered the kitchen, not dressed for the gym as was her usual of late. She was in jeans and a tight tank covered by a cardigan.

"Where have you been?"

"I dropped off the boys. I was supposed to meet Chris but ended up visiting Molly instead. You weren't kidding about that drop-off line thing. What is wrong with people? It's like they all forget how to drive when they're within a five-mile radius of a school. I flipped off at least ten different moms. It wasn't pretty." She rummaged around in the fridge and popped open a Diet Coke. "What's up with you?" She looked me over. "I thought you'd look happier after being with Barrett all night. Please tell me you hit that. Let me live vicariously."

"Vicariously? You mean you and Chris aren't . . .? But I thought—"

"Well, keep on thinking. That isn't happening anymore. Not for now, anyway."

"Oh. Crap."

"Yeah, it's a pity too. He had so much potential."

"Well, maybe you can fix things?"

"I'm not going to hold my breath." She shrugged and rolled her eyes. Turning her back to grab a package of Chips Ahoy! from the pantry. Crap. Cookies and Diet Coke translated into "Clara" meant she was hurting and did not want to talk about it yet. In other words, if Clara was eating her feelings, they were big ones.

"Stephen was just here." I announced, deciding to let her drop the subject. Her eyes got big and she nodded at me to go on as she stuffed a cookie in her mouth. "I agreed to let him take the boys. His mom will be there, otherwise I would have made him wait until—until I was forced to let him take them, I guess."

"Are you okay with all of this?"

"Not really, but I have to be, don't I? This was inevitable. This is divorce."

"I'll be here, Sadie. We'll get through it together and we can always borrow a car, go into stealth mode, and stalk his house for glimpses of the boys to make sure they're okay. Kind of like we used to do to Barrett back in the day." She winked at me, and I shook my head.

"Speaking of Barrett, we planned a movie night with our kids next weekend."

"Oh yeah? You should cook them dinner too. Make your chicken casserole and they'll both fall in love with you."

"That's a great idea."

"Make brownies too. And save like, five of them for me. I don't know if Chips Ahoy! will be enough for the way I'm feeling right now, and who knows if it will get better any time soon."

"I'll make a double batch. I love you, sister." I gestured to her cookies and soda. "And I'm here when you're ready to talk about—whatever."

She smiled at me, but it didn't reach her eyes. "I love you too. I'll go hang with Molly for movie night so you can have the house."

"You don't have to do that. You're family, silly. You're always invited."

"No, it's okay. I haven't been in the mood to be social. I'm not in the mood for anything, really. I'm going to my room to Netflix and mope." I let her go, knowing when she was ready to talk it through with me, she'd let me know.

CHAPTER 19

BARRETT

The week came and went and could have easily been described as uneventful. Unfortunately, Sadie and I hadn't needed to go up to the Bandit Lake site at all. Too many other projects were pushing us in different directions. Plus, I hadn't realized how hard it would be as a parent to steal a moment, even with a kid who was grown. Something was troubling Lizzy beyond what she'd admitted to me, and I was determined to get to the bottom of it. And Sadie's boys were still little, so it was even harder for her to get away.

"Lizzy, I'm going to head to Sadie's house and see if I can help her out with anything before the movie. Come on over when you're done on the phone."

"'Kay, I'll be there in a few," she called from her room.

Tonight was our family movie night. Sadie had arrived home not long ago. I heard them as they walked up the street from the school bus stop. A lot hinged on this evening going well. I wanted to get Lizzy and the boys together and have a great time. I figured if I could cheer Lizzy up and make her feel comfortable here, then she would be more open to me dating Sadie. I was tired of keeping secrets, but I didn't want anyone to get hurt either. Lizzy may not be comfortable with the romance between Gracie and Weston and whatever else it was that was troubling her, but that didn't have to include the entire family, especially Sadie and her boys. We could have our own little bubble right here away from all that drama.

I knocked on Sadie's door. Rider answered, followed behind by his smiling mother.

"Barrett! Come on! You have to check this out. Mommy is making popcorn!" he hollered before he took off for the kitchen.

"Hey." She grinned as her blue eyes met mine.

I whispered back a "Hey" of my own and pulled her in for a quick kiss before following her into the kitchen where butter was melting on the stove and brown paper lunch bags full of popcorn were lined up on the counter next to a huge bowl.

"Look, Barrett!" Rider gestured grandly. "This is our biggest bowl. Sometimes we use it for barf and sometimes we eat popcorn out of it."

"Oh my gosh, Rider!" Sadie covered her face with her hands. "It's clean, I swear."

"No worries, we have one of those too," I reassured her through my laughter. "It smells good in here. You're making more than popcorn, aren't you?" My stomach growled the second I had caught a whiff of whatever she was making.

"I figured we could have dinner together after the movie? I whipped up a chicken casserole and there's a salad in the fridge. Do you think Lizzy would want to have dinner here? And you're invited too, of course." Nervous laughter floated through the room after her invitation.

"We would both love it. Thank you."

"Momma's chicken casserole is yummy, even though there are vegetables in it, which are gross unless they have cheese on them," Rider said as he hopped up on a barstool. "Can I be the popcorn pourer?"

"Yep, are you ready?"

He giggled. Clearly this was a game they played. "Yes."

"Are you set?" She laughed and grabbed the saucepan of melted butter. Rider opened a bag of popcorn.

"Should we ask Barrett to do the salt? Flynn is in his room." Sadie nodded.

He slid the saltshaker to me. "Here, get ready to sprinkle, Barrett." I took it with a grin.

Sadie lifted an eyebrow and smiled at me. "Go Barrett! Shake that salt."

Rider started pouring the bags of popcorn in the bowl while Sadie drizzled butter over the top and I sprinkled the salt. Within a minute we were done.

"I think we set a hot, buttered popcorn production record, Rider." She held her hand out for a high five. When she held her hand out for my high five, I took it, and before I could think about it, kissed the back instead of slapping a high five to it. I couldn't help myself.

"You kissed my mom's hand." Rider narrowed his eyes on mine. "If you want to marry her, you'll need a blue moon and a big-ass diamond. That's the only way she'll say yes to remarriage. She said so. She told it to Auntie Clara."

"Rider!" Her cheeks had turned bright red. Damn, she was as cute as she was gorgeous. And she was too close to me for my own good. Sadie within touching distance was far too tempting. Maybe tonight was a bad idea. I'd be sitting near her for the length of an entire movie unable to touch her when all I could think about was getting her into bed with me again.

"I'll make a note of that." I chuckled, trying to make light of the fact that I really was taking mental notes.

"She's going to need a new husband soon. I know all about divorce now. And you won't get my blessing unless I see a big-ass diamond on her finger."

"Rider! Where in the world did you get that from?"

"From Dr. Simon and from *Shrek*." He shouted as he ran out of the kitchen. "Families give the blessing when people get married and Fiona's family almost didn't like Shrek, remember?"

"I can't even." The flush in her cheeks had spread to the rest of her face and down her neck. "I don't know what to say. We've been talking about the divorce at our therapy appointments, plus I've been explaining it to them ever since Stephen left us. They seem to be okay with it now that a plan to see their dad has been put in place." She buried her face in her hands and turned away.

The coast was clear, so I got up and rounded the island to take her in my arms. "Sadie, baby, look at me."

"I can't. I don't think I can look at you ever again." She groaned. Her forehead landed on my upper chest as her arms snaked around my waist. "He repeats everything. *Ugh!* It was a joke, about the diamond. Clara asked me—"

"There's nothing to worry about. I promise. Kid logic is crazy, we both know that. They say funny stuff all the time, yeah?"

"Yeah, but mine seem to turn it into an art form."

"Leeann left when Lizzy was in kindergarten. I'm a single parent too. I get it, Sadie. Please don't ever be embarrassed around me."

"'Kay, I'll try. Lizzy is coming, right?" she mumbled into my chest.

"Yeah, I'll shoot her a text."

"I'll get the popcorn and drinks set up in the living room." We pulled apart, I texted Lizzy, and Sadie called for the boys to help her with the snacks.

I really needed to get my thoughts under control. All I could think about was Bandit Lake and the myriad ways in which we had fucked each other. I took a deep breath and tried to force tamer mental images into my mind.

"What are we watching?" I entered the living room to find Flynn and Rider armed with NERF guns and shooting at the wide picture window at the front of the house. An array of suction cup darts spelled the word "fart" across the glass, and I laughed. I got the feeling that raising boys was vastly different from my experience raising Lizzy. In fact, I knew it was based on the stuff my brothers and I would get up to behind our mother's back.

"Please don't judge me." Sadie shook her head, clearly mortified.

"This is hilarious." I sat next to her on the couch and grabbed a handful of popcorn. "Don't forget that I grew up with three brothers." I reminded her. "This is nothing compared to some of the things we did."

Flynn turned and faced me with a curious smile. "What stuff did you do?"

Sadie shot me a grin. "Don't give them any ideas. They come up with enough on their own."

A knock sounded at the front door and Rider immediately got up to get it but stopped and asked Sadie if it was okay first.

"You can come with me to get it." They headed to the door, but I decided to come back tonight with a chain lock to install up high on the door to give Sadie some piece of mind.

Flynn sat next to me on the couch. "Rider is kind of a handful sometimes," he announced, grabbing a juice box off the coffee table and carefully stabbing the straw into it. His eyebrows went up as he watched for my reaction. His gaze was disconcerting; it was almost like looking into the eyes of a mini adult.

"Yeah?" I asked, not wanting to agree with him out loud. Rider was an obvious handful, but also funny and pretty clever too. They were both great kids.

"Yeah, and he can't even spell "fart." I had to tell him how. If it were up to him it would say F-E-R-T across the window. He's a good brother though."

I looked away, stifling a laugh, and smiling as Lizzy followed Sadie and Rider into the living room.

"Sit here, Lizzy." Flynn patted the cushion next to himself on the couch. "I fixed you a drink." Lizzy's lips turned up at the corner as she sat down and took the box of fruit punch from his outstretched hand.

"Thank you, Flynn."

"Anything for you," he drawled and attempted to wink at her.

"Oh, my lord above," Sadie said frozen halfway into the living room with her hands full of napkins and drinks and bowls for the popcorn. Shaking her head, she met my eyes and handed me a Dr. Pepper.

"Thanks."

Rider grabbed a small bowl and filled it with popcorn from the sometimes-barf bowl sitting in the center of the coffee table and took a seat against a huge pillow he'd set in front of the coffee table. Flynn also had a pillow and joined him there. "Let's watch *Big Hero Six!*" Rider yelled while cueing it up.

"No, pick another one," Sadie argued. "We watched that twice this week already."

"Too late, Momma. It already started." He stuffed a handful of popcorn in his mouth with a smirk.

"*Argh,* fine," she grumbled.

"No one is allowed to tease her when Tadashi dies. It isn't nice," Flynn announced from his seat on the floor.

"Don't forget that end part with Baymax. She cries at that too," Rider added.

"Spoiler alert," Lizzy joked.

Flynn slid a box of Kleenex across the coffee table toward Lizzy with another wink attempt. "You'll probably need that too."

"Thanks." She met my eyes, and we exchanged a grin. Evenings in our little household of two were not nearly as interesting as this one was shaping up to be.

"Sit by Barrett," Rider instructed Sadie as she began pushing the recliner near the window closer to the couch so she could see the TV.

I patted the cushion next to me with a wink and she blushed. Good thing Lizzy was back on her phone texting her way into the record books, or she would have gotten a huge clue about what was going on between us. Flynn and Rider were oblivious as they stuffed popcorn in their mouths, getting almost as much on the floor as in their stomachs.

She repositioned the chair then took her place next to me. "That's better," I whispered in her ear. The sound of the movie filled the room, hiding the sound of my voice. "I can't be in a room with you and not have you by my side."

Her blush intensified as her thigh pressed against mine. She inhaled a sharp breath at the contact, and I had to actually pay attention to the movie to avoid getting an ill-timed hard-on.

"Can we turn the lights off, Momma?" Flynn asked.

Rider yelled, "Alexa! Turn off the lights!" and the living room lights shut off, sinking us into a darkness we could hide in.

"She didn't say yes, dummy."

"It's okay, Flynn. We can see the movie better this way. And don't call your brother a dummy." Sadie tugged an afghan from the back of the couch, covered our laps with it and snuggled into my side. I draped my arm across the back of the couch and wished I could drop it to her shoulders and pull her closer to me instead. But I refrained.

We watched the movie and munched on popcorn. Sadie cried at the parts the boys had mentioned as did Lizzy, and surprisingly, Rider. Flynn gamely stood up each time and passed out Kleenex.

We didn't touch beyond the sides of our bodies pressing together and our held hands beneath the blanket. It was innocent but it made me feel more than I had in a very long time. It had been ages since I'd done something as simple as sit and watch a movie with a woman.

As I looked around the room, I could see my future in it. Her boys, my girl, all of us together like a family should be. Comfortable, laughing, making a mess with popcorn, eating dinner together and laughing at the word "fart" on the window.

I hadn't realized how lonely I had been until tonight. I had missed a lot by not actively pursuing a new life after Leeann left. I had missed out on having someone to talk to, someone who could understand what it was like to raise a kid on their own. Someone to just be close to and hold hands with. But if I'd gone for it back then, I wouldn't have this magic moment with Sadie right now. It was strange how things worked out as they should. I couldn't imagine being with anyone else.

After the movie and dinner, I waited in the living room for Sadie to finish tucking the boys into bed. Lizzy had gone home while I'd stayed here under the guise of helping Sadie clean up. What I really wanted to do was get my hands on her, maybe talk a little bit, and definitely get a kiss or two before I had to go home to my lonely bed.

"Hey. They'll be asleep any minute. Would you like a beer? A glass of wine?"

"No. Just you for a few minutes. I wish I didn't have to go home. Or that you could come with me. Either would work."

"I know. This night couldn't have gone better."

"Come here," I whispered. She entered my arms, wrapping hers around my neck. "Kiss me," I murmured, and she did, giving herself over to me as our lips moved together. I couldn't stop thinking of our night at Bandit Lake, of being inside her and wondering when we could be together again.

"I want—"

"Tell me," I said against her lips.

"I want so much more than what we can have right now," she answered.

"I do too. We'll get there." And I believed that we would.

I was beginning to think we were inevitable.

CHAPTER 20

SADIE

The week went by oddly fast considering the huge change in my relationship with Barrett. We made sure to text and call, and aside from a few workdays together—which sadly consisted primarily of actual work and only two naughty lunch hour quickies in the Bandit Lake master suite's bathroom—we'd shared a few kisses we could steal in the driveway and some mild flirting. We'd barely had a chance to spend any real time together.

Despite the success of our movie night, Lizzy was falling into a depression. She wouldn't talk to anyone about her feelings, and it was starting to make Barrett nervous. I suggested he make an appointment with the unofficial Hill family therapist. While I obviously felt terrible for her, she was starting to freak me out too—what if she didn't come out of it anytime soon?

But I had other issues to worry about right now. I was packing up the boys to spend the weekend with Stephen and his mother, and I was *not* okay. I needed to cry, and denying the tears was becoming painful.

They were so excited they were bouncing off the walls and thanking me every five minutes for letting them go see their dad. I was excited for them, but it was taking every spare ounce of strength not to break down. What was I supposed to do while they were gone?

"Momma! Is it time?" Rider asked for the bazillionth time.

"No, sweetie. About ten more minutes. Make sure you have everything you want to take with you."

"Why can't you come too?" Flynn asked—also for the bazillionth time—as he packed his new Lego set in his backpack to build with Stephen.

"Remember what we talked about when we were all in Dr. Simon's office?" All the divorce talk and explanations seemed to have flown out the window now that the reality of our weekend separation was imminent.

"Yeah, but I still want you to come."

"I can't. It's Daddy and Grandma's turn to be with you. Understand?"

"Sort of. Mostly. Can I bring my computer to play Minecraft?"

"Daddy said he had one at his house. He bought a new one just for you guys to play with."

He threw himself into my arms. "But I'll miss you so much. Will you come too? I really want you to."

"I can't come, Flynnie. I'm so sorry. You'll be okay with Daddy and Grandma. They have lots of fun things planned for you to do together."

Tears filled his eyes, and I bit the inside of my cheek to get myself under control. "Yeah, but who will take care of you, so you don't miss us? Will Auntie Clara be back before we go?" I bit again, tasting blood.

Come on, Sadie.

"I'm right here, little dude," Clara replied, popping her head in the doorway to my bedroom. "I just got home."

"Will you take care of Mommy when we're gone?"

Rider leaned on the other side of the doorway, next to Clara. "Yeah, make sure she doesn't miss us. Play Minecraft with her. Or get her some Skittles. Skittles always make me happy."

Clara's eyes met mine before darting quickly away. She knew if she showed me any sympathy, I would lose my crap and burst into tears. "Got it. Skittles and Minecraft. What else should we do? Should I take her snipe hunting on Grandma's back forty?"

Flynn burst out laughing, wiping his tears away with his sleeve. "No! Mommy already knows all about snipes. Don't you?"

"You're right, I forgot. But Gracie doesn't know yet," she answered. "Maybe we should take her?"

A horn honked outside. Clara and I met eyes. I inhaled a huge breath as she looked away again, giving me the space I needed to stay sane through this.

"That must be your dad!" Clara cried, clapping her hands once before taking Rider's backpack from his hands. "Come on, y'all! I know you missed him! Yay!"

"Momma . . ." Flynn's eyes filled again, and he threw his arms around my hips, burying his face in my stomach. "Come with us, please?"

I blinked back my tears and bit the inside of my mouth so hard I had to swallow the blood this time. I inhaled the biggest breath I had ever taken in my life, but I still couldn't form words.

There were no words for this. I looked desperately to Clara for help.

"We'll be fine, Flynn. We'll watch a Spiderman movie and eat popcorn. And I'll get pepperoni pizza and all your mom's other favorite things. I won't let her be sad. I promise."

Rider patted his shoulder. "She can't come with us, but she'll be okay with Auntie Clara. They're best friends like we are." He looked up at me. "My birthday Skittles are in my top drawer. You can eat all of them and I won't get mad. See? She'll be fine, Flynnie."

Flynn pulled back and wiped his eyes with the back of his hand. "Okay. Let's go see Daddy."

We headed out through the garage to the driveway. Stephen was parked at the curb, waiting for them just like we'd discussed. When he saw us, he got out. The boys rushed into his arms, and it made me happy to see them so excited. It really did.

"Grandma!" Rider shouted when he saw her in the passenger seat.

"Hey, Sadie," she greeted. "I made my lasagna and a chocolate cake for the boys. We're going to be just fine, honey. No need to worry about a thing."

I smiled at her and mouthed 'thank you.' It was all I could manage. This might be the worst day of my life. I felt foolish and dramatic thinking this way, but it felt like two pieces of my heart were getting into Stephen's car and I didn't know how I would be able to live without them.

"Hug your momma goodbye, boys," Stephen said. He was trying to be kind but damn, I was barely keeping myself together.

I knelt. They ran into my arms, and I kissed the top of their heads.

Rider straightened with a grin then dashed back to Stephen. Flynn started to follow but turned back. "I love you, Momma," he said.

I had to find my voice. "I love you too, baby. You too, Rider." The words echoed in my head, like I was hearing them from under water.

"Love you, Momma!" Rider shouted out the window of Stephen's SUV. "Bye!"

"I'll take good care of them, Sadie. I swear it." Stephen's eyes were soft as he looked at me. He had known me long enough to see that I was about to cry. "You have nothing to worry about. Call me or Mom anytime—it doesn't matter if it's in the middle of the night." I managed to nod. I couldn't answer him through the lump in my throat. "Clara." He lifted his chin to her, then shifted it to me, asking without words if I would be all right.

"I got it," she affirmed. "Take care of my nephews."

My eyes burned. Could a person die trying to hold back tears? My heart felt broken; it physically hurt. I stood there and watched as he drove away with my babies in the back seat.

I couldn't move. I was stuck right here in this terrible moment. I stood there, staring down the street as if they would reappear and I'd miss it if I went in the house and if I missed it, I would never see them again.

"Sadie?" Clara took my hand in hers. "Let's go inside."

I shook my head. What I was thinking didn't make sense and I knew it, but I couldn't stop the thoughts from coming, and I couldn't make myself move.

"Come on, honey. We can't stay out here all night."

"I can't move. I'm being so stupid, but I can't move, Clara. I don't want to do this anymore. Why did I agree to this?" Hot tears squeezed out of my eyes as I shut them tight against the fact that my boys weren't here, and I was the one who had let them go.

"We're going to take this one day at a time. No, we'll take it one second at a time, Sadie. Just one little second, okay?" She wrapped her arms around me, but I remained still.

"I—can't."

"Hold onto me. We can get through a second together. I promise you're going to be glad you did this. They need him, and you did the right thing."

"Did I? I don't know that anymore. I thought I did, but— Do you ever just look around while you're in town? People are all over the place, going about their business without all of this shit we have to drag around with us. Do you ever wonder *what if?* I used to want to escape my whole life, to walk in the rain and feel it clean on my face, let it wash away all the bad choices I've ever made. But then I'd look at my boys and the regrets just melted away. If they're not here with me, then what do I have? I'm left with nothing but the mistakes, Clara. I'm nothing without them."

"That's not true," she argued. "You are so much more than just their mother, Sadie. I wouldn't have made it out of childhood without you. You're the best sister in the world and I won't let you argue about that. You're an awesome designer, you worked your ass off, and now you have a great job, and you did it on your own. Be proud of yourself. But most of all, you are Sadie Lynn Hill. You are a woman who deserves everything."

"I don't know how I'm going to get through this."

"You'll get through it with me, one second at a time. Okay?"

I nodded. Her phone rang in her pocket. It was the special Chris Barrett ring. Her eyes darted to her pocket then back to me. "Get it," I told her.

"I don't want to, but I—"

"I know something is going on with the two of you. Answer it. I'm okay." I wasn't. But that didn't mean I would let my issues wreck Clara's relationship or whatever was going on with Chris.

"Sadie, I'm so sorry. I—" She held up a finger and turned around to answer the call.

Shamelessly, I stayed where I was to listen.

"Okay. Yeah, give me a few minutes. I'll text you. Bye." She lowered the phone and ended the call.

"What happened?"

"I hate that this happened right now," she hedged. "I—I would never leave you alone like this. But Sadie, I'm late. We had a huge fight and . . . it doesn't even matter what it was about now. We haven't spoken in weeks. He wouldn't take my calls, and now my period is late, and I—"

I pulled her into my arms. "You have to go, Clara. If what you had is fixable and you want him back, then you have to go talk to him. I'm going to take tonight one second at a time, just like you said."

"Are you sure?"

"I'm positive. Go. I'll be okay."

"I'll be back soon." She turned away, then whipped back to face me. "No, I can't leave you like this."

I pulled myself together enough to smile at her. "I'm fine, see?"

"I know you're not fine, you big liar. I love you so much, Sadie."

"I love you too. Enough to know that you're not okay either. But you have a better chance of feeling better tonight, so I'm forcing you to take it."

"That is some messed up Hill sister logic, isn't it?" I shrugged with a smile. "I'll be back as soon as I can," she said. "Go out to your patio, get your book."

"That's not a bad idea."

I watched her leave. I meant to go to my patio and act like a freak show back there where no one could see me, but instead I just sat down. Right there in the middle of the driveway. I hugged my knees to my chest and watched the trees lining the street blow in the breeze. I knew the boys were not coming back tonight—I hadn't lost my mind completely—but it felt good to sit here with the cold wind on my face, so I stayed where I was. If the rain couldn't completely wash away the memories of my mistakes, then maybe the wind could blow them away and make me feel good about myself again.

"Sadie?" I looked up to find Lizzy standing over me. "I was getting a snack and I saw you through the kitchen window. Are you okay?"

"Not at the moment, but I will be."

"Yeah, me too. Can't a girl mope out her feelings in peace? I mean, if I want to stay in bed eating Hot Pockets and Sprite, I should be able to do it without the threat of being sent to therapy, right?"

"I don't see anything wrong with it. I'm about to switch to Diet Coke and frozen White Castle sliders for the weekend. And hey, you can mope freely with me. Pull up some driveway and have a seat." I patted the concrete and she sat. "You can talk to me."

She laughed bitterly. "No, I can't. Not about this. I can't talk to anyone about this."

"You can talk about every feeling that surrounds the issue and we can work through it that way. How about that?" This made me nervous. Lizzy was older than my boys and obviously, she was a girl. This might require advanced mom tactics that I did not yet possess. "Or we could just sit together and stare into the evening abyss and let our moods blend into something scary."

She laughed. This time it was real. "I like you, Sadie. You always make me smile."

"I like you too, doll." She leaned her head on my shoulder, so I wrapped my arm around her.

"Everyone thinks I'm hung up on Weston. But that isn't the problem, I'm not. Yeah, I got sad seeing him with Gracie for a minute—mainly because everything was easy back when we were together and now my life is so complicated. And somehow everyone knows what I did to him when I left for college. I literally can't show my face anywhere. And I, um, well there's something else but I can't talk about that, at least not until I decide what to do about it."

"We can talk about anything you're comfortable with. And I get not wanting to show your face, I really do. There's a lot of crap people talk about me, and it has been going around since I was in high school—"

"No one decent believes any of that stuff. You know that, right?"

"Yeah, I know, but the point is, if I cared what people thought, I'd be spending my days huddled in a ball underneath my bed. You're a smart, beautiful, capable girl, Lizzy. Keep your chin up and if anyone gives you any trouble, send 'em my way and we'll handle it all together. You have a friend in me, Lizzy. I want you to know that."

"Thank you. I feel really alone right now, and I hate it. My mom kind of sucks lately and my dad is great but you know him—he always wants to fix stuff and give advice and that's awesome, but all I want to do is get through everything in my own time."

"You need the freedom to be sad without anyone worrying too much. Maybe get a hug now and then. And a steady supply of your Hot Pockets. Yeah?"

"Exactly," she whispered.

"I know, honey. All us girls have all been there a time or two." Her shoulders shook, I knew better than to point it out, so I squeezed her tight with both arms and let her cry.

"You got married when you were my age, right? Because you were, you know . . ." Her whispered question raised alarm bells in my brain. My mind raced with speculative thoughts. *Could she be pregnant? Maybe none of this has anything to do with Weston. Was he her cover, her excuse to be upset and not reveal the real reason?*

I had been right to worry about my mom skills—this was uncharted territory. Super advanced. She should be talking to a higher ranking mom with grown-up children right now. Someone like Becky Lee, not me with my tiny twin boys. "Uh, yes. Yeah, I had just turned eighteen when I married Stephen. But I had a miscarriage soon after."

"I'm so sorry about your baby, Sadie. I can't even imagine," she murmured. "Was it okay? I mean, when you were first with him?"

"It was. At first, I loved him a lot, and he loved me too. At least it felt that way during the early years of our marriage. Are you pre—ummm, why do you ask?"

She didn't answer my question, she just nodded against me. "So why are you out here?" she finally mumbled against my shoulder. Should I push for more information? Should I ask her more questions? I decided to follow her lead. In my experience, pushing never led anywhere good.

"The boys are with their dad for the weekend and I'm not handling it well at all. They just left. Who knows how I'll be later. But could it get worse than crying in my driveway?"

"I'm so sorry. But no matter what, I know you're their safe place, and you always will be. Like my dad is for me." She pulled back to look at me. "That matters to kids, Sadie. So much."

"Oh, honey. Thank you for saying that." Something about those words, especially coming from her, validated my feelings.

We were both crying now. So of course, this would be the exact moment Barrett pulled into his driveway, off from work for the day.

He got out of his truck and headed our way, coming to a stop in front of us without showing one single speck of fear. I respected that. "Y'all want to go for milkshakes and burgers at Daisy's?" We each took an outstretched hand and stood, exchanging glances as we burst into giggles.

CHAPTER 21

BARRETT

They each took a hand and smiled at me. It seemed like I had finally figured out how to read a room. Or a driveway, as the case may be.

I knew Flynn and Rider were with Stephen tonight. Clara had texted me, told me the boys had gone to Stephen's house, and let me know in no uncertain terms that I should get my ass home and tend to her sister.

As for Lizzy? My mother, not so nicely, told me today to quit offering her advice and give her hugs and perhaps offer her chocolate instead of therapy. She said in this case, my time with Lizzy would be better spent loving her rather than trying to fix her. Garrett had laughed and told me to "read the room" again.

So, I read the driveway.

Everyone loved Daisy's Nut House, so why not start there?

"Let me grab my bag and lock up the house." Sadie brushed Lizzy's hair back over her shoulder and smiled at her. "It ain't no Hot Pocket and Sprite, but I think Daisy's with your dad might just be better, don't you agree?"

"Yeah, Sadie." They hugged each other and my heart nearly burst out of my chest.

I watched as she walked away and thought about telling Lizzy I was falling in love with Sadie. It seemed like they had created a bond tonight. Maybe now was the right time.

"God, Dad. I'm so glad you never had the chance to ask her out. How awkward would it be if you did and then y'all didn't work out? She would end up just one more person I wouldn't be able to talk to anymore. She is so cool about everything. I think we could really be friends."

I couldn't let this go. The time had come for her to hear the truth. "Uh, actually —" I looked up from Lizzy's face to see Sadie walking down her driveway, vigorously shaking her head no at me, so I shut up.

"Y'all ready?" she said and clicked her garage door remote to shut it behind herself.

"Let's go," I answered, letting it drop for now but determined to get everything out into the open soon. I couldn't go on this way. Lizzy wasn't a child anymore and keeping this from her wasn't fair to any of us.

Lizzy insisted Sadie sit in the front seat where she promptly turned on the radio the minute she got settled in. Clearly, she did not want me mentioning anything about us to Lizzy tonight. Fine. I'd talk about it with her later, privately, and convince her that we deserved to be happy just as much as anyone else did.

"How are you doing?" I asked over the blare of the radio.

"Clara said I should take this weekend without the boys only one second at a time." She turned and smiled at me. "I'm fine for this second."

"Good. Let me know if it changes." I felt the pull between us, the need to reach out and touch. Not holding her hand right now was wrong. Not comforting her when she was hurting was a dereliction of my duty as the man in her life. I could be a good father to Lizzy and be the man Sadie needed me to be at the same time. Why should I have to choose?

I pulled into a spot in front of Daisy's and walked around my truck to let them out, offering each an arm to take. This would work. I was growing more certain by the minute. They already liked each other.

We sat and ordered. Sadie grew distant, staring out the window. "Is this a bad second?" I asked, smiling when Lizzy reached across the table to hold her hand.

"Why don't you call their dad and see how they're doing?" Lizzy suggested.

Sadie had tapped Stephen's contact info and put her phone to her ear before she could even agree to the suggestion. "How are the boys?" She smiled and it seemed like every part of her body relaxed as she listened to him talk.

"So, how are they?" Lizzy asked after she'd hung up. Sadie's grin was huge as she answered Lizzy and it gave me hope.

"Flynn is playing *Among Us* on the computer Stephen bought for them and Rider is—" She pursed her lips and looked away. "Well, he's had chocolate cake tonight. And Stephen bought them candy, and gave them root beer with their dinner . . ."

"Sugar overload?" I asked with a chuckle.

She looked back at me with a small smile. "I'm starting to think it's not actually the sugar itself. He loves treats but gets excited easily. I think it's excitement overload. Whatever it is, he's currently running laps around the house and listening to Wham! on his iPad. I should have warned Stephen that he's gotten easier to rile up lately, but I was too upset to think of it."

Lizzy burst out laughing. "I love those two! They are something else. I can't wait to see what they're like when they grow up."

"Speaking of that—" I interjected, intending to let Lizzy know the truth about Sadie and me.

"Hopefully we'll still be neighbors!" Sadie cut me off with a glare. "Wouldn't that be nice?"

"It would be awesome!" Lizzy answered before I could get a word in. "I hope they stay as hilarious as they are now. The other morning Flynn told me he infiltrated the Minecraft server of this kid from his class and blew all his buildings up because his stepmom was saying rude things about you and then he started pushing Rider around at recess and knocked him off the slide." She cringe-smiled at Sadie. "Oh man, I shouldn't have said that. I'm so sorry."

"It's all right. It was Jackie, an old high school nemesis of mine. Don't worry about it. Flynn already told me everything that happened. I had to make up an alternate definition for the word "maneater" on the fly because of her big mouth. I called their teacher. She won't be volunteering again." She shrugged. "I don't encourage petty revenge, but I don't actively discourage it either. You reap what you sow, right?"

"Totally, and don't mess with Flynn!" Lizzy laughed. "Or you."

We ordered our burgers and milkshakes and ate while making small-talk conversation and chatting about Flynn and Rider. I didn't broach the subject of Sadie and me being together. I knew by the warning looks Sadie kept giving me it wouldn't go over well.

We finished, I paid the check, and we got up to leave. Lizzy led the way with me in the middle listening as Lizzy described something funny Garrett had done to cheer her up at the office today.

"Oh! I forgot my phone on the table." Lizzy stopped walking to turn back for it.

"I'll run back and get it. Finish talking to your dad," Sadie offered.

"Thanks!" Sadie went back while Lizzy and I headed to the truck.

Sadie's face was stone when she made it back to the truck. "Here you go." Her voice was flat as she handed Lizzy her phone. Something had happened and she was trying to hide it.

"What's wrong?" I asked after she got into the truck.

"Huh? Oh, nothing. Just missing the boys again. Stephen said I should call and tell them goodnight. I'm sure I'll be fine again after that." She smiled then turned to look out the window. This time she didn't bother to flick the radio on to hide her silence.

Lizzy's text alerts started pinging from the back seat. Sadie flinched after the first one. I almost said something but decided to wait until I had her alone.

We made it home. "Bye, Sadie." Lizzy got out and went in the house through the garage.

"I'm going to walk Sadie home. It's dark." I shouted to her back.

"Okay."

"What happened?" I asked Sadie as soon as I caught up to her. "Something with the boys?"

"Nothing happened," she answered. But I knew she wasn't being honest; she wouldn't meet my eyes. "I'm just being a silly mom. I miss the boys. I have to get used to—"

"That isn't it," I insisted.

"What? Yes, it is." She clicked her garage door open and turned to go inside.

"Sadie, why aren't you being honest with me right now? What happened at Daisy's?" She shivered against the cold so I reached for her to warm her up, but she sidestepped me. "Tell me."

"Nothing happened." I'd never seen her like this. Fidgety, looking everywhere but at me. "You know, I've been thinking, Barrett. My life is a huge mess right now and—"

"You said that before, on your patio, remember? I didn't care then, and I don't care now. You could be living inside the eye of a hurricane, and I'd still want to be with you, Sadie."

Sad eyes snapped to mine. "Come inside for a second. It's too cold out here and we need to talk."

"Okay. Fine." Why was the phrase "*we need to talk*" terrifying when uttered by a woman? I followed her into her kitchen.

She spun to face me with her arms crossed around her stomach. "This isn't going to work between us—"

Shaking my head against her words, I argued. "That's crap and you know it. Something happened tonight, I know it. Is it because I wanted to tell Lizzy about us? She'll be okay. I can take care of both of you. The boys too."

"There is no us, Barrett, there can't be. That's what I've been trying to say to you. There is nothing to tell Lizzy because there is no us, not anymore. I don't know what I was thinking. I mean, I'm still married! There is too much going on. You deserve more than what I can give you right now."

"Don't tell me what I deserve."

"Fine. I'll tell you what I have to give. And it's nothing. Not right now. My boys left with their dad, and I broke down. I'm not ready to be in a relationship. I can't, Barrett. I need more time."

"Time? That's it? I'll give you time if that's all this is about. I will wait for you."

"I'm not making any promises. I don't have it in me." Tears filled her eyes. I reached for her, but she shook her head at my advance.

I felt my heart start to break a little bit. The only thing keeping it from flying apart completely was blind hope and the fact that I knew there was something she was keeping from me. I took a step back. "I'll make the promise for both of us then. I will wait."

"I won't hold you to it," she murmured, avoiding my eyes.

"You won't have to. When I make a promise, I keep it."

Her eyes drifted to the door, hinting that I should leave. "I'm tired. I think I need to go to bed."

"This isn't over, Sadie." I couldn't even begin to contemplate that I'd lost her. Not yet.

"My life is a mess right now," she insisted again, like she was pulling reasons to dump me out of thin air. Like she had a list of break-up phrases in her back pocket and was throwing them at the wall to find one that would stick. "It doesn't feel fair to subject you to it."

"Maybe it is, but it's a beautiful mess and I would do anything to be part of it. Nobody is perfect."

"I can't do this right now." She tried another tack, forgetting that I had known her since we were kids. We may not have been the best of friends growing up. In fact, we were barely acquaintances, but I knew her history just as much as she knew mine. When you live in a small town like Green Valley, your life was never completely your own. I could read her better than she thought I could. I knew she was full of crap right now. The only thing I needed to discover was the reason why.

"It's not me, it's you, right?" I suggested.

"Uh, yeah, I—"

"That line is bullshit, Sadie. Try another one."

"Barrett, please—"

"Why don't you try the truth."

"Honestly? I don't owe you an explanation. We never officially declared anything to each other, did we?" Her voice shook with anger, or regret, or possibly sorrow. I couldn't tell. My damn emotions were starting to cloud my judgment.

I bit my lip and looked away. She'd hit me closer to my heart than I liked. Maybe I should quit while I was ahead. "I'm sorry. I'm having a hard time believing any of this."

"I'm sorry too. I'm just not ready to move into another relationship. It's as simple as that."

"Fine. I'll go." Giving up for the moment was the only thing I could think to do. If I pushed too hard, I feared that I would push her away for good and my emotions were about to get the better of me.

Tears filled her eyes. "I really am sorry."

"Don't be sorry, baby." I took one last look at her for tonight and embedded her expression in my mind to contemplate when I wasn't so upset. "This isn't over. Not by a long shot."

CHAPTER 22

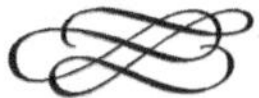

SADIE

I was crying in the kitchen when Clara got home.

"Shit, Sadie! I knew I shouldn't have left. Where's Barrett? I told him to get his ass home and take care of you—"

"I broke it off with him," I sobbed.

"What the hell? Are you crazy? You can't do this, Sadie. You two belong together."

"I won't get between him and Lizzy. She needs him more than I do right now."

"You broke up with him because of the Lizzy-Gracie-Weston love triangle teen drama? No, no, no, that's going to blow over. They're kids! We talked about that. Go talk to him. Fix it. Do it or I will do it for you."

"No. This isn't kid stuff. This has nothing to do with Weston. This is parent stuff. She's hurting right now, in serious pain, and Barrett is her father. Put yourself in her shoes, Clara. You come home from being with your mother—and it was not good for her there, in case you didn't know—and your ex-boyfriend has moved on with another girl and her family is now everywhere you look. At your job, at your home, even in your own family—Willa is her aunt now, Clara, for frick's sake. How would you feel? It's beyond awkward. I can't take her dad away from her. I won't tell him, and you won't either. I talked to her right after you left. The poor thing is a mess." And that wasn't even the half of what was wrong. But I couldn't say anything else—not now, not yet. I needed to be sure of everything first.

"Damn, that poor kid. And you won't tell him what?"

"What? Oh, nothing. I misspoke. My mind is a mess right now. The point is, we grew up without a dad, Clara. And without a mom too, if you think about it. I won't force her to be us. I won't take Barrett away from her."

"Damn it, that makes too much sense. Why are you so nice? And shoot, why am I? This doesn't have to be forever. It will blow over. They're kids, right?"

"I hope I can make him understand if or when it does."

"She'll move on. No one mourns a lost love forever. You'll get him back."

"I also emailed Garrett and quit my job."

"Sadie!" Her arms flew out to the side in exasperation. "What in the actual hell are you thinking? What aren't you telling me?"

"I have another job lined up. When I applied at Monroe & Sons, I sent my resume all over the place. One of the companies emailed me to offer me a job last week. I'm going to take it. Don't worry about the money—"

"I don't give a shit about the money. My god, Sadie! I have loads of money, who cares about that? All I care about is *you*. This is extreme and I don't entirely understand why—"

"There is nothing to understand. I told you everything," I lied. "It's going to be okay. I'm doing this for Lizzy." I wished I could tell her what happened at Daisy's tonight. I needed some good advice, or a time machine so I could go back to Daisy's and never lay a hand on her cell phone so I wouldn't have to know what I now knew. *Gah!*

She eyed me, studying my face kind of like Dr. Simon sometimes did when he was trying to figure me out during a therapy session. "You are not actually Lizzy. You know that right? You're relating to her a little bit too much, I think."

"We are *both* Lizzy. Only we didn't have someone like us to help when we were hurt back then."

"Damn it, Sadie. Stop making sense. You don't have any more logical reasons I can't argue with, do you?"

"Did you talk to Chris?" I needed to deflect. I was not good at keeping things from Clara.

"We're okay. For now, anyway. Don't worry about me. I'll be fine no matter what happens with him. You know me."

"Okay, I'll buy that for now because I'm beyond exhausted. I'll grill you about Chris tomorrow. I'm taking a bath then going to bed."

"I'll be home all night if you don't feel like being alone. Just climb in my bed with me. I love you, sister."

"Love you too. 'Night." She waggled her fingers and went to her room.

When I got to my own room, I spied Barrett sitting in the chair on my patio. Doing the right thing was hard enough without him flaunting his hot self in my face.

"I thought you understood me when I told you that we can't do this right now," I said after opening the French door to greet him.

"Can we talk? Please? I can't accept this. Not when I know you aren't telling me something. Please tell me what changed your mind. If this is about Lizzy, I don't have to tell her—"

"The secret will hurt her. We've barely started with each other. There is almost nothing to hide right now because almost nobody knows about us. If we keep going on behind her back, she'll find out. Then she'll put it all together and figure out how long you've been lying to her, and she'll be even more hurt than she is now, and she'll think she has no one left to trust. You know it's true. She needs you. You need to get her to talk to you, Barrett. Trust me on this."

"That's why I was going to tell her everything tonight. It's driving me crazy that she won't talk to me. I thought since the two of you were getting along so well, it might help."

"I talked to her earlier, and you can't put this on her now. You just can't."

"Damn it, Sadie." He grabbed my face, stepping into me as he hauled my body against his chest and slammed his mouth to mine.

"We shouldn't do this," I panted against his lips. My words contradicted my brain and my lips and the entire rest of my traitorous body as I clutched at him with greedy hands, pulling him closer as I opened my mouth to his seeking tongue.

"Fine. Just give me one more time with you and I'll let you go."

"Liar." I tugged his shirt over his head and kissed the middle of his chest as he shoved me back to the bed, following me down to straddle my body.

He kissed his way between my breasts, tearing at the buttons of my shirt. I shrugged out of it and unhooked my bra as he slid lower, undoing my pants, and tugging them down my hips along with my undies. I lifted my legs and he slipped them off, tossing the garments to the floor.

Wasting no time, he buried his face between my thighs. Involuntarily I arched my back, my knees spreading wide for him. "You're wet for me already, Sadie. Your body knows we belong together even if you won't admit it. You won't be able to fight it forever." His tongue traced a long lick right up my center, swirling at my clit before he kissed his way back up my body to my lips. His mouth was hot and demanding and I wanted nothing more than to surrender everything and give him what we both needed.

"Stop talking, Barrett, I can't—"

He kissed me, shutting us both up. I tasted myself on his lips and moaned.

"Words aren't necessary for us. I don't have to talk to make you want me. You already know you need me as much as I need you. Admit the truth—we belong together."

"Damn it, Barrett. Stop talking." He needed to shut up before I said too much. Before I admitted everything to him. "Just fuck me, please. One more time . . ."

"I'll give you whatever you want, any time you need it." He stood, took a condom from his pocket, and placed it between his lips with a wink. I watched as he let his pants drop to the floor and his dick sprang free. He was hard for me. Long and thick and beautiful and I did, in fact, need it. I needed him. I lifted my arms, beckoning him closer. He knew how much I wanted him. He could see the truth I hid inside of me even when I was telling him lies.

He knelt between my spread legs, lifting me by my ass until my thighs hugged his waist and his cock teased my opening. "Please . . ." I groaned, trying to push myself against him. I needed him to fill me up like only he could do.

"Tell me this isn't the last time," he demanded as he slid the tip inside me.

"Please, Barrett. Give it to me."

"This isn't the last time, Sadie. You're mine. Say it." He gave me another inch and I squeezed with all my might, satisfied when he let out a loud grunt. "Say it." His voice was rough as he ground out the words while giving me only one more inch.

I shook my head. He pulled out and I gasped. "No! Come back."

"Say it," he repeated. His entire body was tense above mine. Every muscle flexed and strained as he held himself back from me.

God, he was beautiful.

His brown eyes—desperate, pleading, full of love—held mine captive. I couldn't look away and I didn't want to. I belonged to him, and he belonged to me. I saw it right there in his eyes and I knew he saw it in mine, so I let my lids drift closed and turned my head to the side.

I had no doubt we were perfect for each other. He was everything I had always needed in my life: steady, strong, and so, so kind. "God, Sadie, you undo me. I can't deny you anything." He gave himself to me, thrusting so deep that we both gasped.

But I couldn't have him, not now. I couldn't take advantage of his feelings this way. And I refused to take him away from his daughter. Putting their relationship at risk was something I would never allow myself to do. What kind of woman would that make me? Selfish, that's what.

It might kill me, but we had to stop. Seducing him into making love to me now would be cruel when I knew I was not going to say what he wanted to hear. At least not tonight.

I scooted backward on the bed, forcing him out of my body as I threw my leg over to sit up to my knees in front of him. "I can't say what you need me to say. Not tonight. This is wrong, Barrett. I won't take advantage of you. And I care about you too much to ever break your heart this way."

Hurt flashed across his expression along with a look that told me that deep down he understood where I was coming from. Maybe I was fooling myself, but that little glimmer in his eyes gave me hope. Right now, we couldn't be together, but a small part of me dared to hope that maybe we could in the future.

I couldn't make love to him tonight, but I cared about him too much to leave him like this, not after I'd allowed him to get worked up to such a state.

I bent low, placing my hands on his thighs as I gazed up at his face. I slid my legs apart and sank lower as I brought my lips to the head of his cock, darting my tongue out to lick and kiss the tip. His head fell back, and his body clenched impossibly tighter, each muscle straining, standing out in stark relief as he kept himself under control.

I wanted to make him lose that control he held so tightly to. I needed to give him something, anything I could, to show him what he meant to me, so he'd remember me while we were apart.

He hissed in a breath as I sucked him deeper, right to the back of my throat. His head snapped forward. His eyes met mine as I swirled my tongue around the shaft, then up around the head and back again and again until his breath grew ragged, his gaze grew frantic, and his jaw tightened with his need to release.

"Touch yourself, Sadie. Make yourself come too."

I shook my head no. "This is for you," I mumbled with my mouth full of him. His hands sank gently into my hair, brushing it back over my shoulders to hold it softly as he bent forward to kiss the top of my head.

"I'm gonna . . ." He tried to pull away, but I moved my hands to his hips to keep him in my mouth. "God, Sadie. Fuck—" His gorgeous brown eyes drifted closed while his full lower lip slid into his mouth as he bit down. His thighs tightened and shook under my hands, so I sucked him harder until he filled my room with the sexiest groan I'd ever heard. It was so deep it was almost a growl, and it did things deep inside of me; my clit pulsed, and I tightened reflexively. I was aching and empty, but it felt so good to hurt this way. I had been tempted to slide my fingers between my legs and get myself off when he told me to, but I was determined to make this all about him, so I didn't. "What are you doing to me?" He gasped and shuddered as he came.

"Mmmm." I moaned, spreading my legs wider and arching my back as if he could enter me from where he knelt in front of me. I was so desperate for him, I could almost feel it. Could I come like this?

"Get up here," he grunted. He hauled me to my knees and reached between my legs to thrust two fingers up inside me. "Ride my hand," he ordered, and I did. We were nose to nose, his panting breaths mixed with mine while I frantically moved up and down on his fingers as he circled my clit with his thumb. "I don't come without you," he whispered against my mouth, dark and full of promise. "What kind of man do you think I am?"

I had no words. I knew what kind of man he was. He was the best kind, the only one I wanted, the love of my life. Tears filled my eyes as my head fell back. I was spiraling out of control, barreling toward an orgasm that was about to shatter me into pieces, just like my heart had shattered earlier when I had to let him go.

"I'm hard for you again." He lifted me by the hips and shifted me until it was his cock I was riding and not his hand. "Take what's yours. Am I making my point, Sadie?"

"Yes, yes, yes," I chanted as I slid up and down, taking him deeper and deeper each time until I was full of him. Body, soul, heart, head—every part of me screamed to let him have his way. "Ohhhhh my god . . ."

"Your body knows what it needs even if you refuse to admit it. Let go for me." His lips met my neck and sucked. He was going to leave a mark again and I loved it.

I let go. My entire body trembled as my legs turned into jelly. He pulled me to his chest, holding me in his strong embrace before laying me down against my pillows.

"I'm in love with you, Sadie," he whispered. He stood and tugged at my covers, tucking me in, wrapping me snug in my quilt before bending low to kiss my forehead, then my lips. "But I know nothing has changed for you." Tears filled my eyes and he brushed them away with his thumb. "Sleep tight, love."

I choked on a sob, my tears flowed in earnest as he smiled sadly, got dressed, then left, closing my French doors behind himself.

"I love you too," I whispered to the dark.

CHAPTER 23

SADIE

I woke up to wretched sunshine. I needed clouds and rain, or maybe a hailstorm to match my mood.

The pounding that started on the door just took the freaking cake. I flipped over in bed, hoping Clara would answer it. I got up when the doorbell started ringing in time with the knocks. Hurriedly, I located my robe and slipped it on.

"What the hell?" I grabbed the baseball bat I kept by my bed and headed for the front door. I was in the right kind of mood to do some serious damage to someone's head.

I heard water running and saw steam billow from beneath the door as I passed the bathroom. Clara was in the shower.

"I'm coming!" I hollered. "Dang it."

I peeked through the peep hole. It was Garrett with his arms full of big manila envelopes and blueprints encased in long cardboard tubes. I threw the door open in surprise. He barged in, glaring at me.

I stuck the bat in the corner by the door. "You scared the crap out of me, Garrett."

"Quiet, Sadie. Barrett called me last night. I know what you did. You dumped my brother and I think I know why." He crossed the foyer into the living room and tossed the blueprints to the couch.

I darted after him. "This is none of your business."

"I don't know what to do about it. Not yet, anyway, and Molly doesn't either. But we're onto the both of you." He answered like he didn't just hear me tell him to butt out.

"There's nothing y'all can do, Garrett. This is between me and Barrett."

He rolled his eyes at me. "Lizzy is troubled right now. Obviously, she needs Barrett's guidance but that's not going to last forever. You're a good woman, Sadie, and a great mother. There is no one else I can see my brother with. You're good for him *and* my niece. Barrett and I talk, Sadie. You're going to be my sister-in-law someday. That means something to me."

I looked away without answering. God, this family was just too good to be real.

"I don't accept this. Look at me." My eyes darted back to him, surprised at the anger in his tone. He was always funny and sweet with me; I was taken aback. Pissed off Garrett was a surprise. I'd never seen him mad before. He held up a piece of paper, tore it in half and tossed it to the floor. "I printed that out just so I could tear it up in your face. I do not accept your resignation. You're working from home until all this stupid kid shit blows over."

"But—"

"Please, let me finish." He held up a finger. "I have a project for you." He tossed a stack of manila envelopes on the couch behind me. "You're gonna let me know what supplies you need to work full time in this house and I'm gonna get them to you. I'll even bring you lunch every day if you want me to. You are not quitting Monroe & Sons. Dad agrees. Mom agrees too. Don't bother calling them to argue because it will be pointless. We're also giving you a raise, effective immediately. I talked to that prick that tried to hire you out from underneath me. If anyone offers you something better, tell me and I'll give you more. You're a brilliant designer and we won't lose you to another company."

"Okaaaaay . . ."

"Now, about Barrett. I think you should talk to him. Tell him everything on your mind and let him deal with it."

"That won't work, and you know it."

He crossed his arms over his chest. "I don't know that. Explain it to me."

"We both know what he's like. He'll analyze, he'll plan, he'll work every detail out so he doesn't have to decide between Lizzy and me. He won't make the choice, Garrett, and you know it. He doesn't want to hurt me, but I will not allow him to hurt her. So, I'm making the decision to take the pain instead of Lizzy. She needs her dad, and I won't take him from her. I grew up without a father. I know what it's like, okay? Maybe someday things will be different, but for now it's going to be my way. No one else has a say in this."

"Damn it, Sadie." He looked away, frustrated.

"Dude." Clara said. Wrapped up in her bath robe and with her hair wound up in a towel, she strode into the living room with a trail of steam wafting behind her. "That's what I said. '*Damn it.*' I'm frustrated by this whole dumb thing too."

"I won't stand for it if any of y'all try to butt in. I mean that. I'm taking myself out of the situation for now."

Garrett sighed. "I won't say a word. But promise you'll let me know if you need anything. Anything at all, and I'll be there for you. Molly too, obviously."

"I won't say anything either," Clara added. "Damn it."

Garrett ran a hand over his face and let out a huge sigh. "Shit, Sadie, I'm sorry for my tone. I read your email, got frustrated, grabbed the plans, and rushed over here without thinking."

"Don't worry about it, Garrett. You may have sounded mad, but you literally just complimented me about my work, told me I'm the right woman for your brother *and* your niece, gave me a raise, and said you'd do anything for me. I really have nothing to complain about."

"Don't forget about him bringing you lunch every day," Clara added. "I was listening from the bathroom."

He laughed. "I'll get out of your hair. Have a good rest of your morning." With that, he left.

I started to go back to my room, but Clara stopped me. "I don't think so." She took my arm and led me to the couch. "Talk."

"I can't. I mean, you have no idea how I left things with Barrett last night. I just want to sleep the rest of the day and not think about any of this."

"Oh, I know exactly how y'all left things. I have two working ears, you know. You didn't put your fan or music on. You two had a grand old break up bang in your room. I had to put my white noise machine on whale calls to drown it out, okay?" She gave me a round of applause.

"Oh god." I was horrified, and so thankful the boys weren't home. Then I felt like crying because last night was the best sex of my life and I'd let him leave. He told me he was in love with me, and I let him walk right out the door like the stupidest almost-martyr who had ever lived.

"Yeah, I believe I heard those exact words come out of your mouth last night, at least once" she teased. "But if I recall correctly, your tone wasn't quite the same."

"Fine. If you stop talking about this, I'll tell you everything." I had to tell someone. I couldn't keep this inside; it was tearing me up.

"Really?" Her chin went back as she side-eyed me. "This was easier than I thought it would be. I was ready to wrestle you into submission and tickle it out of you."

I flattened my lips in mock annoyance. "Pretty sure of yourself, aren't you? You've never beaten me."

She rolled her eyes. "Whatever. I'm pretty sure of what I heard last night," she shot back. "He loves you."

"Yeah. But you don't know—*Ugh!* I don't know if I should talk about this."

"Tell me."

"Lizzy is pregnant." I blurted. "You can't say a word."

Her jaw dropped. "Holy shit. Obviously, it's not Weston's."

"No, it's a tutor from her college. And oh my god, are you pregnant too?"

"No, Aunt Flow is currently in the building and the bitch ruined make-up sex for me and Chris last night, damn it."

"Well, shit. Are you okay?"

"Hell yeah, I'm not ready for a kid yet. Back to Lizzy. How did you find out?

"She left her cell phone on the table at Daisy's when we had dinner. She got a text when I went back to get it for her. I didn't mean to read it, but I did, then all of a sudden, I was halfway through the entire text thread before I realized what I was doing. I have never read anything so fast in my life, Clara. I'm kind of ashamed of myself, but I had to know what was going on."

"Uh, yeah. Obviously. I would have done the same thing"

"She almost talked to me about it in the driveway before we left for dinner. I'm hoping I can get her to open up to me. I assume this is not the kind of thing a girl wants to talk about with her dad, you know? And the teaching assistant? He's four years older than her. Barrett will murder him. I mean, I kind of want to murder him myself. But according to their texts, he loves her. He said he wants to marry her but she's not sure."

"Holy shit," she repeated.

"I know. I was such an emotional mess last night. I shouldn't have broken up with him. But I couldn't think of anything else to do. I can't tell Lizzy that I snooped in her phone, she'll hate me. But I also can't be around Barrett with a secret like this. I'm stuck. What would you do?"

"Don't ask me. I'm obviously the biggest idiot ever with stuff like this. Should we go talk to her?"

"No! What would we even say?"

"Look, when all of this convoluted bullshit sorts itself out I will end up her aunt." She held up a finger. "Shut it. We both know you and Barrett are meant to be, so let's not even debate that right now. Okay, let me think. What would Auntie Clara do for her eighteen-year-old pregnant niece . . .?" She closed her eyes and pondered her own question.

"I've got it!" she bellowed as she shot up to her feet. "Get dressed. You're going to visit Miss Lizzy and bring her your emergency cheer-up cookies. You'll be sweet to her, and she'll tell you everything. And it's not even manipulative because you sincerely want to help her. And also, you're her future stepmother, so it's sort of your duty."

"That's actually a good idea. Peek next door and check if Barrett is home. I'll throw on some clothes, then defrost a plate of cookies." I ran off down the hall to change.

"The coast is clear." We high-fived as we passed each other in the hall. I ran into the kitchen and retrieved a baggie of cookies from the freezer to defrost. Clara met me in the kitchen where we were both huffing and puffing with anxiety.

"This has to work," I fretted as we waited for the microwave to finish defrosting.

"It will. One, the whole Weston thing is a nonstarter. Two, you said she almost told you, which means she wants to confide in you. And three, if you can convince her to tell Barrett then all the problems go away and you two can live happily ever after. But with the fan and music on so I don't have to hear it."

"*Ugh!* I'm sorry. And mortified."

Ding! We looked at each other for a split second before I snatched the cookies, Clara grabbed a half gallon of chocolate milk and shoved it in my arms, and I rushed out the garage door before I could talk myself out of it.

Knock, knock, knock!

"Hey, Sadie." Lizzy took one look at me, eyed the cookies and milk, and burst into tears.

"Hey, I've got you. It's going to be okay."

"Sadie, I don't know what to do anymore."

"I have cookies and milk and I'm here to help," I announced.

She stepped back and waved me inside. "I don't have anyone to talk to about this." She swiped the tears from her cheeks, then led the way into the living room.

"Are you pregnant?" I cut right to the chase. "You kind of hinted about it—"

"Yeah, I wanted to tell you on the driveway, but I couldn't get the words out. You can't tell my dad. No one can know. Not yet anyway. I can't face him."

"Um, I don't know what you've decided, Lizzy, and there's definitely an option you can choose where no one ever has to find out, but most of the available choices are going to be impossible to hide."

"I'm keeping it." Her chin shot up defiantly.

"Okay, then we have to figure out a way to tell your dad," I said gently. "He loves you. Or would you rather tell your mom first?"

She shot me a look out of the corner of her eye. "She already knows. She said she was too young to be a grandmother and I was stealing her thunder. She wants me to keep quiet about it until after her wedding," she announced and flopped back to the couch. "She's never talked to me like that in my entire life and I don't know how I'll ever get over it. She's in Hawaii with her fiancé. I haven't heard from her in weeks."

A cold chill shot down my spine. I knew what it felt like to have your own mother turn her back on you. My heart ached for her. "Are you serious? I'm so sorry. I know how words like that feel. Do you want to talk about it?" I set the plate of cookies on the coffee table along with the milk. I sat next to her on the couch.

"Not now. But I might later. Right now, I'm trying to forget about it. The only person I told was my boyfriend. He wants to marry me and take care of me and the baby. He can do it too, because he's about to become a school teacher. But I'm only eighteen . . ."

"Do you love him? Is he good to you?"

Her eyes lit up. It was the happiest I had seen her in weeks. "Oh yes. He's the sweetest guy I've ever met. Is it gross to say he kind of reminds me of my dad a little bit?" She hid her face in her hands and cringed.

"Not at all. Your dad is one of the sweetest men I've ever met. And you need to tell him, honey. I promise you he will understand."

She huffed out a laugh. "No, he won't. He'll drive straight to Knoxville and murder Ian. He was my tutor, Sadie. We were not supposed to be together. We tried to fight it, but"—she patted her stomach for emphasis—"we got along really well. We kept it a secret. No one knows about us." A wistful smile crossed her face. "And Sadie, I really don't want him to die. And I don't want my dad to go to prison. So do not breathe a word of this to him. I mean it. I'll tell Dad, but not yet. Not until I figure out the best way."

"What about Becky Lee? Do you think she could help?" I suggested.

"Um, no way. She'll go barreling straight to my dad and tell him. I love her, but she thinks everyone needs to know about everything the second she finds out about it. Secrets are not her jam."

This secret was not my jam. Not by a long shot. How could I keep this from Barrett? How could I avoid betraying Lizzy? How could I avoid going insane?

Hello, rock?

Hello, hard place?

Meet your new bestie, Sadie.

I took a cookie from the plate, leaned back into the cushions, and ate it. Then I took another one and ate it too. I had effectively made things worse. Before, no one knew that I knew Lizzy was pregnant. Any choice I made from this moment on would be done with Lizzy knowing I knew the truth about her situation. I wondered how Barrett would feel about me keeping a secret like this from him. I would be upset about someone keeping vital information about my boys from me. If I was being honest and not afraid of admitting the truth to myself, I'd be beyond upset. It could even be a deal breaker.

"I feel better now that I have you to talk this over with. I'm so glad you came over." She smiled at me then took a cookie.

"I didn't like the idea of you suffering alone," I said. "I really feel like you should tell your dad. He's so levelheaded and kind—"

"Yeah, he is totally both of those things, almost all the time. But what dad in the world is going to be okay with their eighteen-year-old daughter getting pregnant by her twenty-two-year-old tutor when she was supposed to be learning about math?"

Barrett would absolutely lose his mind.

And he will never want to see me again when he finds out I knew.

"Lizzy, secrets never work out for anyone. You know that, right?"

She wouldn't meet my eyes. "My grandpa is going to take me to lunch and shopping in Knoxville in a little while. He's the only one who never tries to get me to talk. He just buys me presents and gives me the best hugs. I'm really glad you came over. I feel way less stressed out now. Thank you for keeping my secret and helping me feel better about all of this."

"Uh, sure." I knew when I was being dismissed. I stood to go.

I waited until I was in my house with the doors locked and the music on before freaking out. "I am beyond screwed," I announced to Clara and told her everything.

"There is only one thing to cling to here," Clara said. "Barrett loves his daughter. You've become her confidant when her mother wasn't there. That is a huge deal, Sadie. I know you're keeping a secret. But you are also giving her a safe person to talk to when she feels like she has nowhere else to turn. And also, it seems like maybe she's kind of a brat? Don't you think? We've all been tiptoeing around her all this time because of Weston and Gracie—"

"I don't know about being a brat. She's just young and scared. Plus, no one pushed the issue about Weston with her. We all just assumed that was the problem. Jeez, I may have found the one flaw in that family . . ." I laughed bitterly. "They're the exact opposite of ours and try to protect each other's feelings. Plus, she has no idea how Barrett and I feel about each other due to the aforementioned problem. I hope you're right about him, because if you're not, I'm going to lose everything. And I love him, Clara."

CHAPTER 24

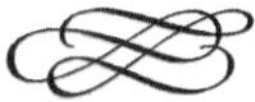

BARRETT

Dice clattered over the wooden tables at Everett's gamer shop, Twenty Sides and Sundry. I had helped him design this space when he first decided it was what he wanted to do. I was proud of how far he'd come with it in the few months he'd been in business.

It was his Dungeons and Dragons tournament day. He was seated at the head of the long table at the rear of the store, and I was holding down the chair at the table in the window at the front like it was my job. I had my favorite bad mood iced mocha from Daisy's Nut House, a dozen doughnuts, and a boiling rage against nothing, because no one was wrong in this scenario. It was frustrating as hell.

Everett's shop looked into a dance studio across the street called Stripped. Each one of my dumbass brothers, except for Wyatt, was lucky enough to catch their woman taking a pole fitness class over there. But not me. I got to watch Suzie Samuels teaching an early afternoon senior citizen class while Clara assisted her. Looked like I'd accidentally discovered why she was always wearing gym clothes. I lowered the blinds with a crash.

Everett had hired Gracie soon after he opened the shop and Garrett occasionally worked here too when he was in the mood to let his geek flag fly. Gracie was currently behind the check-out counter giving me pity looks every time she finished with a customer and had nothing else to do. "Quit it," I said after the latest one left.

"I can't. You're too sad. Your vibes are getting all the way over here and it's making me twitchy because I can't butt into y'all's business like I normally would. Like, I have all these super leading, useful questions that I have no idea what to do with."

"I'm sorry . . ."

"It's not *your* fault." If she was insinuating it was Lizzy's, I didn't want to hear it. I loved Gracie like she was my own blood, and this situation was bizarre, to say the least. "Duh, it's not *hers* either." She grumbled, "Everything about this situation is hella dumb and awkward," then pulled out her phone. To text someone, I assumed.

Okay, then we were in agreement.

What is it with kids and their cell phones? I used to do actual stuff when I was young, like go outside and talk face to face with people.

"Yoo-hoo!" The words trilled from outside the window. I lifted the blinds and of course I saw my mother walking up the street from where she'd parked her car at the curb. The only mystery was why she hadn't shown up at my house at the crack of dawn to wake me up and meddle. "Barrett! I see you, my beautiful boy!" I shook my head at my mother's signature greeting and watched through the window as she made her way up the sidewalk to the store.

"Great," I muttered under my breath. I was not in the mood for talking. I was only here at Everett's shop because being in a bad mood alone at home was worse than being in a shit mood in public. My father, in an effort to cheer Lizzy up, took her and his credit card shopping in Knoxville for the day. The house had felt suffocating the minute they left so I got my Daisy's Nut House coffee and doughnuts and came straight here to spread my joyous mood around.

"You're in for it now," Gracie snickered. "Momma Monroe is about to get this mess sorted right the frick out."

"Gracie, dial it down half a notch," Everett suggested from his table with a grin.

"You're right. I'm sorry, Uncle B. It's hard to fight my nature sometimes." She sighed dramatically before helping another customer.

"No worries, sugar," I called back. This kid was hilarious. Her gift in life was busting chops and I was not about to put a damper on it.

"Barrett! Honey, I'm so happy you're here! I'm delivering treats to the tournament players but you being here too is serendipitous." My mother slid into the seat across from me and plopped a cooler bag on the table.

"What did you bring? Your treats are the best." Gracie shouted from behind the counter.

"Come here and get you one, sweetheart," my mother offered her. "I made my double chocolate marshmallow fudge chubbies for y'all."

"Everyone could use a good chubby, am I right?" she deadpanned.

Everett snickered at his table before catching himself. "Gracie," he said, completely ripping off my dad voice. I was glad to be good for something today.

I muttered, "Good lord," and took a chubby, stuffing half into my mouth to avoid having to make a comment on this ridiculousness.

"I heard the news about Sadie," she whispered. Her eyebrows shot up as she peered at me over the edge of her glasses.

"I don't want to talk about it," I informed her

"Oh, well you're going to, mister. I have a few things to tell you," she fired back.

Gracie snorted behind the counter. My eyes shot to her, and she grinned knowingly. "You better listen to your mother."

"Gracie . . ." Everett warned, using my dad voice again.

"Hey! If she knows even half of what I've heard, then it could be helpful." She addressed me next. "I'm not trying to be rude. I don't like the thought of Sadie being hurt is all. And I am not spreading any gossip around either. This is super delicate information. These lips are sealed."

"It's okay, Gracie." I told her. I wanted to question her about whatever it was she'd heard, but she mimed zipping her lips closed and picked up her cell phone, so I didn't bother.

"I feel sick about the Lizzy situation." My mother whispered, keeping her voice low so no one else could hear. "I don't know if you know this, Barrett, but she won't talk to me anymore. Your daddy is going to do his best to cheer her up today. I told him to just buy her whatever she wanted and take her out to lunch. He's good about not pushing, which, I can admit is not one of my strengths." No, it most definitely was not one of her strengths.

"Don't feel bad, she won't talk to me either." I sipped my coffee and let the Lizzy subject drop. Hopefully my father could make her feel better today.

"I also have an update about Dana. And this bit is not something I heard from her momma." Her hand went to the side of her mouth like she was about to reveal a secret but we both knew she would say it loud enough for the entire shop to hear. "This came from the private detective Sadie's momma hired."

"How do you know about that?" Gracie interjected loudly. "I barely even know about that. I had to do some serious eavesdropping to find out about that. Maybe y'all should ask him about Lizzy." She was clearly both perplexed and impressed by my mother's snooping skills. She also apparently had super hearing and had listened to everything we had just said.

"I have made it my business to get to know your momma lately, sugar pie. Family is everything," she told Gracie. "And in that spirit, I have been going up to the farm stand from time to time with coffee and plates of my Nutty Buddy cookie squares. No one can resist Nutty Buddy cookie squares. And, hello? Two of my boys are with two of her girls. I decided we're going to be best friends and I don't take no for an answer." She pursed her lips before continuing. "She didn't know that about me before. Now she does."

"I have got to see this. I will pay you good money if you let me go with you next time." I glanced over at Gracie, who was elbows to the counter eating up every word my mother was saying about her mother.

"Of course, sugar pie. You can come up there with me anytime you want. For free."

Gracie beamed at her. "Thanks!"

"What about Dana?" I asked. My mother shot me a satisfied smile, happy that she had my full and rapt attention. I grinned at her.

"Yes, back to Dana. Y'all don't have to worry about her anymore. Stephen has broken up with her and it looks like she's moved on, and it might be for real this time. She's at her house in California with some real estate guru over there. But who knows if it will stick or if she'll come crawling back to Stephen again."

"*Ugh*, he's such a tool," Gracie grumbled.

"He is absolutely a tool, Gracie. You are right about that. He was married to the lovely Sadie and treated her abominably by carrying on with a trashy woman like that Dana." She turned her head back to address Everett. "I do not like that woman, Everett. I told you that back when you dated her. Don't you remember?"

"Yeah, I remember, Mom," he called back to her then looked at me. He shrugged. "She was hot," he said in explanation.

"That heifer!" Gracie hollered from right behind me and I jumped. I was so intent on my mother's words I hadn't heard her creep up. "I didn't know Stephen was a cheater until that day at Daisy's. Sadie didn't talk to me about that kind of thing. I can't stand Stephen. He was always such a condescending dick to me, treating me like I was just some dumb kid. And how could he cheat on Sadie? First of all, look at her—she's like a walking, talking Barbie doll, but aside from that, she's awesome and smart and hilarious. She's the best. She wanted to try to get Momma to let me live with her, but I said no because of him. What a dumbass he was."

"She is the best, isn't she, Barrett? Now what are you doing to get her back?"

"Mom, this isn't the time for that."

"It is always the time for true love," she stated as she slapped her hand on the table. "Even if y'all are waiting for Lizzy to come around, you still have to plan your moves."

"Yeah, Barrett. Make a plan," Gracie agreed. "My sister needs someone like you. You would never cheat on her."

"If I make a plan y'all two will absolutely not be a part of it. Zero offense intended. My love life or lack thereof is my private business. And Gracie, for the record, I will never hurt your sister, I can promise you that right now."

She looked at me like I was stupid. "Duh, I know that."

"Well, good. Thanks."

My mother heaved out a put-upon sigh. "Barrett, you're not being very cooperative right now." She shook her head. "You have always been my most hard-headed boy." She looked straight at Gracie. "Next Friday night is the Monroe & Sons employee fried chicken dinner party at your Aunt Genie's bar. I wonder who needs to know about that."

"You are like, serious goals, Miss Becky Lee," Gracie complimented. "You're a puppet master."

"I appreciate the sentiment, sugar, but I'm not quite a puppet master. Though, come to think of it, how nice would that be? No one would question my superior judgement, and everyone would always be happy . . ." She shook herself out of her brief daydream. "Well, unfortunately, all I can do for now is set up the board. Shame I can't move the pieces. You know what I mean?"

"Mom, really?" I huffed out a laugh.

"Hush, you. Where would you boys be right now without my help? You don't even know the half of what I've done for you."

"We probably don't want to know, do we?"

She shrugged delicately. "Well, I'm sure I don't know that answer to that question, do I?" She stood and grabbed her handbag from the table. "Gracie, come have lunch with me. We'll discuss you finally calling me 'Grandma' and talk about chess." She winked at her and held her hand out.

"Heck yes! Tell Everett to let me go for the day." She smirked.

Everett laughed and left his table. "Go on, take the rest of the day off. I got it under control here."

"You're a good boy, Everett." Mom kissed his cheek, took Gracie by the hand, and they left.

The tournament players were still at the table in the back, but the shop had emptied of customers for the time being, so Everett joined me at my table. "What's really going on?"

"Sadie won't see me anymore. She says it's because of Lizzy, but something isn't sitting right. Lizzy is upset, but it feels like it's about more than Weston."

"Gracie is unusually closed-mouthed about the situation," he informed me. "Usually, she can't wait to meddle."

"And Weston?"

He eyed me. "He has nothing to say."

"Smart kid." I chuckled.

"It's just a matter of time. It's gonna be okay."

"I hope so. I'm worried about Lizzy. She won't talk to me. She stays in her room all the time—always with a headache, sometimes a stomachache. I tried to get her to make a doctor appointment, but she refused. She's eighteen so I can't make her do anything anymore. She always used to come to me, Everett. About everything."

"Have you tried talking to Leeann? Maybe she could intervene?"

I huffed out a bitter laugh. "She's in Hawaii with her fiancé and not currently answering my calls. Her only response was a text informing me that Lizzy is an adult and we no longer need to be in touch about her needs. Basically, if Lizzy wants to talk to her, she can call her herself."

"That's typical for Leeann, right?"

"Pretty much," I confirmed.

"All you can do is be there when Lizzy finally decides to talk. Sounds to me like you're doing everything you can."

I was. But it wasn't enough.

CHAPTER 25

BARRETT

Every other month, Monroe & Sons hosted a fried chicken dinner for our employees at Genie's Country Western Bar. Genie was Sadie's aunt on her mother's side, and Willa worked there as a waitress and sometimes bartender. It was the place to go in Green Valley for a wholesome bar experience. Very rarely did fights or trouble break out. This was the place to be for darts, line dancing, live music, and, of course, Genie's famous fried chicken.

Tonight, nearly half the customers were Monroe & Sons employees. Everyone was here, except one. Sadie was the only person I wanted to see, and she was missing. Based on what my mother had hinted at Everett's shop last week, I'd halfway expected her to see her when I arrived, wrapped up in a bow and waiting for me. Unfortunately, this situation was more complicated than what she was used to butting her nose into.

All week long, I'd only caught glimpses of Sadie in the driveway as she loaded up her boys to take to school. Sad smiles and little waves hello were all I had managed to get out of her. I decided to keep my distance and give her some space as I waited for tonight, hoping by miracle or meddling something would change.

I sat in a corner booth with my brothers and Sabrina. I smiled as Willa approached to refill our glasses. We all sank back as she slid a tall glass and a shot in front of Sabrina, then lit the shot on fire. My eyes widened as I watched Sabrina drop the flaming shot in the glass and chug it. "Thanks," she held out a fist and Willa bumped it with a laugh. "This is my first night out in so long, I forgot what it was like in here." Her head fell against Wyatt's shoulder, and he tugged her close with a chuckle.

He whispered, "Let's go dance, darlin'," before nipping at her lobe with his teeth, making her giggle. I watched, full of jealousy, as they headed off hand in hand toward the darkest corner of the dance floor. They had it all, and I wanted it too.

"I know you're wondering where Sadie is." Willa decided to put me out of my misery. She set her tray on the table then plopped sideways onto Everett's lap. "She's spending the evening with Clara and Molly," she informed me as she poured beer in my glass. It drove Everett crazy that Willa wouldn't take a leave of absence or quit and let him take care of her for the rest of her pregnancy—and the rest of her life. "But I'd keep my eyes open if I were you. Don't leave." Her lips slid up in a half grin as she got up, then patted my shoulder and walked back to the bar with her tray.

My eyes lit up as I stood to look around the bar.

Garrett checked his phone. "Sit down. Not yet."

I sat back in the wooden booth. "What's happening?" I asked, for once not completely pissed that my life was subject to the meddling of my family. They could meddle all they wanted if it meant that I'd see Sadie tonight or, better yet, if they could somehow make her change her mind.

My mother stopped to visit us on her way from the restroom back to the table she shared with my dad. "How's Lizzy doing?"

"Fine. She's hanging out with her friends at the movies. At least that's what her text message said."

"Good, she needs to get out more." She smiled then continued her way to sit with my father.

Garrett's text notification went off and my eyes shot right to his phone. I couldn't help it. He chuckled and passed it to me. "Any minute now," he said. They were on their way.

I straightened the collar on my shirt and ran my hands down my chest, anticipation almost driving me out of my head as I waited for her.

I blinked against the dim light of the bar. String after string of lights wound through the wooden beams above our heads and the moonlight shining through the high windows provided the only lighting as I struggled to see the entrance across the dance floor.

Then there she was. I hadn't seen her here at Genie's since we'd been together. She wore her customary tight jeans that hugged every single one of her exquisite curves, turquoise high-heeled cowboy boots, and the same red tank top I'd gotten underneath a few weeks ago. A beaded choker wrapped her throat, and her blond waves flowed like a flaxen river down her back. She was fucking beautiful. Heads turned as she walked through the bar, but not mine; I'd had my eyes on the door waiting for her, and I tracked her movements from the second I saw her come in until I no longer had to squint against the dark to see her. Finally, I caught her eye and stood.

She shook her head, indicating that I should stay away. I sat back down and grabbed my beer, watching as she approached the bar with Clara and Molly. Willa greeted them, taking their orders with a smile. And still I watched.

Never had I been this unsure of myself.

The rest of my life flashed in front of me and if I couldn't get her to see reason, it would be empty. There was no one else for me.

"We're gonna wait right here," Garrett said, his voice was barely audible over the live music and huge crowd.

"Yeah, I'm not going anywhere right now," I agreed without looking at him.

"I'm going to the bar," Everett announced, patting my shoulder as he left the booth.

"He's one of them now more than he is one of us." Garrett laughed.

I forced my eyes from Sadie to address Garrett. "What?"

"He's a Hill sister now. Look at him."

I chuckled as Sadie and Clara sidled up to his sides, each taking an arm as he leaned across the bar to kiss Willa. "Can you blame him?"

"Not even one little bit," he answered, smiling as Molly turned around and blew him kisses with both hands. "Go ask her to dance and send my woman over here."

"You think I should?" Who was I, asking my youngest brother for advice? I wadded up a napkin and tossed it to the table in frustration. I hated being full of doubt like this.

"I know you're hurting, Barrett." His eyes were sympathetic on mine. "I was where you are not that long ago, remember?"

"Yeah. But I've been where I am before, and it didn't work out. What if it happens again? I came this far to fail? Again?"

"Sadie is nothing like Leeann," he pointed out. "For one, Sadie has never tried to run me over with her van. And for another, the flames of hell don't trail behind her whenever she enters a room."

I huffed a shocked laugh. "Point taken, and you're right. They're nothing alike. I'll go." I stood, gathering the courage I must have left somewhere way back in my teen years, since that was the last time I had ever felt as desperate and alone and uncertain as I did right now. My palms were sweating. This was fucking ridiculous. "What if she says no?" My words were almost silent, almost drowned out by the loud music, the boots on the floor, and the crowd. But Garrett heard me over all of it. Or maybe he just knew how I felt.

"You've got this, Barrett. I wouldn't tell you to go for it if—well, just trust me."

I nodded at him then headed across the bar. If I were headed for a broken heart, I may as well just take my shot and let it happen.

I passed an oblivious-to-the-world Wyatt and Sabrina on my way. They swayed together in the corner, not caring that they were out of time to the driving beat of the music. After another stab of jealousy, I flinched as the band started playing "Mercy" by Brett Young.

How appropriate.

I studiously avoided looking Sadie's way as I approached. It might make me a masochist, but if she were going to reject me, I wanted it to be to my face, and not from a shake of her head across the dance floor dismissing me before I could even speak a word to her. We had meant more to each other for me to ever accept that.

As I got closer, Molly waved me close, smiling ear to ear while sipping her beer. "Come on, cowboy. Get your girl," she encouraged.

Sadie turned. Her smile slipped when she saw me. She drew her lower lip between her teeth in indecision. My breath caught in my throat and I shoved the nerves aside as a bolt of determination struck me. If I wanted her, I had to fight for her.

"Dance with me?" I offered her my hand and held my breath.

"Sure," she murmured. A thousand different kinds of relief flew through my body when her palm slid against mine and she smiled at me, soft and tremulous.

I led her to the center of the dance floor. With a twist of our hands, I interlocked our fingers and placed them against my chest as I held her waist with the other and tugged her close.

The sweet scent of her hair flooded my senses as her chin came to rest on my shoulder. Her soft sigh ruffled my hair and my heart kicked up to beat wildly against our joined hands. "I want you back," I stated. "Tell me what I have to do."

"We have to talk first. I've been struggling with something that you need to know about."

"It's too loud in here. Can we finish this dance? Then we'll get out of here and talk the second we get home." What could have been so bad that it made her break things off with me? I couldn't imagine such a thing existed.

"Yes." She stepped her feet apart and I slid my knee between hers as we moved our bodies together to the slow beat of the song.

The hole in my heart started to close as we melted into each other. "My life is impossible without you in it," I whispered in her ear.

"Mine too, Barrett. I can't take this anymore."

I released her hand to pull her into me with both arms. All pretense of a dance was gone as I held her close and brought our lips together for a searing kiss.

I felt another shift between us as she kissed me back. It was just a matter of moments until she was mine again. "Let's go," I whispered against her lips. I was through with dancing. I needed her now.

CHAPTER 26

SADIE

With my arm looped through his, he led me through the bar to the parking lot. My heart raced out of control, but as I passed Clara exiting the ladies' room she gave me a dirty wink that gave me the confidence boost I needed. Once we got home, I would tell him everything. I had to make him understand how trapped I felt, how hard I had struggled with whether or not I should tell him the truth about Lizzy. He had to understand how much I wanted to be there for her, plus how very much I didn't want to betray her trust. And that once upon a time I had been just like her, terrified and pregnant and feeling like I was all alone in the world. I felt terrible about spilling her secrets, but Barrett was her parent, not me. I had to tell him.

"Dad! Hey!" It was Lizzy. Ugly anticipation filled my veins. This wasn't going to turn out good for me; I could feel it. I let Barrett's arm go to hang back with Clara.

"What are you doing here, Lizzy? Who is this?" Lizzy was hand in hand with a someone who had to be Ian. He looked a little bit more boy than man, but he was cute. The way he held her hand so protectively and hovered over her while smiling at her with such reassurance spoke volumes.

"Oh fuck," Clara hissed from my other side.

"Oh my god," I hissed back. I clung to the hope that Lizzy wouldn't let it slip that I knew about her pregnancy, but I knew better.

"This is Ian. He proposed to me, look!" She held her hand out and a tiny, adorable diamond glimmered in the light from the pole overhead. "He's officially my fiancé! I couldn't wait for y'all to meet each other, so here we are!"

"Nice to meet you, Mr. Monroe," Ian said, not realizing the big mess of crap he was about to step in.

"*Married?* You're only eighteen. Why on earth would you want to get married now? Uh, hey Ian." His icy gaze examined him up and down while Ian bravely attempted to keep smiling against Barrett's hostile perusal.

White dots of panic colored the edge of my vision, and an odd thought flew through my mind. We made a strange trio, Lizzy, Barrett, and me. All of us had been married so young.

Would she tell him I knew about her pregnancy?

Did she have any idea at all what it would do to me if she did? *No, she had no clue about me and her dad. We hadn't gotten that far when we spoke the other night.*

"Once I decided what I was going to do, I couldn't wait anymore to tell you, Daddy. Please try to listen and not get mad, okay?"

Clara and I exchanged looks of alarm. I closed my eyes, and she took my hand. The writing was on the wall.

"Ian loves me. Please believe that before I tell you anything else," she continued.

"You're pregnant, aren't you?" Barrett's voice was like ice; his body was too. He was frozen in place. Not one muscle moved except for the angry tick in his jaw as he stared Ian down. "You got my daughter pregnant. How old are you?"

Clara squeezed my hand tighter. "Maybe we should get Wyatt out here or something? Look at Barrett's face—he's gonna kill that boy. Oh god."

"I just turned twenty-two, sir," poor, doomed Ian said. "I love your daughter. I want to marry her, so I can take care of her and our baby. I'm about to graduate, I have a job lined—"

At that moment, Becky Lee and Bill, using some kind of psychic sixth sense parental superpower, appeared behind us as Barrett cut Ian off.

"Quiet," Barrett snarled. "You love her, do you? She's eighteen and pregnant. That doesn't say love, that says something else about you entirely—"

"Dad!" Lizzy burst into tears. Ian pulled her close with his arm around her shoulders.

"Barrett, no!" I cried. All I could think of was what Lizzy told me her mother had said when she found out about the baby and how she may never be able to forget it.

Becky Lee's outraged gasp filled the night. She rushed forward and grabbed Barrett's arm, shaking a finger on her other hand in his face. "Barrett William Monroe, you hush that mouth right now before you say something you can't take back. Don't you dare forget that you yourself were once a boy who got his own eighteen-year-old girlfriend pregnant. And me and your daddy did not react to you this way when you came to us talking about love and marriage and babies and asking for our help. No, sir, we did not. You are going to be a grandfather. Your daughter is an adult. Now you act like one too."

"All right, Becky Lee, take your own advice now. Take a minute, son. Breathe. I think we all need to take a second and calm down, okay?" Bill added, ever the voice of reason.

Barrett ran a hand over his face and turned to me. He reached for my hand, and I gave it to him. He squeezed gently and searched my eyes, looking for comfort, or for something I could convey to him to help him calm down.

Somehow, I knew it would be the last time he would reach for me like this, and I blinked back tears of regret. "It will be okay, Barrett," I murmured. "Everything will be okay."

A small smile ghosted across his face. "You're right." He faced Lizzy and Ian. "I'm sorry, this is—I'm just shocked."

"I'm sorry too, Dad," Lizzy cried. "I should have told you right away. Sadie kept telling me I needed to talk to you, and she was so right but I didn't listen to her, and I made a mess out of everything—"

His head whipped around to face me. Betrayed eyes met mine. "You knew about this?"

I lowered my gaze as I nodded. The pain in his expression was too much to bear. I couldn't look at him.

He released my hand and stepped back, running a hand into his hair. "How could you keep this from me?"

"I—"

"Sadie? How?"

Becky Lee interrupted. "Y'all, let's go inside and give them a minute. Come on." They all left, filing back into Genie's to leave us alone.

Clara hung back, eyes alight with knowing sympathy. "I'll be right there inside the door," she said. "Don't you dare try to leave without me. Do you hear me, Sadie?" I nodded, swallowing the lump in my throat as she backed away and entered the bar. I turned back to Barrett.

He set his jaw. "You knew how worried about her I was. I told you everything. You even recommended your therapist to me, remember? We talked about it all the time, Sadie. I don't understand this. Why?"

"She asked me not to—"

"She's a kid!" he bit out, thumping his hand on his chest. "I'm her father. She needed me. I can't believe you would do this to me when you knew it was killing me not to be able to help her—"

"Please, Barrett. I didn't know what to do. She begged me to keep it a secret, I was stuck in the middle—"

He cut me off. "How would you feel if I kept secrets from you about your boys?" He glared at me. "You'd hate me, wouldn't you?"

Tears spilled over as I flinched away from him. I couldn't hold them back any longer. I couldn't even look at him anymore. I took a step back, stumbling into the side wall of the bar.

Would I hate him if he kept vital information about my boys from me?

Would I?

I couldn't imagine hating Barrett. But I also couldn't imagine him ever being dishonest with me. I choked back a sob. "I'm so sorry. I didn't know what to do—"

He shook his head and turned his back to me. "I can't do this with you right now. I'm too upset to be rational. I am so angry with you. I can't believe you would do this to me! Of all the people in my life, you? You're a parent too." Without looking back, he stalked toward his truck in the parking lot and left me standing there.

I completely understood how he felt. But I also knew exactly what Lizzy had been feeling, because I had been through it myself.

My hand flew to my mouth as I choked on a gasp. This was worse than I could have ever imagined. My heart flew out of my chest as he walked away, leaving me empty and alone in the cold evening air. The blood froze in my veins; I couldn't seem to breathe anymore. And just like the other day in my driveway, I let my knees buckle as I slid down the wall to sit in the gravel.

I don't know how long I sat there before Clara and Willa showed up and each took an arm to lift me to my feet. Willa wrapped me in my coat and kissed my cheek. "You're coming home with us tonight. Momma is going to keep the boys, okay? You don't have to pick them up." I nodded, barely understanding what she said through the haze of heartbreak clouding my brain.

I felt ridiculous reacting this way. I should have been ready for it. It was my own damn fault, after all.

"I got you, honey." Sweetheart Everett appeared in front of me and swept me into his arms to carry me to his Bronco. It made me feel like a foolish child, but since I didn't seem to have any strength left to move, I let him do it. After he set me down, Clara buckled me in and slid to the middle of the bench seat, pulling me into her side as Willa and Everett got in front and drove us to their house.

I woke up hours later in Willa and Everett's guest room with Clara wrapped around my back, snoring softly in my ear. We were spooning, or 'doing spoonies,' as we used to call it, just like when we were little girls, hiding in my bed after Momma had sent us upstairs during one of her fits of anger. The only thing missing was Willa tucked up on my other side. But she had Everett to do spoonies with, so clearly, she was far better off than either Clara or me.

I looked down, laughing when I saw the *Star Wars* T-shirt I was wearing. I barely remembered changing and getting into bed last night. I looked at Clara sound asleep and wearing a brown *Firefly* top. God bless Everett and his huge variety of geektastic T-shirts. I bet he'd never guessed when he married Willa that he would end up having a foursome of nearly identical blonde sisters taking over his collection.

"Hey, y'all awake?" Willa peeked in through the crack in the door. I grinned at her, clad in his *Battlestar Galactica* shirt. "Everett is making pancakes."

"You're so lucky," I said, and promptly burst into tears.

"I heard pancakes and crying." Clara sat up with a stretch. "Come here." She held up her arms and I flopped against her chest and let her hug me.

"Make room for me." Willa joined us on my other side. In the past, I had always been in the middle so I could comfort them both at the same time. This morning was the opposite; they were comforting me, which only made me cry harder.

I was the oldest and should have my shit together by now. But here I was, still making stupid decisions and messing up my life.

I should have left Stephen when I first found out about Dana and rebuilt my life a long time ago. I should have told Barrett the truth about Lizzy immediately, so I didn't have to lose him. I should have . . . *Argh!!*

"Stop beating yourself up in your brain, Sadie." Clara squeezed me tight around the waist. She always knew what I was thinking.

"You were in an impossible situation," Willa added.

"There was no right choice to make, Sadie. You know that, don't you?" I looked up to see Gracie standing in the doorway, looking like she felt a little bit left out. She hadn't been born for most of the Hill Sister Spoonie Years and had been too young for the last few. But she was here now for the Hill Sisters Spoonie Years, Part Two so I held out my arm to her. With a huge grin, she bounded into the room and joined us in our sister cuddle.

"Pancakes are ready," Everett appeared in the doorway to announce, smiling when he saw us all huddled together in the middle of the bed. "How're you doing, Sadie?" he asked softly.

"I'm okay. Thank you all for taking care of me last night." Tears filled my eyes again, but this time they were only half sad. The other half was content, because I knew that no matter how things ended up with Barrett, as long as I had my sisters, my boys, and Everett too, I would always make it through and be okay.

CHAPTER 27

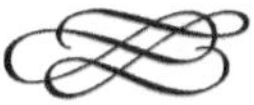

SADIE

The rest of the weekend flew by. I made it through by focusing on my boys and staying inside my house to avoid a potential Barrett sighting. I figured he needed some time alone with Lizzy, and hoped he would also take the time to cool off and think about where I was coming from. I also, in a rare burst of drama, turned off my phone, unplugged the landline, and kept all my curtains shut tight. Needless to say, I didn't hear from him, or any other Monroe aside from Everett. He was his usual sweet self but had zero information to give me a clue about whether or not I should quit hoping Barrett would forgive me. Garrett sent me an email this morning full of sympathetic words and a request that I go to the Bandit Lake house this afternoon for the last official inspection.

Bittersweet memories flew by as I drove the road to Bandit Lake. One of the crews had been out there during the time I had been stuck working from home. I wondered if Barrett would be there, even halfway hoping that he would, but the thought of seeing him made me nervous. His anger at me had been quiet, but it had cut deeper than any knife ever could—especially since I knew I had deserved it. Secrets between lovers were wrong, no matter the reason one kept them.

I drove up the winding driveway with anticipatory nervous energy flowing through my body. It all ground to a halt when I spotted his truck parked to one side. Images of us crashed into my mind as I pulled in and got out. Me on the grass, spinning in the rain; holding on to the staircase as he made me come; him carrying me to bed and all the beautiful things we did that night and throughout the days and nights after. Tears filled my eyes, but I blinked them away.

My life had been filled with bad decisions. Keeping Lizzy's secret from him had just been one more. I wanted to turn around and go home but I had a job to do. I had known what could happen when I started up with Barrett and I did it anyway. We didn't work out, and now I had to deal with it. If I wanted to keep working for Monroe & Sons, I needed to learn how to be around him again.

I shoved open the door and trudged inside. I both dreaded seeing him and wondered how I would ever be able to forget what could have been.

He was sitting on the sofa in the living room but stood up when he heard my heels click over the tiles in the foyer. "Sadie," he said, surprised.

"Hello, Barrett." I wanted to run. I felt like crying. I couldn't do this and turned to leave. I could find another job. I could find another town to live in. I could eventually find another life to live after I somehow made myself forget about him and what I could have had if I hadn't been so damn stupid.

"Hey, wait. Don't leave, I want to talk to you."

I stopped at the door, hand on the knob. "I can't, Barrett. I just can't do it. I'm so sorry."

"Don't be sorry, baby. Please, Sadie, let's talk this out. I was going to come to you this morning, but Garrett said there was an emergency so I came up here instead. There were so many times I almost came to you over the last two days, but I wanted to be sure I had my feelings sorted out before I tried to talk to you. I didn't want to hurt you any more than I already had by saying the wrong thing. Please don't leave, Sadie."

The way he said my name gave me pause. I turned around as a small flare of hope sparked. "Don't say my name like that, Barrett. Not unless you can forgive me for what I did." I held my breath and waited for him to respond.

"You mean what you did *for Lizzy*. She told me everything—about how she felt, what Leeann said to her, all of it. She told me how much it meant to her that she had you to talk to."

"Is she okay?" Worry for Lizzy eclipsed my sorrow. I had to know how she was.

"You are so selfless—here you are asking about my daughter when I hurt you so badly. Yes, she's relieved and she's happy. I spent time getting to know Ian over the last couple days, and I think it might work out for them. They're young, but they have something that I, and I suspect you, didn't back when we were their age. They really love each other."

"I'm so happy to hear that—"

"Sadie. I'm the one who needs to ask for forgiveness.

"What . . .?" I breathed.

"There is nothing to forgive you for. You were there for my daughter when her mother refused to be. You were there when she didn't want me to be. You kept her confidence and made her feel safe, but more than that, you understood her in a way that I never could have. You treated her like her own mother should have done. Sadie, you protected Lizzy at the expense of yourself and I am so sorry I reacted the way I did. My only excuse is that I was in shock. I had been so worried about her for so long and it was killing me inside that I couldn't help her. I couldn't see my way around those feelings. Thank you for taking care of my daughter. Can you ever forgive me?"

Tears filled my eyes. "It's only been a weekend. But all I could think about was what it would be like to live without you, and I couldn't stand the thought of it. I missed you so much."

"I love you, Sadie. I don't want to be without you ever again."

"I love you too. Come here, please." I held my arms out to him. Something about this place, this man, these feelings coursing through my body made me want to bare myself, bare my heart, bare my soul to him and let him have it all.

His voice rumbled, low and rough as he stalked toward me. "I'll do anything you ask as long as you forgive me. Please forgive me. I'll never react to you like that ever again, I swear."

"Yes, I forgive you. Let's forget everything else and make each other feel good again. That's what I want."

"I want that too." He stopped in front of me. We were close but not touching. He overwhelmed my senses—the scent of him, the warmth, the sense that I was back where I belonged. Still, I hesitated to reach out. I needed him to make the first move.

Slowly his hand drifted into the back of my hair and stopped. His warm palm rested at the back of my neck and my breath caught in my throat as his eyes warmed on mine. "I love you." He pulled me tight, banding an arm around my waist as his lips traced over my forehead, my temple, my cheek, then came to rest on my lips where he placed a kiss so tender it brought tears to my eyes.

He released my waist to trail his hand down my chest between my breasts, over my stomach, and lower. His fingertips slid up under my dress and down the front of my panties. He pulled me closer, winding his hand into my hair. "All I want is you forever. And this right now." He flipped his wrist and cupped me under the lace of my underwear, tracing my slit with a fingertip. "I hate the thought of you hurting without me there to make it better. And worse, that I was the one who caused it. Deep down you had to have known I would never stop loving you. Tell me you knew it, Sadie, please."

"I didn't, but I do now." My eyes drifted closed as shivers ran through my body.

"I love you," he repeated. "Look in my eyes and memorize the way I see you. I don't want you to ever forget it. No matter what happens, I will always love you. Always, Sadie." He stroked me gently between my legs as he spoke. "Let me take the hurt away. I'm so sorry, baby." We were about to come back together the way we had started: sexy, intense, passionate in the way we could only be with each other.

"Barrett, I have never in my life felt like this. I love you so much I don't know what to do with it. I can't—" Tears spilled from my eyes, and he kissed them away.

"I love you," he repeated. "I will die loving you."

"Take my clothes off." I breathed.

"You do it. I want to watch you give yourself to me. Then I'm going to give you everything I have."

I took half a step back and untied the belt of my wraparound dress to let it fall in a pool of black silk to the floor. It felt decadent to be dressed in so little while he still wore his clothes from the office. I grabbed his tie to pull him in. He kissed me once, deep and claiming, slanting his mouth over mine while his hand at my neck drifted around to my throat.

Then he pulled away from me with a sharp intake of breath and sat on the chaise lounge in the entryway to watch me just like he did at Genie's when we danced. Looking at me as if I were the only thing he wanted to see.

The lights were off but the descending sun shining through the paned picture windows glowed in fiery shades of red and orange to make him look dark, almost sinister, as he sat there shrouded in the shadows cast by the frame of each window. His palms went to his thighs and his chest heaved as he waited for me to undress for him.

I inhaled a deep breath as anticipatory goosebumps rose over my flesh. I wanted him. I felt hot pulsing waves of desire pool between my legs, and I swear I almost came from imagining what we were about to do.

I reached around and unhooked my bra, sliding the straps from my shoulders with a shrug. The red lace caught on my nipples and the sound of his low groan lit me up inside. "Do you like that?" I asked.

"Yeah," he ground out. I let it fall to the floor and turned around. I wasn't quite sure what compelled me to bend over and pick it up, but I did it anyway, then spun to toss it in his face with a low laugh. "Get over here," he growled, eyes wild and flaring like he wanted to consume me.

Gentleman Barrett had disappeared again.

"Come and get me," I teased.

In one quick movement he was on me. Arms crossed around my waist, mouth at my throat, kissing me, sucking on my skin, bending me backward to bite teasing little kisses over my already sensitized nipples. His arms tightened around my waist, and his hands squeezed my ass. "You're mine, Sadie," he groaned into my skin. "I can't wait to get inside you again. I've never felt this way about any woman ever, not in my whole entire life. I'll never let you go again."

"Barrett . . ."

He pulled back, his eyes burning into mine. "Don't say my name like that unless you want me to fuck you. Because I will."

"Barrett," I moaned. "Please."

"Please what? Tell me what you want, baby. Tell me you want me, tell me you love me, and I'll give you anything you ever ask for."

"All I want is you, god, so much. I love you."

He slid his hands to the back of my thighs and lifted. I wrapped myself around him, burying my face in his neck as he walked us toward the ground floor master suite, the place where we first began. I heard him slip his shoes off as he strode across the living room and down the short hall. "Hurry," I urged.

"Damn it," he growled as he fumbled with the doorknob. He set me down. His eyes were crazed as they met mine. "It's stuck."

"This house really is cursed," I said with a slightly hysterical giggle.

He grinned and slid his hands down to my waist, hooking the scrap of thin lace I wore with his thumbs as he sank to his knees in front of me. I could feel the heat of his breath at the apex of my thighs as he lifted my leg to rest over his shoulder.

I whimpered, "Oh my god," as he sank his tongue inside of me then slid it up to lick and suckle my clit into his mouth. "Barrett," I breathed. "Ohhhhh . . ."

Just like everything else in his life, he was perfect at this. He gripped one of my hips with a broad palm, holding me steady against the door as he entered me with his fingers, gliding them in and out as he circled the tip of his tongue around my clitoris. "You feel like silk," he murmured against my most sensitive skin.

I felt myself pulsing around his fingers and I cried out as my hips involuntarily writhed against his mouth. I was out of my head with lust and love and feelings that were about to overwhelm me. I wanted to scream out his name; I wanted to pull him further into me by his hair. Or shove him to the ground and grind myself on his face.

I was about to come, and I needed to so badly. I had missed him so much. My head whipped back, banging against the cursed door but I didn't care. Nothing could hurt me, not with Barrett's head buried between my thighs like this, giving me mind numbing waves of pleasure.

I arched my back, my palms slapped against the door as he placed my raised leg back on the floor and gripped my ass in his palms as he drove his face hard between my legs. He licked into me, fucking me into a restless insanity as his tongue drove inside and his nose pressed to my clit. My entire body shook as I carefully slid my feet, still in my heels, to the sides to widen my stance and tilt my hips forward. He grunted his approval as he used his thumbs to spread me apart and suck my clit back into his mouth.

"Don't stop, don't stop," I chanted as I inched closer to an orgasm that threatened to break me into pieces and send me flying.

"Mmm." He hummed into my flesh as he did what I said and kept at me with the same steady pace that was driving me wild.

"Right there. A little bit harder, just like that . . ." He sucked harder, exactly where I wanted him to, exactly like I told him to. "You are a great freaking listener," I encouraged. The soft laugh he let out felt so good, I squirmed against his genius mouth that was hitting the exact right spot.

Heat surged up my spine as he maintained the relentless swirling suction I had requested. "Faster," I begged, and good lord, he went faster but it wasn't enough. I needed him inside me. "Barrett, I need you," I murmured, grabbing his hair, and pulling him away from my greedy flesh.

"You have me," he panted.

"No, I want you inside of me." He stood and spun me to face the door. I heard his zipper slide down and his belt buckle hit the floor. In one smooth movement he filled me, all the way, until I felt his hips flush against me. "Yes," I breathed.

His chin rested on my shoulder. The silk of his tie tickled my spine as he pressed hard against me. "How do you want it?" he asked.

"I don't care as long as I have you back." I felt every inch of him as he pulled out of me, ever so slow, all the way to the tip, before driving back inside with one quick thrust. It was brutal; it was beautiful. It was everything I'd ever wanted. I was his and I would never, ever put us at risk again.

He repeated that slow withdrawal. Then grabbed my hips to drive back inside me once more. "Yes?" The question was whispered in my ear through his panting breaths. I could swear I was floating on air, not standing pressed up against a door, naked, save for a pair of high heels.

I moaned and placed my palms against the door for leverage as he fucked me. "More," I demanded, pressing back against him and spreading my legs wider, taking him further into my body. I needed all of him. I couldn't get enough.

"You're amazing," he grit out, grinding himself even harder into me. "I love you so much." We were pressed so close together, I swear I could feel his cock pulse in time with his heartbeat at my back.

He pulled out abruptly and stepped away. Afraid I'd done something wrong, I turned to face him. "I want to feel you against my skin," he said as he tossed his tie aside and tore at the buttons of his shirt to remove it. "Nothing should be between us. Not ever. It's just you and me, Sadie. From now on."

I nodded, crazed with want, and needing nothing more than for this night to last forever. "You and me," I repeated.

"Come here." He reached for me, and I went, entering his arms like I belonged there. And as I looked into his eyes, I knew for certain that I did. We were made for each other. We fit, and we were perfect.

He walked us backward, kissing me all the while, to the couch in the great room where he let me go and sat, sinking back into the cushions. "Take me back," he said, gesturing to his cock. Long and thick, it bobbed between his legs like a welcome invitation.

Of course it was just as gorgeous as the rest of him. I licked my lips as I straddled his lap. "How do you want it?" I murmured into his ear before kissing his neck and darting my tongue out to taste the salt of his skin. I could feel him hard as a rock at my entrance and I was more than ready for him to be mine again.

"Any way you want to give it to me." He looked at me like I was everything he'd ever wanted. His eyes were locked to mine, jaw clenched tight with desire, chest heaving, abs clenching and unclenching in a rippling wave as he held himself still for me. His palms pressed to the cushions at his side as he waited for me to take him. He was like a wild animal pacing a cage, waiting to be let out. "Sadie, please . . ."

That word. *Please.*

I reached between us to hold him steady and sank down to reclaim him inch by inch. He arched up as I ground myself down, both of us moaning as we reconnected. There was no better feeling in the world than being with him like this.

"You're so beautiful." He yanked me close for a plundering kiss then bent me backward over his lap so he could lavish attention down my neck to my breasts, sucking each nipple into his mouth in turn as I rode him gently, making us one again.

"You make me feel beautiful." I gasped, enraptured as he held me close and whispered sweet words in my ear until we fell over the edge together.

Barrett ran his fingers through my hair as I rested my head against his chest. "I'm going to miss this house," he said, breaking the satisfied silence we'd fallen into. "I fell in love with you here."

"Maybe we can rent it for a weekend every now and then. There are a few rooms left that we haven't made love in."

Languid kisses drifted over my cheek to my neck where he buried his face and hugged me tight. "We have the rest of the evening for that," he whispered against my skin. "I don't want to let you out of my arms tonight."

"Good, because I'm staying right here." I cuddled into his strong arms, sinking against his chest with a sigh. "You're mine, Barrett and I'm never letting you go."

CHAPTER 28

BARRETT

I had a big-ass diamond ring in my pocket—four carats, oval cut, rose gold—and I hoped like hell Rider would approve because I was bound and determined to marry his mother. I also had the woman herself sitting shotgun in my truck. She didn't know it, but we were on our way to a spot I had heard of located just above Milton Overlook.

I had thought of proposing to her at the Bandit Lake house, out on the dock perhaps or maybe in a boat on the lake. But I couldn't have all our memories tied up in one place, so I decided to take her up here to make a new one. I drove over the twisted roads, spiraling up into an area of the Smokies that only locals could traverse with confidence. The trees grew dense as the road narrowed. I chuckled as Sadie studied my profile, her eyes narrowed in suspicion along with the road as she sang along with Adele. *Hello,* indeed.

"Now will you tell me where we are going with that picnic basket you packed up so carefully and all those pillows and blankets in the back?" Sadie grinned from her seat after finishing her duet and switching the music off. "I can always turn it back on and try to serenade-slash-torture our destination out of you some more with my terrible singing."

"Baby, I love it when you sing to me. I guess I never mentioned that before."

"Aw, be still my heart." Her giggle was like music too. I turned to give her a smile and steal another look at her gorgeous face.

She was luminescent, cast in the golden hue of the setting sun. We were driving through the magic hour when the sun met the horizon and the colors of the day flamed out in one last blaze of glory over the tops of the trees. But we weren't here to see the sunset. Tonight, we were here for the moon.

This morning, her divorce became final, and tonight was a rare blue moon. Both were clear signs that it was high time I made her mine forever.

I came to a stop and carefully backed my truck between the trees into the brush at the side of the road.

"Hey, are we above the Milton Overlook? I know this spot. It's gorgeous up here. I used to drive up here to watch the sunset and be alone." I nodded, letting my lips tip up in a grin. "But what are we doing here now? The sun just finished setting, silly. Are we going to have a picnic in the dark?" She teased and poked me in the side.

"Something like that." I threw the truck in park and got out. "Stay there." I opened the back door and started tossing the pillows and blankets into the bed of the truck.

She hopped out and slammed the door. "Let me help."

Soon enough we had a little nest set up. I grabbed the basket and set it down, then helped her climb up to sit on the tailgate.

"Well, it's dark, Barrett." I could hear the laughter in her voice as she pushed me back so she could kneel in front of me between my legs. "I can think of plenty of things to do in the dark besides eat whatever is in your picnic basket."

"We'll get to that. After."

"After what?" She giggled, placing her hands against my chest then sliding them up to wrap her arms around my neck.

"After you look up, baby." It was dark out here like she said, but it was bright enough that I saw it when her mouth tilted up at the corner in a perplexed smile.

She tipped her head back anyway. "Is that—?" She dropped her head to face me, then tilted her had back again for another look. This time, her jaw dropped along with her head as she met my eyes. "Flynn said it was a blue moon tonight, but I forgot until just now. You brought me here for the blue moon, didn't you?"

"Among other things."

"Oh, Barrett . . ."

"Don't say my name like that unless you want me to marry you. Because I will."

"Oh my god, I am so into you right now." Everything had clicked into place. I could see it in her eyes. She threw herself back into my arms and I caught her with a laugh while I dug around in my pocket for the ring box.

"I have something for you. Sit here." I shifted her to sit next to me and held the red velvet ring box in front of her. "Sadie—"

"Oh my god." Her hands steepled under her chin.

I chuckled and started again. "Sadie Lynn—"

"Oh god."

One more try. "Sadie Lynn Hill—" I opened the box and she gasped.

"Barrett! That's the biggest diamond I've ever seen in real life." Her head shook side to side as she examined the diamond. "It's too much. I can't take that. All I need is you. You didn't have to buy something that big for me—"

"I know I didn't have to. It represents how much I love you. The way I love you, Sadie, is huge, it's out of control, out of my plans. Every time you look at the ostentatious beauty of this ring, I want you to remember this moment and that I love you more than the world." She held out her hand as tears flowed down her face. It fit her perfectly. "If I could, I would buy you a diamond just as big as my love, but this was as close as I could get. Now, I have something to ask you. May I?"

Her frantic nod was the only answer she gave.

"Sadie Lynn Hill. I knew a long time ago that you would always be the most beautiful woman I would ever see, but now that I know you, you're more than that. Your smile lights up my life. I don't live without you, Sadie. I just count down the minutes until I can see you and then my life begins again. The way you love your boys and my daughter is beautiful. As a mother you are fierce—your love comes effortlessly, and I couldn't ask for a better woman to be in Lizzy's life. My heart is full when I am with you." Tears, shimmering in silver rivulets, ran down her cheeks. I brushed them away with my thumb.

"I love you so much," she murmured.

"I love you too. I want you to be my wife. I want to spend the rest of my life with you. Will you marry me?"

"Yes, I will marry you." I kissed her ringed hand then pulled her into my arms. I knew that she'd be there forever.

"I'm so happy, Barrett. How do I be this happy?"

I held her as she cried against my chest. "Hold on to me. If we don't let go of each other, this will never go away."

"I'll never let you go. It might get annoying how much I'm never going to let you go."

"Never. I want you right here. Always."

CHAPTER 29

SADIE

"The happy couple has arrived!" my future mother-in-law announced as Barrett and I plus our collective children arrived at the Monroe house in town for Thanksgiving dinner. Barrett was loaded down with the eight different pies I made—two pumpkin, two pecan, two apple crumble, one buttermilk and one peanut butter—while I carried the giant chocolate sheet cake I had also made. And the boys each carried a platter of the assorted cookies that, you got it, I had made. This was my first Monroe family event as an almost-official part of the family, and I was nervous. So I stressed baked the heck out of my dessert assignment.

"Oh, my gracious, honey, that's a lot of desserts. I love it! Come inside and let's set those up on the dessert table in the breakfast nook. Boys, put those cookie platters on the coffee table in the living room, then go play. Your cousins are already in there." My heart leapt at the word cousins. We'd been coming to the Monroe gatherings for the better part of the last year, but the thought of being a part of a family like this for real was overwhelming. My boys would grow up the way I had always dreamed of.

I ran into Molly on the way to the breakfast nook through the kitchen. "Good lord, girl, look at all that pie. I'm skipping dinner and diving headfirst into dessert."

"I went overboard. I couldn't help myself. My baked goods make people like me."

"Are you kidding me? I, along with everyone here, already love the crap out of you. But the sight of that buttermilk pie just made me fall in love-love." She took the cake from my arms and set it next to the pies Barrett was carefully arranging on the table. "Okay, whip it out and let me see it. I heard it was big."

"That's what she said," Gracie yelled from her seat in the living room. She had already seen the ring currently weighing my hand down up close and personal last night at my house. When Barrett and I returned home, I had a house full of sisters waiting to congratulate me. The best part was that my mother had been there too, just like she was here tonight.

"Damn it. You beat me to the joke, Gracie," Garrett grumbled as he passed us by on his way to the living room. "Congratulations, future sister. Welcome to the family."

"Thank you," I called after him, then held my hand out so Molly could examine the big-ass diamond Barrett had installed on my finger last night.

"It's gorgeous," she said.

"Thank you." I beamed and Molly hugged me, then went off to join Garrett. I smiled at her as she walked off and when I turned back around, I was surrounded.

This was a full house, and I couldn't help but wonder how many times I would end up sticking my hand out for people to admire Barrett's handiwork.

Ruby took my hand next, tilting it side to side so the ring sparkled under the light. "That is something else," she admired. "Barrett has good taste."

"No, I have good taste," Rider insisted. "I told him what to get."

"You sure did, bud," Barrett agreed, finished with setting up the pies. "I couldn't have done it without you."

"Damn right," Rider said and held his hand out to Barrett. Barrett smacked his palm with a chuckle then wrapped me in his arms.

"Rider, give me a break and watch your language tonight, please." I closed my eyes and prayed for patience.

"That's my fault. Sorry." Clara cringed next to me. "I'm working on my foul mouth, okay?"

"Once you know bad words, normal words are just not fun to say." Rider shrugged then ran off to the living room with the other kids. After kissing my cheek, Barrett let me go and followed him.

"He has a point," Bill said with a laugh. "Let me see that ring, sugar." I gave him my hand and he smiled. "I'm so happy you're joining us, Sadie almost-Monroe." My eyes got misty as he pulled me in for a hug.

"Thank you," I whispered.

"My turn!" Becky Lee nudged her way between Bill and me and wrapped her arms around me. "I just adore you, Sadie. I couldn't be happier about this."

"I adore you right back and I'm thrilled. I can't believe this is really happening." My cheeks were beginning to ache from the constant grin I wore tonight but even though I was happy, a tear still fell and made its way down my face.

Becky Lee smiled softly and swiped it away with her thumb. "Oh, honey." She pulled me in for another hug, then she and Bill headed back to the kitchen to continue with the dinner preparations.

"Sadie." Lizzy entered the room, eyes shimmering with tears. "I'm so sorry. I didn't mean to hurt you. I had no idea about you and my dad."

"No, no, no." I pulled her into my arms. "No apologies, doll. Everything is okay now, shh."

"But I have to apologize to you. I messed up so many things since I got back home, and I need to be responsible for it. I was so selfish and oblivious to everyone but myself and I hurt you and my dad. My head has been a mess ever since I told my mom about the baby. I couldn't get over what she said, and I was afraid my dad would be mad like her if I told him, so I kept secrets and hid out in my room. You were the only one who figured me out and yet you're the one I ended up hurting the most, and I'm so sorry."

I hugged her tighter. "It's okay, sweetheart. I understood exactly how you felt. Please believe that."

"I do believe you." She swiped the tears from her cheeks. "You understood me when I didn't even understand myself."

"What did your mom say, Lizzy?" Gracie asked softly. She'd had her fair share of mean words thrown at her, too. Plus, her drama radar must have *pinged* from the living room because she sure got in here fast to mix in.

Lizzy pulled out of my arms to talk to Gracie. "I told her I was pregnant, and she said I was stealing her thunder and to keep my mouth shut until after her wedding. She's back home now and she wants to have lunch tomorrow to talk about me being her maid of honor—"

"She said what now?" Clara stormed in through the kitchen entrance to yank up my hand. She pointed my ring out to Lizzy as if she hadn't known it was there. "Listen up. Your dad is marrying my sister. That means you're about to acquire some mean-as-shit aunties, sugar pie. And we would be glad to have your back. We can look the other way if you want us to, or we can become very involved. But regardless of what you decide, we'll be here."

"Oh snap," Ruby exclaimed, her mouth dropping open.

"Yeah, and your soon-to-be-stepmother is the fiercest of all of us. So just say the word," Gracie informed her.

"You're not alone. I'll be by your side every step of the way through this pregnancy if you want me to be Lizzy," I offered.

Willa chimed in. "We're here, and we're not going anywhere."

Gracie grinned and lightly shoved Lizzy's shoulder. "Check this out—technically I'll be your aunt too. Weird as hell, right? I won't make you call me by my official title, but I'd like to be your friend."

"I would love that." Lizzy sniffed, now realizing that she wasn't alone, and she never really had been. "Hey, where's Weston?"

Ruby laughed. "He's hiding upstairs in Wyatt's old room playing video games with Harry. I'll let him know he has nothing to fear anymore."

"Oh god. I'm so embarrassed. Thank you, Ruby."

"It's all good. You really don't have to worry about him. He's a marshmallow inside, remember? We'll all be friends again, I promise. But, enough about that, let's see your ring." She snatched Lizzy's hand up.

"I love it," Gracie said. "It's dainty and perfect. So what's your last name going to be? If you decide to change it."

"Reed. Eliza Kay Monroe-Reed. I kinda love it. He's with his parents this Thanksgiving. But next year he'll be here with us, and we'll have a baby!" She giggled. The three girls wandered off, talking about Ian and her engagement and the baby.

"Well, that was just wonderful," Willa said. Then she added under her breath. "She seems happy, for real. But, as the voice of pessimistic reason . . . we'll be here for her if it implodes too,"

"Absolutely." Clara added. "Reality sucks."

I shook my head. "I'm not saying anything negative. They have something we never had. Real love."

"Dinner is ready, y'all!" We spun to the sound of Bill's voice calling us to the table. We all took our places in front of the pumpkin-shaped place cards with our names on them. A mixture of Hills, Monroes, Logans, and Coopers surrounded the massive table that Becky Lee had been justifiably smug about tonight because every single adult member of this family fit comfortably around it. The kids were at a smaller but equally decorated table in the living room.

Barrett tugged me hard into his side. "I love you," he murmured. "Right here, right now, this is part of my dream coming true, Sadie. Having you with me means everything. I want you to know that."

"I love you too." He kissed me and I blushed as a round of applause filled the room.

Then platters and bowls went around the table along with laughter and conversation. The subject of the Bandit Lake house came up and the various and sundry things that had gone wrong there.

"What are y'all going to do when you aren't working in the same place every day?" Molly asked.

"Don't worry about that, Molly. If they seem lonesome for each other, I'll just crack another tile or break a window for them to fix," Bill said with a laugh.

"What? That was you? I thought it was just some punk kids." Barrett laughed. "Sadie thought it was aliens, didn't you, baby?"

My blush deepened as I shook my head. "I—"

"Uh, it could have been aliens," Molly defended me. "They could have body snatched Bill and made him do it. Maybe there are alien matchmakers living in Bandit Lake. You don't know."

"God, I love you." Garrett grinned at her and kissed her temple.

"I don't know about aliens, but I could always rearrange the wires in the breaker box again." Everett leaned back in his chair with a smug smile and a wink.

"Yeah, and we could cancel a few more furniture orders if it comes down to it." Garrett shrugged.

"What . . .?" Sadie breathed. Her eyes widened as she realized just what kind of family she was marrying into.

"Well, I *had* to change the locks on the master suite," my mother announced. "Y'all tore that room up. That bedding was expensive and white and y'all left it on the floor by the fireplace. You don't do that kind of thing to white velvet. You just don't." She shook her head as she tutted her disappointment.

Wyatt snorted. "Busted," he said.

"I just died." Sadie said. "You are now communicating with the ghost of Sadie Hill." She leaned into me and hid her face against my shoulder.

"Mom—really?" Barrett huffed a laugh as his cheeks turned pink. We exchanged a glance and shrugged. Ultimately, the embarrassment was worth the cost of everyone finding out we were together.

"But, y'all, what about the Sandersons?" Lizzy asked. "Aren't they mad that their house isn't done yet?"

Becky Lee cleared her throat delicately. "Oh, did I ever mention to y'all that your Great Grandmother Betty was a Sanderson on her momma's side? No? It must have slipped my mind. Anyhow, that house passes from woman to woman down the family line and it's mine now. And everybody knows you can't sell Bandit Lake property. So, I guess I could use a couple of tenants . . ." Her eyes drifted around the table landing on each one of us in turn. Her smile was the smuggest one I had ever seen on her face as she winked at Barrett.

"I freaking love this family," Gracie announced.

Barrett and I exchanged shocked glances. We both knew who would end up renting that house.

Becky Lee blew me a kiss while Bill chuckled next to her. "Well done, my darling," he whispered and took hold of her hand.

"Grandma Becky Lee can we have pie now?" Mel, who belonged to Wyatt and Sabrina, asked. The kids had gotten restless. Apparently, Mel had been elected as head child, since she was standing at Becky Lee's side, surrounded by every little kid in the family except for Cora, but that was only because she was spending the evening strapped to Wyatt's chest sleeping in the baby carrier he wore.

"Have y'all finished your plates, yet?" I laughed because she knew they hadn't. We could all see the half-filled plates sitting in front of their empty seats in the living room from here.

Most of them shook their head no. My two looked everywhere but at Becky Lee to avoid answering.

"Just a little piece for each of you then. Head over to the dessert table y'all."

"I'm all about that pie. I'll help you dish it up, Becky Lee," Molly offered.

"Becky Lee, they should finish dinner first, don't you think so?" Sabrina asked.

Becky Lee laughed and shook her head no. "I'm sorry, sugar plum, but I'm not allowed to say no to them on a holiday. Once you graduate to grandmother status you are required to operate under a different set of nutritional guidelines. Am I right, Samantha?" She addressed my mother, who was apparently going to be her best friend, like it or not. I loved the idea; she could use a friend and someone besides our therapist to help her come out of the bitter, angry shell she had kept herself in over all these years.

Momma laughed. "That is correct. I reread the rule book last night." Laughter and a joke too? Combine tonight's progress with the last few Sunday dinners we had together and the future relationship between my mother and us Hill girls would continue getting better and better as time went on.

"Before we get to dessert, I want to make a toast." Becky Lee stood and held her glass aloft. "Bill and I are the luckiest parents in the world. Our four beautiful boys have all, with my help, of course,"—a collective smile and loving laughter spread around the table—"chosen the most wonderful women to bring into this family and I am so thankful. To each one of my new daughters, I love you. And to my boys, you are my heart. And to all my grandbabies, and I mean every single one of you—by marriage, by blood, and now a great grandchild on the way—thank you for helping me reach the ultimate trifecta of grandmotherhood. I will love you and spoil all of you rotten all the way into infinity. Cheers!"

We cheered and clinked glasses. We talked and we ate and then ate some more as Thanksgiving rolled along well into the evening.

Finally, Becky Lee had had enough. "Y'all, it's time to cut to the chase." Her eyes landed on me then Barrett, clearly, she was about to fish for information. "Barrett, Sadie, when is the wedding?"

EPILOGUE

BARRETT

Spring

"This time you're ready, Barrett. I can see the difference in you. Your heart is in your eyes, son and I am so happy you found her. What did I tell you?" My father's grinning face greeted mine in the doorway of one of the upstairs bedrooms in the Bandit Lake house—my house.

"You were right, Dad. Sadie is everything I need, and this time it will last forever."

"Are you ready?" Garrett poked his head in the door. Dad and I exchanged a smile at his inadvertent joke.

"It's time," Wyatt added from behind Garrett. "We have to get outside before it's too late."

Everett wasn't with them. He would be walking Sadie down the aisle, then joining me at my side as a groomsman.

"Yeah, go on and I'll catch up."

They left. I waited a few seconds so I could have the house to myself as I walked outside.

The house was finished now. And as I'd told Sadie a few months back, I could build a home, but without her it wouldn't be beautiful. Looking around I saw the magic she had created in every room. It was stunning. But it was nothing compared to what she had done for my life.

From the top of the stairs, I could see almost the entirety of the ground floor. Memories filled every inch of the space. And as time went on, we would make even more, enough that I would have to build more rooms to hold them. But today would be the biggest; we were getting married here.

My hand slid along the dark stained oak bannister as I descended. Sunlight shone through the windows as I stepped through the living room to the rear of the house and out the open back door and down the sloped lawn that led to the lake.

In front of the dock off to one side of an arch wound with lavender flowers and white roses stood Garrett and Wyatt, along with Flynn and Rider. White wooden chairs holding our families lined both sides of an aisle carefully delineated by lavender petals and flameless candles.

The music started once I took my place and, one by one, Sadie's sisters and Lizzy, each dressed in a pale hue of purple, walked down the aisle to join us.

I looked toward the setting sun as it burst through the cotton candy clouds floating in the sky above the house. Their colorful beauty deepened through the sun's burning descent and, for a brief moment, hovered there, making the house shine bright like a beacon against the deep green of the surrounding trees.

My breath caught in my throat as Sadie came through the door on Everett's arm.

She was dressed in creamy white silk with a delicate crown of lavender woven through her hair and glowed brighter and more beautiful than the setting sun above us.

Simple. Elegant. Stunning.

My Sadie. My love.

Tears filled my eyes as she approached. I didn't blink them away or hide them. Her sons needed to see exactly how much I loved their mother. And my daughter needed to see the kind of love she deserved.

"I'm gonna marry you right now," she mouthed through the glorious smile on her face. And I laughed through my tears.

"I love you," I said out loud. Even though she knew it, I had to tell her again.

In front of our families, we tied our lives together, vowing to love each other every day for the rest of time and beyond.

AUTHOR'S NOTE

Please do not google blue moon dates and email me about it.
Yes, I took some creative liberties with astronomy.
Escape reality with me!
Let's pretend that Sadie and Barrett could get engaged beneath a blue moon.
Love you!

ABOUT THE AUTHOR

Nora Everly is a life long reader, writer, and happily ever after junkie. She is a wife and stay-at-home mom to two tiny humans and one fat cat. She lives in Oregon with her family and her overactive imagination.

* * *

Newsletter: https://www.noraeverly.com/newsletter-1
Website: https://www.noraeverly.com/
Facebook: https://www.facebook.com/authornoraeverly
Goodreads: https://www.goodreads.com/author/show/19302304.Nora_Everly
Twitter: https://twitter.com/NoraEverly
Instagram: https://www.instagram.com/nora.everly/

Find Smartypants Romance online:
Website: www.smartypantsromance.com
Facebook: www.facebook.com/smartypantsromance/
Goodreads: www.goodreads.com/smartypantsromance
Twitter: @smartypantsrom
Instagram: @smartypantsromance

ALSO BY SMARTYPANTS ROMANCE

<u>Green Valley Chronicles</u>

<u>The Love at First Sight Series</u>

<u>Baking Me Crazy by Karla Sorensen (#1)</u>

<u>Batter of Wits by Karla Sorensen (#2)</u>

<u>Steal My Magnolia by Karla Sorensen (#3)</u>

<u>Worth the Wait by Karla Sorensen (#4)</u>

<u>Fighting For Love Series</u>

<u>Stud Muffin by Jiffy Kate (#1)</u>

<u>Beef Cake by Jiffy Kate (#2)</u>

<u>Eye Candy by Jiffy Kate (#3)</u>

<u>Knock Out by Jiffy Kate (#4)</u>

<u>The Donner Bakery Series</u>

<u>No Whisk, No Reward by Ellie Kay (#1)</u>

<u>The Green Valley Library Series</u>

<u>Love in Due Time by L.B. Dunbar (#1)</u>

<u>Crime and Periodicals by Nora Everly (#2)</u>

<u>Prose Before Bros by Cathy Yardley (#3)</u>

<u>Shelf Awareness by Katie Ashley (#4)</u>

<u>Carpentry and Cocktails by Nora Everly (#5)</u>

<u>Love in Deed by L.B. Dunbar (#6)</u>

Dewey Belong Together by Ann Whynot (#7)

Hotshot and Hospitality by Nora Everly (#8)

Love in a Pickle by L.B. Dunbar (#9)

Checking You Out by Ann Whynot (#10)

<u>Architecture and Artistry by Nora Everly (#11)</u>

Scorned Women's Society Series

My Bare Lady by Piper Sheldon (#1)

The Treble with Men by Piper Sheldon (#2)

The One That I Want by Piper Sheldon (#3)

Hopelessly Devoted by Piper Sheldon (#3.5)

It Takes a Woman by Piper Sheldon (#4)

Park Ranger Series

Happy Trail by Daisy Prescott (#1)

Stranger Ranger by Daisy Prescott (#2)

The Leffersbee Series

Been There Done That by Hope Ellis (#1)

Before and After You by Hope Ellis (#2)

The Higher Learning Series

Upsy Daisy by Chelsie Edwards (#1)

Green Valley Heroes Series

Forrest for the Trees by Kilby Blades (#1)

Parks and Provocation by Juliette Cross (#2)

Story of Us Collection

My Story of Us: Zach by Chris Brinkley (#1)

My Story of Us: Thomas by Chris Brinkley (#2)

Seduction in the City

Cipher Security Series

Code of Conduct by April White (#1)

Code of Honor by April White (#2)

Code of Matrimony by April White (#2.5)

Code of Ethics by April White (#3)

Cipher Office Series